Blind-Man's Buff

A Novel

by William R. Polk

Panda Press
2013

First Panda Press Edition 2013

Copyright © 2013 by William R. Polk

All rights reserved under International and Pan-American Copyright Convention.
Published in the United States by Panda Press 2013

All photographs are courtesy of the author.

The Library of Congress has catalogued this edition as follows:

Polk, William Roe 1929-
Personal History/William R. Polk, 1st edition

ISBN: 978-0-9829340-4-3

Editor: Milbry Polk
Cover Design: Mary Tiegreen
Design & Production: Eliza Polk

www.williampolk.com

For Cooper

My lifelong friend

'Tis all a Chequer-board of Nights and Days
Where Destiny with Men for Pieces plays;
Hither and thither moves, and mates, and slays.
And one by one back in the Closet lays.

The Rubaiyat of Omar Khayyam
Edward Fitzgerald Translation

NORA

POLYGRAPH? SURE.

I've taken so many of them, I don't need you here to ask the questions. My name is Nora Adams. I was born in Nebraska. My father was in the insurance business. I went to college in Chicago, Northwestern, and studied economics. I drink coffee. I was never a member of the Communist Party. I am not a Lesbian.

You'll see, when you ask all the questions, the needle won't jigger. So far, I am telling you the truth, but of course, it is not "the truth" that counts here.

That is not the reason I am being fired.

Ok, have it your way, "separated." But I know why. They called it "snooping." But wasn't that what I was trained to do? Anyway the stuff is still so highly classified that I can't even read the report I wrote. I don't think that is what really bugged them. I think it was when I tried to contact that Russian general to find out his side of the story.

Of course, you don't need to look startled. I know I should have gotten permission first, but I figured they would say no. And anyway I reported it all in detail and in writing after I spoke to him. Pretty much a waste of time, matter of fact. He was a real pro and anyway I don't think he knew what I really wanted to find out.

That Afghan, whatever he really was, knew more, but we sure misjudged him. Talk about deep cover! He was a master.

And I did track down almost everyone else. Not all of them directly, of course. Some were dead before I had a chance...and now it's too late. I guess almost all of them are dead now. Convenient, isn't it. Oh well, that's the way the game is played. I don't know why I am still alive since I know more than anyone else. Lucky to be just fir...retired, separated. What difference does this polygraph make now? At least to them. But, for me, it is necessary, you know, retirement and all, clean reference...pension. Those things count too.

Of course I realize this room is bugged. I am not naïve. But, listen carefully to the bug, you people. I said my father was in insurance. And in a way I am too. All I found out is written down so it wouldn't do any good to, how do they put it, "terminate me with maximum prejudice." In fact, as long as I am alive, the story is safe. With me dead, it might all come out.

But no need to tell you all this. I am really speaking to the people who will listen to the tape recorder. I know you are just a technician, or so you told me. The funny thing is that some of "them," the ones who will hear the bug were my old colleagues. I can't talk to them any longer. The ones that are still alive, that is. The others from SY I don't know of course, and you don't need to know – probably aren't even cleared to hear the real story. I guess I can't ever hope to tell the real story. Or what I think is the real story. Just bits and pieces of it. My little piece of it was like the pebble that set off the avalanche. Yeah, I know that sounds dramatic. But that's where the war really began.

Funny thing...I guess you have to say it began, strangely enough, not in Afghanistan but in Oklahoma...that's where I really got to know Ernest.

Ok, put on the suction cups...

ERNEST

ERNEST CROWNOVER MORE THAN FILLED THE CHAIR. It creaked ominously as he eased his shoulders against the back. Quickly glancing around himself to be sure no one was there to watch, he moved over to the sofa. That day and in those strange surroundings, he was uncharacteristically nervous. Uncharacteristically, that is, about everything but his size. That had been a life-long hazard. There was just too much of him to fit in offices.

Yet he was not a fat man. It was just that everything about him was out-sized. His cupped hands lay in his lap like soup ladles. His legs bent awkwardly and had overflowed the space between the long coffee table and the chair. Conscious of the danger his big frame posed for furniture and bric-a-brac and filled with memories of disasters in other rooms, Ernest had learned to 'ease' rather than to sit. He was always easing himself in and out of situations. The simple fact was that he was just too big, too heavy for the indoors. He felt more at home on construction sites or behind the wheel of a pickup truck. A tent or a trailer offered up no sacrificial furniture, no 'elephant traps' as his mother once joshed him after he had gone through a cane back chair in an aunt's parlor in Oklahoma. A drafting board and a transit were built for his kind of man; a coffee mug was just right for his big paw.

He simply didn't fit inside of houses. But it wasn't just avoiding breakage that drove him out of doors. He loved the open spaces. True, he felt safer outdoors but more than that he felt at peace and, yes, clean. His one sadness, in truth little more than a joke with him, was that the beautiful highways he built so pridefully quickly filled with dirty cars driven by careless people. But, he was a practical man and thought or worried little about such things. He built them because they should be built and he knew how. Let others keep them clean and functioning. He had no use for the 'knee-jerk liberals' and less for the 'bleeding heart environmentalists' — even when he was surprised to find himself agreeing in what they wanted for the great outdoors.

He was a builder, not a regulator. He respected government because government gave him the money to build his roads, but he hated its red tape, chaffed at its rules and shook his head in wonder at its conflicting imperatives. His favorite peeve, actually more a joke on them rather than a peeve against them, was the rule that a grader had to have a warning horn that sounded automatically when you backed it up ('the Feds say') but you could not make all that noise ('the County says'). He lived with the county, went to church with them, argued with them, drank with them while the Feds were the foreigners. It was the amusement of his retirement years that he had finally become a 'Fed' himself.

That turned out to be not bad either. What really mattered to him, in addition to hunting and fishing and other extensions of himself into the outdoors, was that he was 'contributing' in his own way, building good, honest roads that were of obvious use to people. He didn't make that workaday satisfaction into a virtue — and he would have been embarrassed to write it out like that — but it just made him feel better to live that kind of a life. He didn't condemn others for what they did or try to change them. The world was big enough for all kinds, he had long since discovered. He liked the variety or, as he put it, "the big and the little, the sweet and the sour." But his life was his own, and he did with it (or rather had done with it all those years in the Oklahoma Highway Department) pretty much what felt comfortable. It was his fear of losing that sense of involvement in retirement that drove him to the bizarre, even crazy (in the opinion of the neighbors) decision to get a job in the U. S. Government aid program overseas.

"Over there" as they said. "What in Christ's name are you going to do over there…I mean with all those foreigners and all? Hell, how will you talk with them? Like a bunch of wetbacks. Good thing you're a big ol' bastard. At least they won't run over you."

Ernest would just laugh. He never argued with anyone. Laughter was a sort of argument with him. But he went right ahead and applied for the job. To him it was a Godsend. A last fling before he really retired. No, he didn't want to admit that even to himself. It was a new career. He was starting all over again, young and fresh, but with experience. This time, he wouldn't waste a minute of youth. He wouldn't ever retire. He would just get better at what he was already good at. Real retirement was, of course, impossible, even immoral. What would he do? A man can't fish all the time. Why, he'd just die if he didn't do something useful.

His wife knew that too. So she silently stood by him or, more exactly, vocally stood apart from him, hearing the female versions of disbelief from her friends at church parties and bridge games. "Well, Ernest and I want to see the world, you know, and this is a wonderful chance. I mean, we've paid all those taxes and all. We…we just thought we'd like to get a round trip out of it." A joke, she had learned from Ernest, won more debates than logic.

When an opening — a 'slot' — in Afghanistan came up, and Ernest got a letter offering it to him, they had to rush to the local library to dig out a map. They were appalled. Afghanistan practically sat in the lap of Russia. It was just a big gully coming out of the Chinese mountains. And it was so far away. Worse was to come. When the librarian, curious about their interest, handed them the Encyclopedia opened to a page headed "Afghanistan," all they found was a jumble of incomprehensible events in which bandits with unpronounceable names were always murdering one another.

Ernest's big frame sagged under the withering gaze of his bantam wife. Suddenly, his big paw shot toward the page. There were the magic words, probably thrown in to fill out the space allotted by the editor, "the landscape is cut through with countless gullies. High in the mountains, many of these flow with water from the melting snows and are filled with trout. In the far north, the high valleys and plateaus are famous for the 'Marco Polo' long-horned sheep." Smiling back at his wife, he said, "see, it can't be all that bad."

Mrs. Crownover, Lucy May to their friends, found no such succor. But, at the last minute, just as they were about to depart, she got a welcoming note from the Oklahoma-born wife of one of the men working in the AID mission. Armed with the note and her unflinching admiration for Ernest, she went happily to the already-foreign airport in Oklahoma City and on into the wilds.

For Ernest, Afghanistan was, as he said, "a whole new ball game." Hardly pausing to unpack, he breathed in the high mountain air and was off like a young man again. Soon his pickup was a familiar sight all over the country. He visited every construction site, American, Russian, Afghan. All the same to him. He wasn't noisy or intrusive, but he loved to watch earth being moved — whose shovel did the moving was of little moment. He rarely commented and then only when asked. What he said, in Oklahoma American, was rarely precisely understood but somehow he communicated. Sometimes what he suggested was an obvious improvement. Sometimes it wasn't tried. But always he evinced a sense of decency, solidity, even, although he would never have thought of using the term, brotherhood. It was no big thing and he was under no illusions that it would change the world or even last beyond his visit, but it made him happy and that was reward enough.

Before he had been six months "in country," as the embassy people put it, he could drive almost anywhere, along the dusty roads, stop in front of a camp or work site, or even a truck stop, and be greeted and invited to drink tea. Learning to like tea was the real struggle. Forty years on Oklahoma construction sites had filled even his veins with coffee, as he chuckled to himself. Here tea was the password. Drinking it, he could 'howdy' with any Afghan.

It amused him to think what the fellows back home would have said if they had seen him squatting...Yes, he even learned to do that...with a bunch of...what would they have called them? Wetbacks? Wogs? Niggers? And God alone knew what they were anyway. The new words tumbled around his mouth in confusion. He could hardly pronounce them. Tajiks, Uzbeks, Mongols, Pathans, Turcomans. He couldn't tell them apart. But he really didn't care. To him, they were road men. And, in that and that alone, was the secret of brotherhood. Religion, language, place. Those things caused trouble. But a campfire at first light. A shiver under a great coat as the warmth of a bed roll was lost. The shared sight of an early hawk on the prowl. Above all, a glass of tea. Those were the real passports opening the frontiers of outdoorsmen.

Having moved over to the solid looking sofa, Ernest tried to put his mind to musing on these familiar and comfortable things. But still he was uneasy. As he glanced around the bare room, he noticed the lack of windows and took in the heavy, padded doors. He had been told the room was the outer office of Thomas Worthington Smith, Second Secretary (Political) of the Embassy who wanted to see him. He had been surprised. He had never met Smith before and could not imagine why Smith would want to see him. And who was he anyway, really? Never appeared in the part of the embassy Ernest knew.

"More phony than a $3 bill," he thought to himself. But what of it. Just like the Uzbeks and Tajiks. It didn't make any difference to him what label Smith wore. Smith had invited him over for a coffee and that was nice of him. So Ernest came. It was not in his nature to be impolite or distant. Nobody ever got hurt drinking a cup of coffee, he always said. "Or even a glass of tea," he had learned to say. While he waited, he looked over the magazines on the coffee table. What a weird selection, he thought. *Motoring Magazine*, the *TWA Ambassadors Magazine* (probably, he figured, the relic of one of Smith's trips), a very old Rotary magazine, and an issue of *Time* that must have been left over from the last Administration. Smith must not have many visitors, he mused.

"Coffee?"

Ernest jumped at the sound of the voice. He felt as though he had been caught peeking in secret papers. Being that kind of office made you feel that way even if all you had been looking at was an aging copy of the *Rotarian*. It gave him the willies.

"Yes, black, thanks," Ernest managed. He even managed a quick smile. He smiled easily. It made everything easier, but that wasn't why he did it. It was just automatic. "People don't bite," his mother used to say to him; "they want to like you. Sometimes they just need a little help. Smiles go miles." And he believed her. The years in the Highway Department had occasionally made him doubt her adage, but usually he got along with little trouble. Smiles weren't all, but they certainly helped, and smiling, in any event, was just part of his nature.

Again left alone as the woman walked out of the room, Ernest studied the room. 'Studied'. That is what he would have said if anyone had asked him what he was doing. His speech was laced with expressions from North Texas. What he saw brought up all his feelings about 'g'ment'. "Even way the hell out here in Afghanistan," he had come to believe in the few months he had been around the embassy, "the cement that holds the country together isn't the Constitution. It's government-issue furniture. Every one sits on the same chairs, reads to the same light and walks on the same linoleum."

In this room, the furniture was the same as in "his" part of the embassy complex but the atmosphere was not. Over where he worked, or at least checked in after his time in the field, the doors were never closed. People were moving around, talking with one another. The sun and wind and, of course, the dust poured in through open windows. Papers and maps and plans were scattered over tables and on easels. And the walls were pasted with notices and pictures and even postcards.

"Hi, gang. You'll never believe what I did in Paris! But, you guys be good, OK? At least till I come back. (Ha!) See you soon. Cheers, Al"

Plants bloomed in luxuriant color on the desks of wilting secretaries and the normal intercom was a shouted,

"Hey, Tom, there's this Afghan on the phone who wants to know how he can get hold of some hybrid seed like we was experimenting with down on the Helmund. You better talk with him. I can't hardly make him out. Must have learned his English in Haaaavad! It'id take an Aggie like you to figure it out..."

Then laughter and cat calls would sound from all the nearby offices.

But this room was silent, bare, windless, suffused with a perpetual gloom, and virtually sealed off from the adjacent embassy. In it, Ernest felt numbed and trapped, like an animal. And the stale air made him feel unclean. *The Rotarian* didn't do a very good job taking his mind off this feeling.

Claustrophobia came easily to him, and it had him by the scruff of the neck when one of the sound proofed doors abruptly opened and out stepped a young fellow he had seen around, even seen early out jogging – or as Ernest called it, "loping" — around the back roads near his house early in the morning. He had never spoken with him, but knew him by the name of Jack Farnsworth.

As Farnsworth turned toward him, Ernest saw that his face glowed with anger and he was just finishing what he must have been saying inside the office, "...not even that." Abruptly he broke off. There was a moment of silence, as Ernest lumbered to his feet. Then, over Farnsworth's shoulder, Ernest could see Smith standing behind his desk, telephone in hand but not to his ear, his face set in a forced smile.

Whatever had just happened was obviously over, but it must have been a corker, Ernest thought.

Instinctively, built in by years of admonitions from his Mother and now second nature, Ernest smiled and started to hold out his right hand.

He always offered his hand, to everyone, always. It never hurt anyone to say, "howdy." or "mornin," but, seeing the glare in Jack's eyes, he froze, and the message raced down his nerves, stopping his thrusting arm in middle passage.

Jack had seen Ernest rise out of the sofa, like a big brown bear in a forest clearing, it took him a moment to change emotional gears. Furious with Smith, furious with himself...just plain furious, Ernest was the first thing he had seen. And Ernest was the last thing he never dreamed of seeing in that office.

The two men stood, lost for words, and then Ernest heard Smith saying, "Mr. Crownover..."

Half turning from Jack, he threw up the smile and said, easily, "Ernest. Everyone calls me by the name my Mother gave me."

"Ernest. I'm delighted to see you. Thank you so very much for coming over. Let me introduce you to Jack Farnsworth. Won't you come right in."

Ernest was not one to let the moment end on mindless anger. He reached out again for Jack's hand and that time he caught it. It was not so much an offered shake as a grasp. Jack's hand almost disappeared inside Ernest's and stuck there.

But Jack was in no mood for conviviality or even politeness. Besides who the hell was Ernest? He was not one of them. Or was he? He couldn't know about the issue between Smith and him. At least Jack hoped so. It had to be very secret. His life depended upon that. Worried and confused, his hand still caught, Jack turned back toward Smith, started to say something, paused and thought better of it, and twisting back again to Ernest, said with affected calm managed, "glad to meet you, Ernest." Then, gingerly extracting his hand, he turned away and walked out a different door than either of them had used before.

Smith waited a moment as Ernest stared at the closing door. "Angry." It was not a question.

"Yes. A silly matter. You know how it is," Smith waved the matter lightly aside. "Vacations, promotions, assignments. Younger people are always upset with routine and discipline. Do please come in."

Ernest listened without expression. He heard echoes behind the words, but they were not his affair. He had not spent a lot of time around the embassy, but what time he had spent showed him that if you wanted to hear gossip or get involved in quarrels, it could become a way of life. So, like a hunter, he listened, smelled the often stale air and watched for what might be of interest or value but tried never joined in. He didn't like this patch of the woods, anyway, he had already decided.

With Smith behind him, Ernest bent his head and eased through the low Afghan doorway into Smith's office. As he had guessed it would be, it was climaxed by an American flag. The Red and White hung in an almost permanent crease down the mahogany pole. Before it, like an altar, was the requisite imposing desk with its carefully placed "In" box, piled high with the ritual offerings of office, and the empty "Out" box that bore witness to the efficiency of the man's secretary. One more detail and he had the whole picture. The Government-issue water jug with two glasses on the small round plastic tray. They were the give away — no matter what the title said, it meant that Smith was a big shot in the embassy.

In his first days in the embassy, Ernest had learned that you didn't need to read the 'stud book' to find out who the important people were; all you had to do was look for the water jug and the flag. That was the spoor for the hunter.

"I'm sorry about that...the scene out there." Began Smith. "Aw, its the altitude. We all get a bit testy up here."

11

"It was just a little matter…" "And none of my business."

"No, I certainly didn't mean to imply…"

"You didn't, Mr. Smith. I did. I don't believe in prying into other folks' affairs. I put alota store in the old saying that high fences make good neighbors. Now, what did you want to see me about, Mr. Smith?"

Smith frowned. He was not about to have this hick tell him how to be polite and he certainly wasn't going to be interviewed. "First, would you like some coffee?"

"Your little lady took my order out there," he replied, tilting his chin toward the then closed door.

"Okay. Fine. Please sit down."

Ernest settled onto the sofa, another, bigger and newer than the scruffy ones over in the offices he knew. Completing his rapid inventory of the room, he sank down onto the leather-like cushion. Only two items remained on his check list: one was nearly personal. It was the obligatory collection of pictures on the table behind the desk, wife and children. There they were, but all were, at first glance very young, obviously, to judge by Smith's age, taken long ago, packed and repacked from God-knows-where around the world. They smiled limply for all time from behind their glass fronts. Amazing, he thought, how much all families look alike in those photos. No real point in removing the pictures Woolworth's had put there to sell the frames. What a guessing game it would be if one could gather all the family shots in this embassy up, mix them around and then try to match them up with the living people. Almost as interchangeable as the furniture, he mused.

Then his eye moved back to the wall. There it was. The last item. The patent of office. The official appointment. In this office, his lair, Smith was a senior official. Out there, in the other office he kept in the overt part of the embassy, he was a minor flunky, a second secretary, hardly more than a name in the phone book. That open office "out there" had none of these signs of power and symbols of office. But it existed and gave official status — 'cover', a word Ernest used in another context — to Smith for Embassy receptions and telephone messages.

Actually, even that wasn't true: it existed for politeness sake. To maintain pretenses so as not to embarrass. Smith was not, could not be, "under cover." His counterparts among the Russians, Chinese, Afghans and, of course, the British well knew who he was and, in general, what he did. Each, in fact, made sure that the others knew. That was part of the game. A big part of the game. Whole battalions of men and women kept track of the movements, the careers, marriages and divorces, fortunes and failures of members of the fraternity. As a senior member of a major service, Smith figured in everyone's secret *Who's Who*. He didn't try to hide the reality — it was actually not only useful but even crucial to his work. Everyone knew the story of the Russian defector who had tried for several hours, before his own service caught him, to find the senior American intelligence officer in Tokyo. No, far better to be obvious or at least reachable.

But, of course, there are things everyone does but doesn't talk about. Everyone goes to the toilet, but normally that is not a major topic of conversation. Polite people don't usually question one another about their private actions. Espionage is just another one of these. For Smith to be listed in the phone book as "Second Secretary, Political" and to maintain an office in the "other" part of the embassy kept up pretenses. It was polite. It didn't force anyone, or at least anyone who didn't want to, to think about it.

'So this is where the spooks are,' thought Ernest. "Cream?"

"Black, thanks."

"Sugar?"

"Just Black."

"You're from Texas, aren't you?"

"Oklahoma. Right on the Texas line. You were close. And you?" Ernest wasn't going to let a polite chat turn into an interview.

"Memphis.

"Been out here long?" Smith wanted to do the questioning. And to direct the light chatter that served to get both parties ready for serious talk.

But Ernest didn't know the game. He wasn't used to interviews. So, he joined when he was meant to follow. "No, just a couple of months. You've just arrived, haven't you?"

"Yes, just a couple of months ago. Oh, thanks, Miss Peterson."

The secretary had slipped in and was silently on the way out of the door almost before they noticed. All Ernest saw was a faint shape pulling the door closed after her.

'Funny,' Ernest thought to himself, 'I must be getting old. I always notice pretty girls. Especially, pretty ones like that. Spooky place. Spooky people too.'

"Ernest," said Smith in a more abstract tone, fingering the handle of his cup, not really trying to pick it up but swilling the coffee around inside of it, "the reason I asked you to come by today has to do with your work."

"My work? Are you interested in road work, Mr. Smith?" "Well, yes... in a way."

"Well, that's real friendly of you. Do you want to come out to see one of the sites I'm working on? I'd be pleased to have you. You're the first fellow in the embassy..."

"Yes, I would love to see what you are doing...But, I have a couple of things I must say first."

"Like I say, 'it's your nickel.'"

"No matter what happens today," Smith said, staring meaningfully in a well-practiced gesture into Ernest's eyes, "no matter what we say to one another, I must ask you to protect its confidentiality. And you may rely upon my discretion. Do you know what I mean?"

"Translated into Oklahoma, I guess it comes to 'don't go blabbing.'"

"Right. I am sorry to sound like a school teacher, but this is a small post and, as you know, people love to talk. And each of our agencies has its own rules and customs."

"How do they say it in the movies, 'my lips are sealed.'" Ernest melodramatically pulled his big hand across his mouth. "Fact is, we're just having coffee. To be honest, I wouldn't know a secret if it bit me. It's pretty hard to be secret about bulldozers and graders, my line of work, you know. I'm just a country boy, Mr. Smith. Frankly, I suspect you got the wrong Crownover. I'm Ernest Crownover, the road man..."

"I don't think so, Ernest. But let me go on."

"...like the feller said, 'don't go trying to make a silk purse...'"

Smith had tired quickly of Ernest's banter. He immediately suspected that the good ol' boy talk was put on for his benefit. That didn't surprise Smith. He was accustomed to men using speech or mannerisms as shields to protect themselves or their thoughts from others. Much of his skill lay in penetrating these shields. With real targets, it was challenging, even fun, but with a marginal case like Ernest, it was just annoying, perhaps even a waste of time. He looked at his watch. Ernest followed his eyes. He had seen the gesture before. It was typical of certain levels of government officials and showed both impatience and status.

"Yeah, Mr. Smith. I agree with you. It *is* getting late. I'm off a job up near Kunduz and I've got to get over the pass on the Hindu Kush before nightfall, when the curfew starts up there, to get to the site before they pour the concrete on a culvert. They're good ol' boys, but if they don't get it just right, it'll wash out in the spring rains. And all that work'ill go down the drain."

"Down the drain, that's a good one," said Smith a forced chuckle. "Okay. What I wanted to say, Ernest, is that you get around the country a great deal and…"

"Sure do. I guess I have seen about as much as anyone in the Embassy." "That's just it. You really are our expert on rural…on the provinces."

"…try to see as much as I can. Fact is, I enjoy it. I'm not much of a deskman, never have been."

"Right. I fully appreciate that. I'm not either. I wish I could travel like you do."

"Nobody likely to stop you. Nobody stops me."

"But, it's difficult in my…"

"Aw, Mr. Smith, we both know, some fellows travel and some don't. I don't mean to be impolite. But our last AID director, you know the one that just got fired, why he never even got out of…"

"But, in my position…"

Ernest paused, chuckled and uncharacteristically allowed himself a cheap shot. "Why that was just the words he used."

"Well, be that as it may, the fact is that our positions…"

Ernest warmed to his theme, enjoying watching Smith caught off balance. "Fact is, I've never seen a bunch of people who move around less than the folks in this embassy. Well, of course, we don't have the roads finished yet…there're pretty dusty."

Smith winced. "Be that as it may, the fact is that I am not a liberty to... to travel...to go around the country..."

"Sorry, Mr. Smith. I didn't mean to pry. I'm sure you've got good reasons...It's just that I hear everyone say the same thing and it's such a big, such a beautiful country that I..."

"Ernest," said Smith firmly, again glancing at his watch and determined to take the conversation in hand at last, "I imagine that you have a pretty good idea of what I do in the Embassy."

"Not much." He paused as it dawned on him that his words meant something else than what he meant. Then, embarrassed, he went on, "I mean, not much of an idea. Not a very clear idea anyhow."

"Well, of course we all work for the same Govern..."

"Well, I tell you, Mr. Smith. I'm over here just to help these folks build some roads. That's all I know about. I don't know their language, couldn't possibly learn it in a coon's age, and I don't give a hound's howl for their politics. But, I like 'em. And they seem to like me. There's hardly a camp up and down the main roads...or even the little country roads...that I don't stop to drink coffee — no, here it's always tea — and pass the time of day. They always welcome me, share their bread with me. Oh, it's not much, mind you, but it's what they have..."

"Ernest, that's just it. You really have gotten to know this country and its brave people."

"They just know that I mean 'em no harm."

"Heavens, Ernest, neither do I. We are all over here trying to help preserve their liberty, trying to keep the Communists from taking over the country. You and I are working for the same Government, for our country. We are in this together." In a melodramatic gesture, Smith started to point

17

toward the flag but then, as not quite sure how he had judged Ernest, ended by merely looking at it.

Ernest waited, in his turn, not sure what he was supposed to say.

Then Smith went on. "Of course, not all of them are sophisticated, not all of them are loyal. And their enemies are smart. That is why we need to know, why we must know…"

Ernest found his voice, and, shaking his head, broke in. "Mr. Smith, I guess this will sound country to you, will make me sound like the hick I am, but I just don't believe in drinking folks' coffee and eating their bread and prying into their affairs to spread…"

"For Heaven's sake, slow down. I'm not suggesting that you…"

"…spread stories about them. Anyway, fact is, I can't even speak to them.

"They's not one in a hundred who speaks English. And those guys are the worst. Why they even claim I don't speak English!" He chuckled mirthlessly trying to reduce the tension he felt.

"Ernest, what I want is something entirely different."

"I'm sorry, Mr. Smith." Politeness took over as it usually did with Ernest. "What is it that you want from me?"

"It's very simple," Smith replied slowly and evenly. "I'd just like you to keep your eyes and ears open and let me know if you see something unusual…"

"Gosh, Mr. Smith. For me that's a big order. The whole country is unusual to me! That's why I was happy to come out here. Its wild and beautiful. Nothing like it. Why, never a day passes that I don't see…"

"Okay, okay. I'm sure that's true, but, of course, I would let you know what we are most interested in at any given time."

"You mean, I would sort of go to work for you?"

"Well, no, not exactly. It would be more informal. Frankly, you would be more valuable not working for us. But, of course, I know that you would have some extra expenses and perhaps we could…"

For the first time, Ernest winced and struggling upright from the deep cushion of the sofa, he leaned toward Smith. "Mr. Smith, let me stop you for a minute to tell you about myself. I retired from my job in Oklahoma two years ago. I had worked hard and done a good job. I've lived a wonderful life. Done exactly what I set out to do. I like working with my hands, you know, really getting into it. And, I'm proud of what I did. You can see it. You can drive down it, even fish behind some of it. I built things, mostly roads and dams and bridges and culverts, along with a few houses. Built my own, in fact. My daughter…she and her husband'er living in it now. Those things I understand. But what you…I don't mean to be impolite. What your people are doing just isn't, well, just isn't my line. Probably I'm wrong, probably I'm just an ignorant old cuss, but I don't think I like it very much either. You see, Mr. Smith, I came over here to build roads because these poor people…Oh, hell, that's really not true. To be honest, I came over here because I couldn't stop, couldn't stop building roads. They've been my life. I guess I was scared to quit. And, I talked myself into thinking that I could help. But, to be honest, I knew they could help me, let me get in a few more years of real life. I know I'm not saying this well, but what I'm trying to get across is that it's been a fair trade. We really are helping each other.

"I just wouldn't do anything to spoil that."

"Okay. I understand what you're saying, and believe me, Ernest, I agree with you. But remember. Roads are neutral. They will carry anybody. And we don't want, can't have, Russian tanks racing down them toward India."

"Hell, Mr. Smith. I don't know nothin' as we say down home about the Russians. Never seen 'em except out on the construction sites..."

Smith saw his chance. Ernest had set himself up. "Ernest, That's just it. That's what I've been trying to say, and now you've said it better. Don't you see, you are the only American who really sees what is going on. Why you are the only real expert in this whole embassy."

Ernest looked uneasy. He had felt the ice give under his foot before and recognized the danger. But then he grinned. He felt a grudging admiration for Smith: Ernest had often using the same tactic to get some upstart engineer to build a culvert his way.

Smith didn't catch the grin and went ahead with his ploy. "That's just what we need to know. About the Russians out on the roads. How many are there? Where are they? What are they doing? How do they get along with the Afghans?"

But they weren't talking about culverts, and the worry returned to Ernest's face. "Well...I...I don't know..."

"You talk about unusual things. And you know about roads. But, did you know that our pals, the Russians, have built into that wonderful road of theirs that comes down from Herat to Kandahar...I bet you have driven over it a dozen times. Well, did you know that they built at least five sections that are strong enough so jet fighter-bombers can land on them? We found out about that from...well, let's just say, we found out. No, as a matter of fact, I'll tell you, we found out from aerial photographs. Of course, the Afghans don't know about it. How could they? They're not trained in...they have no capa...They just see that the Russians built a good, straight stretch of road. They couldn't imagine MIGs landing there. But, for a man of your experience, well, it would be most unusual to see the amount of concrete they are putting into that road. And, you would do the Afghans a favor by letting us know... so we could warn them."

Ernest shook his head, obviously impressed, even stunned. Airplanes landing on the highway…unbelievable…why would they…he sat back and gazed at a spot on the ceiling for a moment. Then his eyes fell again on Smith. He blushed. What he had said sounded very naive, even plain selfish. He looked down at his big hands, feeling foolish and a little cheap.

Smith recognized the signs. He had been over this trail, after bigger, more sophisticated quarry many times before. It was time, he thought. He made his move. He called it the 'end game', a favorite term he had borrowed from chess. He had the board all set up. Now the winning move.

"Ernest, I know you will retire next year and that this has been an expensive assignment. For all the extra work and trouble involved, I think we could arrange to offer you…"

Ernest suddenly sat bolt upright. Behind Smith's voice he heard echoes of tense encounters with contractors angling for special extracurricular deals. He wavered no longer. It all suddenly came clear to him. But, instead of speaking, he looked keenly and deeply into Smith's eyes. At last he spoke in an almost sad voice that betrayed the temptation he had momentarily felt.

"Mr. Smith. This'll sound old fashioned to you. But I really wouldn't feel comfortable about that sort of thing. I guess it's silly. In construction work, it's called a bribe, and I'm just a little too old to start sticking my hand in the pot now. I don't mean to be impolite. I'm sure you didn't mean it like that. I don't work with words enough to make it sound right. But I think a lot of what I hear about, pardon me, not from you, but around this embassy, is a… to put it in Oklahoma…a load of shit. Roads and dams and bridges are real. Gossip and high politics and spying and…"

Smith knew he had lost it. Just as he had the fish up to the boat, ready to lift it in, the line broke — no, the fact was that *he* broke the line with that clumsy remark about money. He should have known. He was furious with himself…and sick and tired of playing folksy patriotism with

Crownover. Anyway, 'screw it,' he thought. 'Now to get the old bastard out of here without wasting more time.'

Leaning back in his chair and smiling broadly, he almost laughed, "Okay, Ernest. Tell me, on a more serious note, do you get in any fishing on your trips?"

Ernest broke off in mid sentence like he had been slapped. Then he laughed out loud, looking full and clear into Smith's eyes. It was only a second, but it seemed much longer.

"Pretty good, Mr. Smith. I'm sorry. I didn't mean to be impolite. Got me going, I guess. You don't need a lecture from an old hick like me. Okay, let's get together sometime to talk about fishing. There isn't really very much of that either, come to think about it. The streams mostly go dry in the...but I'd be wasting your valuable time chatting about fishing. Besides, that's really secret. Thanks for the coffee."

With that, Ernest heaved his big frame off the sofa, and Smith noticed that he had not touched his coffee. Balancing surprisingly lightly on his big feet, he held out his hand to Smith.

"Well, for now," started Smith with the bailout, "let's just say..."

"I'll remember. We hardly even met." Ernest turned toward the door, but Smith got there first and opened it. With an awkward wave, Ernest had started toward the outer door.

"No...use this one, if you don't mind," said Smith, opening the middle door, the one that led out, out to the "other" side of the Embassy. Ernest paused for barely a moment, half turned and tossed back, "See you around, Mr. Smith."

"Thank you for coming in…" he just managed as the door closed silently on its well-oiled hinges. "Stupid son of a bitch," he growled at the secretary. She looked up from her typing and her mouth involuntarily opened as though to ask a question. "Stupid son of a bitch, I said." Smith turned and walked into his office, slamming the door behind him.

WAR GAMES

"LOOK AT 'EM GO!" Leaping up from the pillow the provincial governor had ostentatiously provided for his diplomatic guests. Malcolm shouted in unison with the turbaned men and enveloped women arrayed on the small hill. Then turning quickly to Nora, he hoarsely confided, "Thank the gods they are going and not coming!"

Almost hidden by a cloud of dust, forty horsemen thundered past, flaying one another with their quirts as they struggled to get a hold on the headless body of the nearly fully grown calf.

"Really savage…and ugly," Nora shook her head disdainfully.

"Oh, come on, Nora, let yourself go," Malcolm shouted over the din. Buzkashi is the way the Mongols prepared their soldiers for battle." He settled down on the ground next to Nora.

"Well, fortunately, that was a long time ago. I wish they remembered other things than how to kill one another, she sighed."

"Think of it as polo. You like polo don't you. Well this is just polo and wrestling but set to war. The idea was to train the cavalry, what the Mongols were famous for, not to be afraid of banging into the enemy."

"Well, polo is bad enough. But this is mayhem," Nora rose to her feet, brushing off the dust, and prepared to leave."

"You can't do that," Malcolm said, firmly taking her arm. "The governor will be terribly offended. His deputy told me that he had never invited any foreigners to his party. Anyway, the show is really quite a spectacle!" The now genuinely excited Malcolm stood up and yelled between the cheers of the crowd. Then, bending over Nora, he half yelled above the din, "You won't see this sort of thing anywhere else. These men are deadly serious…for them this is not a game. For them, it is preparing for combat. No, it already is combat – like we train our troops with live ammunition. Sure, it's rough, and as you say, even savage. They occasionally get killed, and practically all those I have seen have broken bones and deep cuts from their whips. They are Afghanistan's gladiators." Then he paused. "Oh, my god, they are turning around and coming straight at us."

"Look at the Governor. If he turns tail, so will I," Nora was not joking. Her faced showed real panic.

Immediately, seeing the oncoming riders, the squad of soldiers in front of the governor brandished their rifles and waved hats and scarves frantically, trying to make the riders wheel again. One fired a shot. But the mob of horsemen was unwilling or unable to stop. On they came, and the soldiers panicked and fled toward the little hill. One was not quick enough and disappeared under the charging horsemen. The governor too turned and ran higher up the hill, losing his turban on the way, and the audience, watching the phalanx of horsemen rushing toward them, screaming in terror, tumbled over one another trying to get out of the way.

"Don't run," Malcolm shouted, grabbing Nora's arm. "We'll get trampled in the mob if we do! Just stay here beside me. But don't sit down! We may have to jump up and run."

Then, just in the last seconds before they would have charged right into the midst of the crowd, already half way up the hill, the horsemen wheeled back. Immediately, at the foot of the hill, a fight broke out. Horses reared and crashed against one another as riders lashed them…and struck out at one another.

"They didn't even look at the audience," Malcolm shouted above the dying screams of the crowd. "For them, the soldiers, the audience and the governor are just like a bunch of foot soldiers, despised infantry, just as they were to the Mongol horsemen. Of no account! Just to be ridden down. Before they went on to sack the city. In those days, the foot soldiers were often chained together to keep them from running away. You can see why."

"Well, I'm no foot soldier!" Nora gasped. "And, I'm not chained. Let's get out of here before they come back!"

"Take it easy," Malcolm soothed, as he pattered her arm. "They will be going way over there, across the field," he pointed toward another low range of hills. "That's the goal…that's where the game is won…Getting that calf across the goal line. They aren't interested in us. And, they know that if they come back, the Governor's soldiers will shoot to kill. They will surely be punished for running away this time. They won't take a chance again. We'll be okay.

"Anyway, we can't let our side down. The governor invited us and we can't just walk out on him. Not many Americans get invited out here in the wilds to watch buzkashi. It is a real honor. It took me quite a time to arrange it. I had to pretend that the ambassador was coming."

Nora scowled and shook her head. But she sat down again.

Just then, they saw two horsemen, fighting over the calf, using their whips on one another and their horses, and as they were struggling, another horseman slammed into them at full speed, knocking both of them, himself and all three horses to the ground. Immediately, grabbing his opportunity, another horseman made off with the body of the calf, furiously lashing his horse into a dead run while hotly pursued by a dozen others.

"God, those three men on the ground just couldn't be alive after that," Nora almost screamed as she jumped to her feet.

But one of the three men, struggled upright and leapt back on his struggling pony and, lashing it back on its feet, rushed off after the melee now disappearing into the plain.

"I don't believe it. I was sure he would never walk again," said Nora.

"The Afghans say that the rider, the *champandaz*, is solid bone, not a bit of soft flesh. He has to be to live very long. He has to be practically indestructible. Or at least that one is. The other two haven't moved…at least not yet.

"My God, the Afghans are a tough people. They never seem to even think about giving up. And mercy is something only Allah can dispense. I sure would hate to have them on my tail!"

As they watched, two of the soldiers scurried out onto the field.

Looking carefully at the surging mass of horsemen and gaging their distance, two of the soldiers scurried out onto the field. Grabbing one of the downed riders, they jerked him up upright and then slapped him across the face.

"God! Hasn't he had enough? Why are they slapping him around?" Nora was shocked.

"In their eyes, he doesn't deserve any compassion. He is just a fallen gladiator. The governor doesn't ape the Roman emperors in turning his thumb down to have him finished off, but he gets no sympathy. Anyway, I guess they have to get him out of the way before the horsemen come raging back."

In less time than it took to tell, the clot of horsemen was galloping back toward the hill, but this time, they seemed to be in control of themselves and their horses. No one was using his whip on the others. And one man rode out in front of the others. Bending low in in his saddle, he saluted the governor. The calf, over whose body they had been so viciously fighting a few minutes before, was nowhere to seen.

"He won," smiled Malcolm. "Oh, my lord, look," he blurted out, "he's the one who just got knocked down. See his red headscarf! That old devil made it. How he did it, I can't imagine. He looks like he is at least sixty years old.

"Now he will get his reward. "

"I would think that just being alive after all that would be reward enough. I think it is for me! I thought we were going to get it ourselves as they came roaring up the hill."

"Me, too," laughed Malcolm, "but he will get a reward – about the equivalent of fifty cents -- from the governor. Of course, in Mongol times, he would have been rewarded more lavishly. He probably would have been given a slave girl."

"Always the spoils of war, eh?" said Nora.

As they watched, one of the soldiers ran out toward the horseman with a small leather pouch. "It will be full of tiny coins," Malcolm explained. "Not much for us, but perhaps more for him. Anyway, it is not the money but the honor that he will think counts."

Just as he was explaining, Malcolm looked around and saw standing just beside them a young Afghan in a Western suit.

"Why, hello Hafizullah. I didn't know you followed the *buzkashi*," said Malcolm.

"*Salam*," replied the young man, looking carefully around himself as though he expected the riders to fall upon them.

"Let me introduce you to Nora Adams. She is...ah..." He paused as though trying to recall Nora's official title, her 'cover.' Then, he recovered, going on, "She is the second secretary of the commercial office at the American embassy."

"Nora, this is Hafizullah. Hafez for short. Hafez has recently come back from America. He was a Fulbright scholar at the University of Colorado. Are you getting readjusted to life in Kabul?" Malcolm smiled at Hafizullah. "Of course, it's quite a jolt. I remember how it was for me, coming out of college."

"Well, yes, I guess so, I mean, coming back," replied Hafizullah somewhat hesitantly. "Of course, it is very different. I mean over there, in school, life was so easy, so different. I had a lot of fun. The girls were so pretty, you know, and everyone was very nice to me. But, of course, they didn't know anything about me. No one had ever heard of Afghanistan. No one could even say my name. Sometimes, they just called me "Joe." They thought I must be a Mexican or perhaps an Egyptian. That was about all they knew about the world, just those two countries. I spent a lot of my time, explaining."

"So that was a fair trade," laughed Malcolm. "They taught you engineering and you taught them geography."

"I guess so," he hesitated. "Anyway, it is all over with now."

"So what are you doing now? You haven't come over to the Embassy to see us since you got back."

Hafizullah looked around again and edged closer to Malcolm. "You know, there are a lot of people here who don't like foreigners, Americans and Russians now and the British in the old days. And they are very suspicious of those of us who have gone abroad to study with any of them. I feel it every day."

"Well, I guess you will just have to put up with that. Maybe, being an engineer now, they will like what you can do for your country."

"You sound like one of my professors. But it is not that easy."

"Nothing ever is," smiled Nora, joining the conversation for the first time.

Hafizullah look closely at her but said nothing. It was clear that meeting one more foreigner was for him an extra burden. And, avoiding her, he turned to Malcolm, "funny...when I called the Embassy to ask for the Commercial section, the operator told me that there was only one person there and he had been reassigned."

Nora blushed while Malcolm jumped in to change the subject. "So tell us, what is your biggest problem in settling in?"

"To be honest," Hafizullah started out, "it is corruption. I mean there has always been some...a lot, in fact...but now there is more money and more to gain.

"The truth is that I have been offered a share too. After all, things here are governed by family ties. Not like America. So my uncles and my cousins are willing to help me...willing, in fact, to use me to get more for the family. Do you know what I mean?"

"Well, yes, every country faces that problem. It is not easy to handle. I don't have any advice. But where is the worst, do you find?"

"I don't know if it is the worst, but the customs is where I work. And my Mother's brother is one of the senior men. So he pushes the choice jobs over to me when he can. But I feel kinda funny about it.

"There are other problems. I can't talk about them...particularly to you...everyone is very suspicious. I've gotten suspicious too. We all think about spies all the time. And we don't trust one another either."

Nora winced and sat down again on her cushion, pretending to examine the contents of her handbag.

Looking down at her and then glancing around at the other nearby Afghans, Hafizullah almost whispered, "Well, nice to see you." Then in a much louder voice, as though to make sure he was overheard this time, he continued, "It was a good accident meeting you. Maybe we can get together again soon." With that he turned and quickly walked away.

When he was out of hearing, Nora sighed, "Wow, that was very uncomfortable! I hope I didn't screw up your contact with him. I feel like a leper."

"It couldn't be helped. And you weren't even wearing your leper's bell. Let's not worry about it. But, you should remember the old Afghan saying about foreigners."

"About foreigners or about my kind?"

"To the Afghans, there is not much difference."

"So what's the saying?"

Malcolm laughed, "It is from the old days of the British invasions and the Great Game. It goes like this: 'The first Englishman comes to hunt. The second Englishman comes to draw maps. The third Englishman leads an army. So it is better to shoot the first Englishman.'

"I am just glad you are a woman. The secret police – the ones Hafizullah was glancing around to see if they were watching him – would probably never believe that you were…that you were…how shall I put it, here to draw maps. I am just glad that your colleague Jack was not here too.

Nora didn't reply but just shook her head.

Malcolm went on, "now that everyone has cleared out around us and nothing out here can be bugged, tell me about Jack. I have never exchanged more than a 'good morning' with him. But, you must know him quite well. What kind of a fellow is he, anyway? He is a real loner, I guess."

Nora thought for a few seconds, nodding her head and looking off in the distance. Then she took a deep breath and spoke. "You would be surprised that I really do not know him very well either. But, I'm sure you're right: he is pretty much a loner. I see him in the office, of course, but almost never out of the office. We aren't invited to Embassy functions, as you know, or at any other embassy. And, out of the office, he spends a lot of time, jogging by himself. In the few talks we manage – you know our bosses are obsessed with security and we have different clearances -- I have the impression that he is very much a 'black and white' person, not much subtlety in him. But, he is a determined professional at everything. He works very hard at everything he touches. He came out here already having studied Dari, but quickly threw himself into learning all the other languages. I understand – I can't follow it – that he is very good at that terrible language, Pashtu. I tried it and gave up. It is a jawbreaker. But Jack never would give up. I understand he even is learning the language or dialect of the Hazara people up in the Hindu Kush mountains."

"Sounds to me like a very lonely man," mused Malcolm.

"Probably. I don't think he spends a lot of time pondering man's fate," Nora agreed. "I have tried to penetrate his reserve, without much luck. He is a very private person. But, for the first time, we are being thrown together next weekend. We are going up to the north."

"What on Earth for?" laughed Malcolm. Don't tell me it is to buy carpets."

"As a matter of fact, it is," smiled Nora. "Don't ask me any more."

"Okay, I don't want to know more, but if your people can't come up with a better line than that, they ought to be fired."

THE BARRIER

"I DOUBT THAT WE FOOLED THAT OLD FOX," laughed Nora.

"Which 'old fox' do you mean?" Jack glanced quickly at her for just a second as his eyes roved back and forth from the narrow road to the temperature gage on the dashboard.

"Your old fox, old Abdul. I bet he would have given a year's salary to know where we were really going. I can hear him now – 'Jack Beg...where are you *really* going? Not somewhere dangerous, I hope. Please be careful. The countryside here is very dangerous and the mountains are worse. Please let me help you. Let me go with...' she mimicked his voice, pleading and whining.

"He's a wily old bird," Jack replied. "But he never would have talked like that. He would have died before he would beg. He is as proud as an eagle, a real Afghan. And, we wouldn't have fooled him very much. He saw our sleeping bags, jackets and the Jerry cans of gas we put in the Jeep. He would have known we weren't going down toward Pakistan. But he would never have asked outright. After all, he's been with us – me and my fore bearers, so to speak, for generations. I am sure he must know, or at least guess, pretty much what we do. But don't read too much into his 'inscrutable Oriental" looks. He's just a good Pathan servant. No more. I mean, I like him and all that, but let's not go Kipling over him."

"Okay, but Kipling was often more than somewhat right. And, anyway, it's more fun in Kipling." Nora yawned and gazed out of the window. "Let's talk about something more beautiful. I know you can't look around while you

33

are avoiding potholes in the road so I will act like your eyes.

"Looking back over my shoulder, as you turn to your right around this curve, I can almost see Pakistan. The plains down there are a muddy brown streaked with yellow where the sun has already caught the hills. And off to the east…" Then, lulled by the swaying of the Jeep as it rounded each curve, she fell silent, and, glancing quickly at her, Jack saw that she had dozed off.

Jack also struggled to stay awake. The road was demanding and that helped, but he wished Nora would play her part in keeping him alert. Without exactly meaning to, he swung the car more than he needed to avoid a rock in the middle of the road. That woke up Nora, which he guiltily admitted to himself he had meant to do. And, coming out of what must have been a dream, Nora shook her head and abruptly turned to him, saying, "are you ever lonely?"

"Well that's a revival," laughed Jack. "I thought you would never wake up. Fat lot of company you are! But, what on Earth brought that up? Aren't you?"

Nora rolled down the window, letting in the chill mountain air and stretched. After what seemed a minute, she shrugged, "I guess so. I like to think of myself as a liberated women, of course, but I admit I have a secret nesting instinct. I guess everyone, or at least every woman does. Perhaps being alone increases the desire for companions, children, you know, a house with a little patch of garden, even the PTA, Junior League, the whole bit. I wonder about that sometimes. I realize, of course, that I probably would feel trapped if I really got those things. But…well, I don't know. And anyway, this game of theirs isn't really, deep down and honest, isn't mine. And I don't imagine it is completely yours either. It makes our lives so, what is the right word, transitory."

"Yeah, we're always moving from pillar to post – or at least from post to post. Rather good, that, don't you think?" Jack laughed.

"I'm being serious, Jack," Nora frowned. "It's not only the moving, it's always being 'transitory,' It's what happens when we get there. I always feel such an outsider, you know, not being able to talk much with other people, not even with the other people in the Embassy. And I feel a bit like a leper when I am around them."

"They don't make it very easy, do they?"

"They certainly don't. Not even inviting us to the regular Embassy functions."

"Thank God for small favors. I would rather be whipped than having to make small talk with most of them. At the least, I would become an alcoholic surviving their receptions."

"Well, sure…I guess that's right, boring, boring, boring. But still…"

"It hurts?"

"Sort of…"

After a pause, Jack mused, "I know what you mean, and maybe it is just defensive of me, but I've worked out my own two-bit philosophy on loneliness. What to hear it?"

"How about the dollar, seventy five cent version?" laughed Nora. "We've got time. And, up here, we are all alone. How many Americans do you think ever get up here? Two? Three? I doubt that there are more. I only know of one other."

"You mean old Crownover, the road man from AID you got me talking to?"

"Yes, I thought you shared a love of the outdoors. So I set up a drink for you to get to know one another. I don' think he mentioned it, but I guess you know that Smith tried to recruit him?" Nora said. "I watched the first act in that play. I was there when our boss ushered him into the office. He looked for all the world like a spider in his web luring in the flies."

"Smith's secretary, Jane, my good friend who keeps me informed, told me a bit about the last act. Smith got turned down flat. She said he was furious. He doesn't like to lose. Thinks he is a master of the craft, which to be honest, he is. But this time, he felt maybe not outsmarted but certainly out-somethinged. I would loved to have heard that conversation!

"The master fisherman – I can't see him as the spider – trying to reel in his catch and then losing it."

"But you know the scene. You must have seen it before," Nora replied. "But you were about to reveal your answer to life's woes. I am dying to hear it."

"Don't be sarcastic and I will. What I mean...well, while you were dozing, I was thinking about our life and jobs. I agree with you that in some way we are not really part of it. I mean, for them, it is both a game and a profession. I am beginning to think that it is really not that, or at least may no longer be that, for me. Of course, they play to win and work hard to learn the craft – I did too. And not to brag, I was damn good at it. I always was top of my class during the training. I guess I was a sort of junior Smith. Like Smith, I had become a sort of professional athlete, a kind of intelligence gladiator, to mix my metaphors. That is Smith now and me before.

"But, something began a while ago...I don't know exactly how or when...it just sort of happened. I began to feel less and less a part of the game.

"And there is another funny – curious – wrinkle in this. The pros have a lot in common, no matter which team they are on or how hard they fight against one another. I guess that must have been true of the real gladiators too. They understand one another. Or at least they understand one another better than they do other people.

"Do you know what I am trying to say?"

"I think so," Nora replied and then asked, "But what made you think of all this now?"

"I don't know. Maybe it's just being up here and getting the perspective of these mountains. They really do make us look small, don't they? But I think it was partly set off by the short exchange I had with that Foreign Service stuffed shirt, Malcolm, at your house the other day."

"Don't be too hard on him. He is doing his job, like we are doing ours. He knows that if he keeps on the straight and narrow he probably will end up as an ambassador, which will never happen to us. And to give him credit, he really is trying to learn about the people here. You can't say that about many people in the Embassy. He took me to a buzkashi a week ago. I hated it, but he really got into the spirit of the thing."

"I can't imagine him mixing with all those smelly people," scoffed Jack.

"Well, be that as it may. I won't try to defend him, but let's get back to your thoughts on our predicament. Perhaps, you – we – work in a sort of void. Does that bother you?"

"I don't know. I don't think so, at least not all the time. Does it bother you?"

"No," Nora shook her head. "I don't think so. I take them as I find them. I don't like many of the Embassy types and would hate to go to their endless cocktail parties. But, I guess I am somewhere between them and you, emotionally I mean. I guess I really like the profession and try to be good at it, but I think there is more to life than it."

"For me, it used to be 'life.' It was not a game. I really never got a kick out of dealing with the opposition, even out of beating them. Of course, I don't know any of them, but I know a lot of our guys I feel uneasy around. And almost always I feel uneasy around our cousins, the Brits. Fact is, I feel uneasy around the Embassy types like your friend Malcolm. Hell, I seem to have lost touch with everyone. It's so hard to talk with anyone when so much of your life is hidden and so much of what you spend your time snooping into is important or interesting only because it is secret. Christ! I remember once reading a directive on how crucial it was to find out whether they – whoever 'they' were at the moment – used pins or paper clips on documents. Can you imagine a conversation with normal people about things like that? For Christ's sake, the poor bastards think that what we do is romantic and we won't share the gory details because it is all so wonderfully fascinating. And we can't talk. Even about the trivia. So where are we? Sorry for the diatribe!"

"Well, life is mostly about trivia," soothed Nora.

"Yeah, I know. Most of them don't have much to talk about either, promotion panels and precedence and the protocol of the minister-counselor's cocktail party and all that crap! But they seem to enjoy it. I guess I live alone too much," Jack shrugged.

Nora had been taken aback by the intensity of Jack's words. After a few minutes of silence, she replied, "I do too, Jack. I mean, live alone. I guess really everyone does, in a way, but, of course, it is worse for us."

"I hope so," sighed Jack. It would be terrible to think that everyone was so alone."

"Maybe," Nora continued, "the real question is where your particular 'alone' is. I wonder if we have…I don't think we have…the same one. Mine, or at least a lot of mine is just make-believe. Daydreams. Talk about trivia!"

"Don't run yourself down, dear Nora. My Mother used to say that there are plenty of other people who will do that job for you. Think of your daydreams as a sort of flywheel that enables us to keep going, despite the trivia. For me, it isn't the daydreams, although there is that too, but rather the occasional missions – like this one."

"I thought we were instructed not to talk about that," Nora shot back.

"Yes, you're right. Anyway, I really don't understand it and could not tell you very much."

"You can't be serious or else you are lying through your teeth," Nora laughed.

"Well, you're right. No talking about that. So let me tell you a silly tale of my youth."

"Humor is always welcome."

"It isn't exactly humor, but it makes a point I was trying to say about aloneness. It taught me that aloneness is not just the result of being alone – and certainly not 'alone' in the way we are talking about – it's knowing that you are."

"I don't follow. What do you mean?" Nora looked puzzled.

"My story. You see when I was still a student in college and had already been interviewed for this job – work, profession, trade, sport or whatever we decide to call it – anyway I had finished the preliminaries but was not yet inducted, I decided I would do something I could not do again, visit the dangerous haunts of the enemy, before the gates slammed shut behind me. I sort of felt then more like it was a priesthood than a job and so I would be taking vows with no more flirting with the devil and no visits to the land of sin and damnation. So I signed up for a college tour. I didn't see a lot and don't remember much of what I saw, but I will never forget one minute or maybe one hour in Leningrad. Nothing really happened. After all, I was just a green kid. But I got a special feeling of being alone that must have been like what someone feels at a conversion. It was terribly exciting. I felt like I was invisible, apart, somehow higher, more aware, more special than anyone around me."

"I know what that feels like," agreed Nora. "It's the other end of loneliness. It's very special. And almost everyone tries to find it, I guess. I must be what people feel when they join the Church or The Party. Or maybe even just by living in a neighborhood and getting married. But I haven't met many who have really found it."

"Specially in marriage," said Jack.

"I wouldn't know about that. Are you still bitter about it?"

"A bit, I suppose," sighed Jack, "but that is another conversation. What I mean is that being a spy – we might as well call it that. Being a spy is to make a lifestyle of being alone – really to make a virtue of it. Instead of being depressed or frightened at walking down that Leningrad Street, watching everyone hurry about their affairs and thinking 'where can I hide,' I was exhilarated. I *knew*. They didn't. I wasn't alone. They were. I was above them all. There was an almost physical sense of it.

"Sometimes, of course, it can be terrifying. You feel like you are printed in another color, set off from everything around, terribly obvious. You think to yourself, 'Christ! Everyone can see me.' And, in a funny way, you want them to try, to know it's you, to see how special you are. But, they can't. Only you can. And, I think, that is what gives you the feeling of being the ultimate insider. Everyone else is flawed, blind. You alone can see. You know.

"I'm sure all this is old hat to you, but you asked for it."

"I did, indeed. I have had some of those feelings myself. Say, by the way, did you ever read Kim Philby's book?"

"Yeah, there's some of that in the book. I don't know how much he realized it. I guess he must have. He was maybe the greatest spy of all time and he lasted so long. All the stories about his getting drunk make me suspicious. And we know that he hinted to many people that he was a spy. I think he wanted to test to see if they could see. And he must have gotten his kicks out of finding out that they couldn't. Even the counterintelligence chief of the CIA was his pal, almost his cover. He was the ultimate test and Philby won. He was the only one who *knew*."

Nora started to speak and then paused. After a moment, she said, "You know, I always had the feeling that he tried to escape by getting drunk."

Jack shook his head. "No, I don't think so. The liquor was only a dodge. He was a real pro. He got his kicks by flirting, skating close to the edge, as close as he could without falling off. He must have been on a constant high, I'd guess."

"And to hide it all so long from the Agency and British Intelligence! Incredible performance." Nora shook her head. "I wonder how many others have hidden it. A sort of life-long high…"

"Yeah, that is the real payoff. I guess that feeling of seeing and hearing more is what makes it so much more fun to deal with our own kind. Even with the opposition, like Philby did. Two carpenters can really talk about wood! But with us – and you and I are part of 'us' at least this far – it's being able to see hidden things, being able to read the signs."

"But, I understand from what reading I have done in psychology," Nora replied, "everyone needs to find some way to let down. Liquor might also have been that for Philby. Love affairs too. I hear he had quite a few. And to use your analogy, even the carpenter has to sometime lay down his tools."

"Well I guess we all try, but it is harder for us. The carpenter can drink a few beers with the boys, make love to his wife – or someone else's – and dream about buying a farm. But how the hell do you retire from this game?"

"I guess that's another interpretation of my daydreaming," rejoined Nora. "But Philby? Do you suppose he ever *wanted* to retire? And what about our good friend Thomas Worthington Smith? Do you suppose he dreams about reentering Memphis society? 'What did you do *over there*, Tom. Were you in banking? Did it take you long to learn Spanish? And did they have a good golf course…'

"Memphis will be the acid test. I don't see him passing it. He'll never do well in the Rotary Club. He'll never feel comfortable with insurance men like my Father. And he will keep on avoiding journalists like the plague. Everyone will just seem superficial – 'intelligence blind,' as you put it -- to Smith. He will always be reading more into casual conversations than they could imagine."

"You're making my point," Jack laughed. Our game is like heroin. Once addicted, you're hooked. It's too strong."

"Right out of a Gothic novel," sighed Nora.

Again they both fell silent, each plunging down the dark alleys of his own thoughts. Then, as they rounded a particularly steep bend, they came to a narrow defile between massive cliffs. Across the road angled a long metal boom, like a fallen telegraph pole. Signs in Dari, English and Russian warned the driver to stop or be shot.

Jack already had the Jeep in second gear to cope with the last steep incline. Taking his foot off the gas pedal, he allowed the mountain to bring the car to a halt just before the barrier. But he left the engine running because the temperature gage showed that the radiator, overtaxed by the long climb and the thin mountain air, was near boiling. Anyway, just as in Kabul, he reckoned, the guards would raise the barrier when they saw the green diplomatic license plates on the car. So they would be stopped only for a minute or so until the guards woke up and put down their tea glasses.

While he waited for this to happen, he ran his eyes over the sparse scene. Next to the boom was a windowless gray stone building that, he guessed, served as a combination guardhouse, bedroom for the commander and jail. Two scruffy Afghan soldiers sat idly on a faded carpet, by a spindly bush, drinking tea. They paid no attention to the Jeep. Annoyed, Jack honked his horn.

The soldiers turned and gazed indifferently at the car. Languorously, one put down his tea glass, stretched and scratched the back of his neck. Only then did he shamble over toward the car. But just before he got there, he saw the green diplomatic license plate. Seeing it jolted him as though an electric shock had hit him: he jerked upright and saluted. Then still saluting, he dashed back to the hut. Although the soldier had not made a sound, his comrade, watching the scene, dropped his tea glass and jumped to his feet, hitching up his trousers and buttoning the collar of his burlap-like tunic as he rose. No sooner had he affected this martial stance than the first soldier emerged from the low doorway of the cabin, cradling a Kalashnikov sub-machinegun in his arms. Now properly decked out, both soldiers managed a parade-like attention.

They were just in time because right after them, also hastily buttoning up his somewhat more fashionable tunic, came the commanding officer. With an exaggerated version of parade-ground precision, he walked around to Jack's side of the jeep, saluted, bent over to see into the window and then, in halting English, obviously rehearsed for just such an occasion, said he would be honored if Jack and his lady would join him for tea.

This invitation caught Jack in the dilemma common to Westerners in Asian lands: how to be polite but to maintain that aloof stance which, all westerners believe, the native would interpret as power. Also, squinting at the waning sun, Jack wanted to use the remaining daylight to find the "jumping off place" – the place designated in his instructions when he must begin his mission – before the mountain shadows obscured it. So, without getting out of the car, he declined the invitation with as much flourish as he could muster in a combination of Dari and English.

By his fourth or fifth refusal, it had become clear that the officer's invitation was motivated by more than politeness. The invitation to tea was really a mantle covering an order to provide information. It had to be accepted. But, of course, the officer would not be so crude, especially before this august figure in the car with the green diplomatic plates, as to demand

43

or even to ask them to stop, but he too was caught in a dilemma: he could not let them pass without filing a report. So finally he managed: "Surely you will honor me for just the few minutes it requires to sip tea in my humble headquarters."

Of course he would! Reluctantly, Jack got out.

"Would the lady also join them?" The officer invited.

"Of course, the lady would be delighted," Jack responded but left unsaid, "if she must."

All this was conveyed in phrases of infinite delicacy and formality in the language each affected to compliment the other, Jack's Dari and the officer's English."

Nora was suitably demure, affecting an Oriental modesty that Kipling would have approved, but which she did not feel, she alighted as the second soldier, now also burdened with his Kalashnikov, opened the door for her.

Glancing at them, between unctuous phrases of welcome and gratitude for hospitality, Jack wondered if the poor fellows would have to stand at attention all the while as they sipped tea. But it was quickly clear that the officer regarded them less as guards than as his cook and washer. Curtly, he sent them running to fetch water, a pot and glasses. Then with belabored dignity, he turned to escort Nora to the rug recently vacated by the soldiers, and, spreading his arms in welcome, he invited them to sit.

Knowing the rules, Jack and Nora kicked off their shoes and stepped onto the *kelim*. Faded and dirty it was, but symbolically, it was the officer's "tea garden," and they respected it out of politeness. The officer did precisely the opposite. As though anxious to show his Western or modern liberation, which such a traditional gesture might compromise, he stepped onto the rug without removing his heavy boots.

A long exchange then began in the traditional style. "You are most welcome," began the officer in halting English. The questions and answers were inane but were calculated both to the pass the time while the tea was prepared and to open a polite exchange. Done in the elaborate Persian manner, thrust and parry could go on for hours without either party revealing anything of significance – or danger.

"How are you?"

"Well, praise God."

"Are you well?"

"God is merciful."

"Is your health good?"

"Yes, thanks to God."

"Was your trip from Kabul pleasant?"

"All trips in your beautiful country are happy."

"Do affairs go well in Kabul?"

"Ah, yes, all is well in Kabul."

And on and on. In the Persian, the vocabulary of asking and answering is almost infinite so that what in English is repetitious in Persian is poetic. The effect is like the splash of water in a Persian garden fountain, slow, soothing, pleasant. Nothing personal or specific and certainly nothing to do with the real matter under consideration, "why are you and this woman up here anyway?"

At last tea arrived. The soldier who brought it had trouble holding the bent tin tray level enough to prevent the china pot from falling off, keeping his machinegun from pointing too often at the officer or the guests, and saluting all more or less at the same time. He was not helped by having to balance on his extra large and untied boots. And the officer, seeing catastrophe in the soldier's next step, muttered a vicious curse, grabbed the

45

tray and contemptuously waved him away. Then putting the tray on the *kilim* he poured a small amount in each glass, swilled it around to wash it. Next, filling each glass half full of sugar, he topped it off with more tea. It was an Afghan rite that at that very moment must have been repeated thousands of time all over the country. In its different way, the tea ceremony was the equivalent of the litany of question and answer. Tea replaced conversation as the glasses were refilled time after time.

Tea and conversation both exhausted, Jack senses that the time had come when he could leave. The officer could not hold them longer. The liturgy of polite society had been honored; now, to make them stay, the officer would have to raise the stakes, risk insult and drop his mask. Jack decided to test. Would the officer dare? Lazily he rose to his feet, pulling Nora to hers and with exaggerated politeness began to thank the officer for his generous hospitality. He stepped off the rug and put on his shoes. Then, starting toward the car, he mimicked the Afghan manner, bowing and urging the officer to visit him in Kabul.

Panic dilated the officer's eyes. 'How could he stop them? Those green diplomatic license plates. Diplomats. Immunity. Was he an ambassador? From which great power? A whispered complaint to a high official – whom this foreign gentleman surely saw every day – and his career would be ruined. Even an official letter of complaint! Would they go that far? 'But the alternative hell yawned before him too: 'He must file some sort of report. What if he did not and they were robbed or kidnapped or murdered. Prison would be the mildest of possible punishments. It had happened before. God forbid! Why didn't such people, foreigners, just stay home? What was there for them up here on this Godforsaken mountain anyway? He must try again.' So, seizing Jack's hand and in the softest of tones, he implored, "Please honored sir, tell me what I must say in the report."

Jack played his part. Looking grandly over his shoulder, down the long road to the capital, where his good friend the King must now be reflecting with gratitude over their last heart-to-heart conversation, Jack said, in an even lower, more confidential voice, "camping. Camping near Kunduz. To buy a *kelim* from the nomads for the American president."

Relieved to hear almost any answer, no matter how unlikely, the officer bowed low, "Ah, thank you. Thank you. A thousand times welcome to my humble post. When next you come, I will slaughter a lamb and we will feast together. You shall not pass here again without staying with me."

Jack smiled grimly, thinking how much he hoped that he would not have to accept that invitation.

But as he slammed the car door behind Nora, the officer again repeated, "You shall not pass here again without staying with me."

Jack started the engine and engaged the gears on the now-cool engine. As they pulled away, he translated the last bits of the conversation to Nora and said, without joy, "I don't relish the idea of trying to get by here again. I hope Smith has this covered."

Nora scowled, "Of course he must have it covered. How else can you get back? This is the only way over the mountains."

"Oh, of course, Smith must have a plan." Jack went on. "It's just that I won't have those beautiful green license plates and I wouldn't like to test Afghan hospitality on their wrong side of their law. Like being found hidden in the back of a trader's truck. Don't kid yourself, those fellows look like hobos, but they are tough and ruthless. Like the Afghan cowboys, the *chapandazs*, you like to talk about. These mountains are their natural element. I sure wouldn't like to test them…"

"Don't talk like that, Jack," Nora shot back. "It's silly! You told me that Smith is going to have you picked up in Kunduz and that you'll be back in Kabul the day after I get there. You're just getting a kick out of being melodramatic – like you told me you did in Leningrad when only you knew.

47

Like all men. You actually love the game, don't you?"

But Nora's face would have given her away if Jack could have taken his eyes off the road. She was worried. 'The whole mission didn't make sense. It violated all the trade-craft she had been taught. Why two obvious Americans? Why not local agents? Why way up here, so obvious? What was Jack supposed to do anyway? As a foreigner, he would be immediately spotted. And why such a silly cover story? With Kabul full of rugs, why would anyone drive up here to buy one?' Even to her, not knowing all the details admittedly, the plan seemed full of holes, gaps so large that even a novice in operations could hardly have made them. And whatever else he was, Smith was no novice.

Then there was the barrier. How could Jack get to Kunduz? He had to pass this way. And that barrier was real. To try to cover her thoughts, Nora began to read aloud from the guide book she found in the glove compartment, "Just to the West of the road…the giant statues of the Buddha, carved from the rock face, before the arrival of Alexander the Great in 324 B. C., tower over a hundred feet over the traveler…

THE RENDEZVOUS

JACK AWOKE WITH A START. The dial on his watch gleamed greenly. Rubbing his eyes, he made out that it was 4:00 AM. The stars were fading into a pale opalescent sky. As he slid out of the sleeping bag, a cool breeze caressed his naked body. After carefully surveying the still-dark campsite, he paused and looked down at Nora. He was sure that she was awake but she pretended to be asleep. He was glad. It seemed better that way. No goodbyes. And, anyway, he thought, he now had no time for goodbyes.

Despite his talk about disillusionment with the service, Jack felt elated. He thought he could almost hear the adrenalin coursing through his body, but he smiled to himself deciding it was really just the cold wind blowing down the mountains. Still, as he felt his muscles tense, he liked the sensation. How much better than sitting at a desk in Kabul. Or Cleveland!

'But, still,' the nagging thought came back to him, 'it all made no sense, no matter how many times he had run it through his mind. Everything he had been taught in those endless lessons back in Langley and down on the training grounds seemed to be violated by what he had been told. And even more by what he was not told. The mission seemed so unlikely. Why, for heaven sakes, use an American when a local could have done it so much less conspicuously. And the planning! It almost seemed as though there was no planning. Instead of carefully rehearsing each move, he was given almost no guidance. And what he was told sounded so amateurish. Granted, he realized he did not know the whole plan, but still…'

Then, snapping out of his reverie, he took a deep breath of the freezing air. Choking down a cough, he stretched his arms and twisted from side to side, bent his knees and flexed his back. His muscles felt stiff but tense. He liked the sensation. It seemed to clear his mind. All that jogging was paying off.

With his little routine finished and as silently as possible, he tiptoed on bare feet across the cold gravel to the Jeep. Easing the handle down he opened the door. When it creaked, he glanced back at Nora. Her sleeping bag was zipped up and she had not moved. He turned back to the Jeep. On the seat in front of him, was his gear. What there was of it! The night before, he had laid out the few things he had been allowed to bring so he could make a quick start in the early dawn. Once again, as in the argument with Smith back in Kabul, he puzzled over the spartan selection — no field glasses, no compass, no weapon to defend himself even from wild dogs. Astonishingly, Smith had insisted on checking him out just before they drove away. Just a flashlight and even that he had virtually smuggled. He shrugged. *They* had their reasons as usual, he thought ruefully. It seems a set-up for failure, but he would do the best he could…despite them.

Feeling the wet surface of the jeep, he was glad he had put his clothes and shoes in the car. At least he would not start out soaked with dew.

Leaning against the Jeep, he pulled on his trousers and shirt, then he turned and sat down behind the wheel to slip on his socks. He smoothed them carefully onto his feet. As a hiker and jogger, he knew that feet were the most important part of his preparation. He laced his boots and tied them with a double knot.

What he could do, he ruefully thought, he did well. But he had little to work with. His pockets were empty and he had no backpack. But he had nothing to put in them, even a canteen. Or even a chocolate bar. He felt his jacket pockets for the large dark handkerchief he had remembered to bring – Smith didn't notice that. Nor had Smith seen his pocketknife. No keys, not even any money. But, curiously, Smith insisted he take his passport, even checked twice that he had. How silly, no foreigner ever traveled even around

Kabul without his passport. He shook his head in silent anger. How stupid not to have…"oh well," he muttered half aloud, 'ours not to reason why…'"

His preparations had taken just a minute or two. Finished with them, he checked the ignition to make sure that he had left the key. Fearing to make a noise, he pushed the door as tightly as possible without closing it. Then he stepped back and looked over the car, nudging the tires with his toe to be sure that they had not gone flat in the night. He thought with satisfaction that he had topped up the gas tank from one of the Jerry cans and had parked the car facing down hill. At least in the little ways, he had done what he could to protect Nora. She had had done her job, providing a sort of cover for him. She was a great girl, he thought, and he was fond of her, but, more, he didn't want to risk her blowing the whole mission if she got stuck here on top of the mountain. Then the question arose again, did she know more of the mission than he did. But he decided as he had each time he thought of it that Smith would never have told her more than she needed to know. Shaking his head, he silently laughed: what a lot of mistakes that "need to know" rule caused. Anyway, she had no part in what would follow. At least, unless someone's security people began to ask questions.

Even if the battery was dead, he told her the night before, she could coast to a start. She was a good driver, at least on the Kabul streets. And driving down would not be difficult. All she had to do was to rejoin the road which was more or less at the bottom of the hill, drive into Kunduz and turn the car over to a part-time employee of the mission. In the briefing, the only one they had together, Smith said the driver would take her straight to the airport where a seat was reserved for her on an Afghan Airlines plane to Kabul. Trying to put a joke into those bare instructions, Smith had quipped, "How did our British cousins say it, 'a piece of cake."

Satisfied with his inspection, Jack looked back at Nora and soundlessly blew her a goodbye – or good luck — kiss. Then, looking around the ground by the Jeep as well as he could in the pale starlight to be sure that he had dropped nothing, he muttered under his breath, "nothing much to drop…

Stupid sons of bitches." With that he was off.

Opposite the gentle slope by which he had crested this hill, to the northeast, by the gray half-light of the false dawn, Jack could barely make out what appeared to be a deep, rock strewn valley. Imposing upon the little he could really see what he had learned from the map and U-2 photographs, he knew that it led toward the junction of Russia and China. Flexing his still cold legs and rotating his shoulders, he set off briskly along the ridge toward what looked like a path down into the valley. At first the going was easy. By the time the first blood-red glow had capped the murky eastern mountains, Jack was striding down the barren hillside.

Far below him, still shrouded in a blue- black shadow, he could make out – or imagine — the road that was his destination.

Slipping and sliding on the loose gravel and sand, he was glad not to have the leisure to think. It was hard enough just to avoid twisting an ankle. Where he could, he cut across the wide bends of the sheep trail to save time, now running, now jumping, sometimes sliding, often falling on the loose gravel and stones, but always keeping an eye on a small point of light, a pale flame, flickering far below.

That would be the bonfire, he thought, at which the truck, *his* truck, would be stopped. In his mind's eye, he could already see the scene clearly: the driver and his gaunt, yellow-faced crew, huddled against the cold, in a tight circle around the fire, dressed in that universal uniform of the poor of Asia, cast-off British army great coats that were at least a generation old.

But there were newer ones, he laughed to himself, remembering his shock at seeing whole villages of Afghans dressed in surplus army uniforms. Many were still festooned with insignias of rank, some even with campaign ribbons on the chest. Imagine the consternation of the Soviet intelligence, he had then written in his diary, 'we have identified elements of the 82nd Airborne at Kunduz and the 1st Cavalry in Mazar-i Sharif...' Some entrepreneur must have bought those surplus clothes by the division issue. But, probably his drivers would be too poor to have these fancy new clothes. Anyway they were probably less warm than the British army issue. The Brits, after all, had been in these mountains long enough to fight three wars.

He looked down at the point of light. Tea...everyone on the roads was drinking tea at this hour. Glad to be awake, glad to be away from the cold gloom of night, glad to be off the hard ground, glad for warmth, even if it had to be poured in. He could almost hear the crackle of the fire and smell the acrid smoke from the mixture of dung, brush and diesel oil. No sight or smell in Afghanistan was more familiar or more evocative: little glasses, unwrapped from a cast-off head cloth and still crystalline from the unmelted sugar of yesterday's tea, scalding hot from today's tea, but held unflinchingly in the cup of the hand. "These Afghans feel no pain," Westerners cited it as proof that normal feelings here meant little. "Out here, life is cheap." They said.

Pausing to get the sand out of his sock before it got down into his boot, he thought back to the barrier that had stopped them on the drive up from Kabul the day before. For him, the memory was vivid.

When they got stopped at the checkpoint, he was glad they had at least been allowed to use an embassy car with diplomatic license plates. The checkpoint seemed almost a joke to Nora. Even before they got out of the car, Nora had laughed about the slovenly little detail of soldiers who hardly bothered to get up. When the soldiers had just gazed indifferently in the direction of the car, Nora had snickered, "must be high on hash." When they at last came to life, one had almost tripped over his untied boots. Nora had burst out laughing, "Charlie Chaplin couldn't have done it better."

Jack had nodded. But he was not amused. He had heard enough stories about the brutality of the army. "The soldiers do look ridiculous," he had cautioned Nora, "like they hadn't had a good meal in a week. They're certainly scruffy and dirty, but don't let that fool you. One word from the officer and they would have shot me without a moment's thought with their Kalashnikovs. More likely even, they would have cut my throat with their daggers. Slowly. And with relish."

When they got back in the car and drove off, he commented, "Don't be fooled by appearances. They are tough. And brutal. It's all very well, sitting here behind those green license plates, but for anyone out here, walking and on his own...well, that would be a different story. But don't worry, they would have been more gentle with you. Women's rights. Of course, they could not have left you alive as a witness. But it would have been quicker, kinder..."

Nora just flinched. And didn't reply.

Jack had laughed, but he could not get out of his mind the officer's "invitation" -- "You shall not pass by here again without staying with me." Grimly he was thinking how much he hoped he would not have to accept that invitation. But, then, he reflected, Nora had been right. Better not to dwell on what was, after all, just speculation. Anyway, he couldn't afford to dwell on that conversation. The path was too rough and it was still dark. Just to prove the point, he stumbled over a dust-covered rock and went flying into a pit of sand and gravel, skinning his left hand as he landed and filling his shoes with sand. "Shit," he almost yelled out as he settled down to unlace his boot.

Picking himself up, he glanced nervously at the eastern skyline. Dawn was approaching. He had to hurry now. He had to be in place before the sunlight hit the valley.

But caution took told. Who would the men in that truck be? Who were they working for? How many would they be? What, really, did he know about them? Could he be running into a trap? Perhaps *his* group had been apprehended and replaced by the enemy. It had happened before. Often, during World War II when the Gestapo took the place of the underground reception party and even when Philby set up a KGB reception committee for the Agency's men wading ashore in Albania. It could happen. But there was no way to prepare for that. 'And anyway,' he reassured himself, 'at least on issues like that, Smith was a real professional, with years of successful work behind him. Almost a legend in the service. Infuriating, no doubt, but no fool.... Still...'

Then he shrugged. 'How silly we all are about these poor nomads. Poor bastards, they're just cold and hungry. Carrying me along is just another way to earn a meal. Hunkered down in the tattered finery of a forgotten army, each man would be staring vacantly into the fire. It was one thing for romantics with full bellies read their stares as speculating on the mysteries of man's fate. Wonderful parlor games, of course, but hunger and cold were very different.'

Preoccupied momentarily with these thoughts, Jack almost tripped again. Reality drove philosophy out of his mind.

Then, almost before he realized it, he was only a few hundred strides away from the campfire. Abruptly, the land had leveled toward the road, and his mind, freed from the task of staying upright, turned toward the second task, how to make contact with the truck and its crew.

His instructions on this had been very clear, in fact, they were the clearest part of his whole brief: the truck, the only one he was to approach, would appear at first sight to be just like any other. It would be as covered with gaudy designs and slogans as the tattooed body of a sailor. But, above all these it would sport a plain pale blue panel. Blue, Smith had said, was not a common color for Afghan artists and yet it would not be too noticeable. "Remember, the panel will be plain blue without a trace of writing proclaiming the 'Unity of God' or the 'Wonders of His Will,' so it will be virtually unique...And visible from a long way off."

"Visible from a long way off, my ass!" Jack muttered. "I can hardly see the damn truck. How will I ever be able to see that blue band until I am practically next to it at high noon? Why couldn't they have picked some intelligent signal, like lighting two camp fires or putting up a small flag?" Or, of course, it would have been so simple, he thought again, as he had argued with Smith, to let him carry a small pair of field glasses.

Smith's answer, like his answer on the compass and the pistol was just "no..." amplified, for politeness sake, to "you won't need it."

Crazy business, Jack thought as he did lying awake nights before the mission.

Now, more worried about being seen than falling, Jack bent over and crept forward across the open ground. He would have to get very close in the wasting dark, lie down and wait for more light. Then, suddenly, he froze. Suppose they had guard dogs! Guard dogs, he knew, were common among the nomads and were legendary for their ferociousness. Worse than wolves, for being accustomed to men, they were bred to be killers. He had heard enough terrifying stories about that danger: Afghan guard dogs were more dangerous than lions or African wild dogs. Worse, even, than men. He wet his finger to see if there was any breeze that might carry his smell toward the camp. Gratefully, he knew from the cool he felt on his finger that he was down wind. His scent would carry away from the truck.

Back in Kabul, Smith had spoken rather grandly of 'lying up' nearby. He should 'lie up' until he had checked the truck panel. To go to the wrong truck would abort the whole mission since any other driver would immediately report him to the police, anxious for a reward and terrified of the punishment that would come if he did not.

"Lie up." Jack had mocked silently to himself. It was the sort of verbal cover desk men loved to use for what they didn't want to say. Used to hide simple things like flopping down in the dust and staying still was a joke. Like the other two-bit expressions it had become a habit. You didn't obliterate a village; you carried out a surgical strike. You didn't murder; you terminated with prejudice. Romance again. How they all loved it! Tigers lie up by their kill, but Jack wasn't feeling very tiger-like right then.

Beyond the guard dogs and the frightened men, he wasn't happy at the prospect of being interrogated by the Afghan security police who might not be too impressed by the niceties of diplomatic immunity. "Way up here" by the Soviet and Chinese frontiers, where smuggling was a way of life and death, security police probably would not even know what diplomatic immunity was.

"Why," he asked himself, for the thousandth time, was Smith so absolutely determined to use an identified American officer for this mission? It seemed so unnecessarily obvious. You didn't even do that for simple jobs in Kabul. You used a cutout, an Afghan who could be disowned if caught and who, in any event, would be far less likely to be caught. He understood Smith's reply but, especially way out here and right now, it seemed even less convincing than when he heard it from Smith's lips.

"And, God Almighty! Talk about a flimsy cover story! A camping trip with his girlfriend. Two young Americans out for a lark up by the Soviet frontier! Out to buy a rug from the nomads. For God's sake! How could Smith or the people back in Langley think that would wash? Afghans were not stupid. Anyway, it was so unnecessary. He could think of any one of several local contacts, agents with whom he had been working for months, who could have done the job without any fanfare or danger.

Danger, that had been the red herring: once that word came into the con- versation, he could not reason with Smith since whatever he said made him sound like he was trying to protect his own skin. Sure, he wasn't looking for a commendation for bravery, particularly posthumously, but it wasn't really his skin that worried him, it was just that it all seemed so irregular, so unnecessary, so obvious.

But Smith had seized on his use of the word 'danger' and threw it in his face. He repeated it time after time in their exchanges even when Jack didn't and then, having set up a straw man, knocked it down. "The worst that can happen, Farnsworth" — Jack noticed that suddenly he was not Jack but Farnsworth to Smith – "is embarrassment, embarrassment for the Embassy. The Afghans would never hurt an American or any foreigner. Particularly not one with diplomatic status. They have been taught by generations of dealing with the Great Powers not to play too rough. No, their game is to encourage the foreign agents to have at one another so as to leave the Afghans alone. You don't need to worry.

"But, I warn you," he had continued sternly, "don't get caught. Both you and I will wish the Afghans had got us instead of the Ambassador. He is at the end of his career and isn't going to let anyone put a blemish on his clean record. He would boil us in oil."

As annoyed as he was, Jack had had to laugh at that image: Smith in his best Brooks Brothers suit standing like a naughty school boy getting dressed down by the irate ambassador — and not being able to tell him the truth. "You see, Mr. Ambassador, one of our men, unauthorized of course, on a camping trip with his girlfriend up by the frontier...hiding behind a rock...yes sir, he was...no sir, I was not...well, I didn't think...you see, Mr. Ambassador...yes, of course, I know about the President's directive, that you are the chief of the whole mission, including the Agency personnel, but I didn't think you wanted to know about <u>all</u> the things we did...well, now, of course, I understand, but before...well, I realize...but...yes, sir, yes, of course."

It would be almost worth getting caught for that, he smiled, afraid to laugh.

The minutes passed. His eyes caught and held the truck. Nothing but the outline was clear even so close. He crept closer. About fifty paces from the truck, he found a small outcrop of rock at the base of which a scraggly bush desperately fought for life. Moving cautiously lest he dislodge a rock or trip and fall, he settled down to wait for just the bare minimum of light to be sure about the truck markings.

As he settled down, he reached out with his left hand to break off a twig that exactly lined up with that top panel. His right hand automatically went down to steady his body. With a sudden jerk, he pulled his hand back. Something else was 'lying up' beside him. It was all he could do to keep from jumping up. What if it was a snake? Vipers were said to be common in this area, and this was the right season for them. Vipers, he knew, are silent. They give no warning. Sometimes, it is said, the victim doesn't even feel their bite. Just a little pinprick and then nothing to worry about...he could almost feel the snake slithering along beside him, crawling up his pants leg. Cautiously he twisted and looked down where his hand had been, just in time to see a small lizard scurry out of the bush. It stopped, craned its head and looked up at him. 'My turf, not yours,' he imagined it thinking.

There it was again. His turf, not mine. Exactly. That was the nub of the problem: why someone so obviously alien had been put in this silly position? A lot of good his Eastern Turkish language skills were now. Oh sure, they could dress him up like a hippie, but even a hippie would look a little foolish hiding behind a rock up here on the Soviet frontier. Anyway, none of the hippies – "world travelers" they were called in Kabul — ever came up north. The hash was cheaper in the south where they could find banks and an American Express office to draw money from home. To people living in the little villages near Kunduz, struggling with all the diseases of the Earth, bilharzia, dysentery, you name it, near the brink of starvation, even the hippies seemed rich and privileged, exotic and obvious despite their affecting local dress, so Jack would stick out of the landscape like a mountain. He might as well be in cowboy clothes swinging a lasso from a white horse.

Faster than he realized, the light crept into the valley. He must not move now. How did the Muslims determine the legal beginning of day, he mused. It was when you could distinguish a white from a black thread? It was at least that light now. Every minute it was getting brighter.

Daylight was now flooding into the valley. With startling clarity, each rock, each miserable, dwarfed, spindly bush leapt forth as though etched on the desolate scene. But, he realized, as clear as each outline was, colors were still indistinct, drained, bloodless. This was the impossible time: if he waited even a few more minutes he would certainly be seen but, for the life of him, he could not be sure about that panel. He strained his eyes toward it. Then, almost without turning his head, he surveyed the road. Good thing he did.

Far down the valley, he could make out a cloud of dust rising as another truck inched its way toward him. Before it could get close, he would have to move...or vanish. Squinting toward the truck panel, he realized, this time without too much doubt, that it was blue, devoid of writing. It *was* the truck.

Jumping quickly to his feet, he hailed the men by the fire. "*Salaam*," he called the standard greeting in Dari. He had been told to use that greeting because it would not be expected. He, and the truckers, would have been more at home in Turkic. That was their native tongue and for his Soviet work, his specialty. "*Salaam*," he repeated urgently. It didn't seem to work. Either they were too taken aback by this apparition which arose from nowhere virtually amongst them or something was wrong. He glanced from them to the truck panel and back again.

Silently, without getting up, they twisted toward him, staring but with no hint of emotion. Behind those expressionless masks for which the Mongols are famous, they might have been examining a piece of cloth in the bazaar. "*Khoda hafez*," Jack called out. Not a regular greeting, it was part of his signal. But it should have come after he got a reply. Silence. Just stares. Once more, "*Khoda hafez*." He glanced at the approaching plume of dust and then strode forward, covering the distance before the men, still stiff from the night cold, could get to their feet. Instinctively, they pulled apart their great coats the faster to get at their weapons. Jack ignored the gesture and, walking up to the oldest man, held out his hand. He suddenly realized the primitive meaning of that gesture, to show that he had no weapon in it.

The old man, that would be Qol Khan, he desperately hoped, eyed him suspiciously for a moment and then, bowing slightly, said "*khoda hafez.*" A second later, in halting English, he said, "you come afar."

At the words, Jack took a deep breath, relaxing slightly. "Far is near for some," he replied in English, as the instructions had said he must.

"Then, quickly, into the truck," the old man said urgently in Turkic, pointing toward the plume of dust down the road.

Without another word, Jack put his foot on the iron platform, cluttered with extra Jerry cans of diesel fuel and a grease-stained tool box, and hoisted himself up to the high bed of the truck. As he rose, he eyed once more the telltale blue band around the top. It was there. It was his truck. He was safe. Then he plunged into the murky, foul interior.

Right after him, two of Qol Khan's team leapt in. Speechless, since they probably knew neither Turkic or Dari, they signaled him to lie down. Jack looked with revulsion at the piles of untanned and still bloody sheepskins at his feet. The two men squatted and patted the skins. Finally, failing to get his message across, one of them hit Jack sharply on the leg and with the flat of his hand patted the skins once again. The other peered out of the tent flap and, turning around toward Jack, pointed out the flap and drew a finger across his throat.

Jack lay down.

Immediately, the two men began to toss the skins of freshly killed sheep over him. The smell was overpowering and made him gag. The stench of the wet wool, "green" skins and blood was blended with diesel fuel, urine, sweaty clothes and what must have been vomit. Vomit of some previous passenger. That thought made him try to struggle upright. He opened his mouth to protest, but words would not come. Who would listen anyway? His discomfort was the least of their problems. If he were caught, he might be sent away with a slap on the wrist, but they would be shot...or worse, much, much worse. And they knew it. He was not then an ally, even if a friend of their British or American patrons. He was a bomb, ready to explode in their midst. And they were going to make sure that bomb was not likely to be found, even if they killed him in the process. The best way was to bury him as deeply as possible under material so foul that no inspector would care to dig too deeply into its stench.

Almost suffocated, Jack sank into the miasma. When he breathed, he wished he had not. The effluvium seemed almost a solid thing, crawling into his lungs like a slug, wet and hairy. He tried to breathe only in short, shallow gasps, but after a few was forced, like a drowning man, to inhale normally again. It was an agony, made the worse by the contrast so fresh and recent with the sharp chill of the mountain air.

With great effort, under the crushing weight of the skins, with one of the Mongol boys probably sitting on top, he managed to pull his right arm forward and, like the little lizard he had seen under the bush, he burrowed a hole for his mouth and eyes toward the air. He gasped for air with the effort.

Then he thought, 'what if they decided to kill him?' It would be so easy. Just a hand pushed in among the pelts. He could almost feel the knife, probing his side for the rib cage, then slowly pushed home as he screamed a muted cry. They wouldn't even need a knife. They could just smother him — they almost had already, without even trying.

Or, how easy it would be to just sell him to the Russians. After all, in the old days, there was a lively traffic in human beings across this frontier. He had read stories of earlier travelers in these parts who had disappeared to rot in dungeons in Bukhara or Samarkand. The Agency would never protest.

'Disappeared on a camping trip, probably killed in an avalanche, Search discontinued...'

In fact, the Agency would probably deny ever having heard of him.

And the Russians. Ah, that would be different, he thought. "Now, once more, Mr. Farnsworth, what did you say you were doing on our frontier? Who were you in contact with in Russia? Names, Mr. Farnsworth, names if you don't want..."

These distant fantasies were suddenly crowded out by a nearer reality: flies. As the day had dawned, not only men and lizards but flies had come back to the ceaseless struggle for survival. And this stinking pen was their garden. Big green flies; in squadrons, they buzzed like hornets over the skins, gorging themselves on the rotting flesh and congealed blood. Finally, with unerring instinct, they found his air hole. Defenseless, with arms pinioned, and his whole body paralyzed, he watched one green fly advance relentlessly toward his eye. It was a monster in miniature — and miniature was the scale of his world: one tiny air hole from the feted hell around his inert, useless body. Reality was reduced to fly and eye. In that reality, the fly was enormous, magnified by the lens of his eye and given power by his incapacity. He could make out each hair, its twitching arms, and its unflinching eyes. Like a shark, it homed in on him.

At terrible cost, he sucked in a lung full of the stink and rot and blew out as hard as he could. The fly retreated but did not go away. Then, only a moment later, it advanced toward the inviting wet of his eye. He blew again. This time, it merely stopped. Half an inch away, with one eye closed, he could see it, like a great hairy monster, rubbing two of its legs together like a chef sharpening his carving knife. Then it moved onto his nose and crawled slowly up toward his eye. He blinked and tried to toss his head. But he couldn't move more than an inch. The fly paused. Then, satisfied, it moved on again, probing his shattered defenses. Carefully, it explored each eye, tasting the tears that had welled in the corners. Then, remorselessly, it crawled down and into his nose. He sneezed. The fly retreated. But a second later, it was back. Again he blew as hard as possible. This time it hardly paused. It knew...

Just then, he heard the grating scream of brakes and the choking rattle and gasps of a truck motor. That would be the other truck he had seen just down the road. With a shock, he realized that what had seemed hours of torture was mere minutes.

Greetings, slammed doors, and other muffled sounds were all but drowned by the nearer buzzing of the flies. Numbed and stifled, almost suffocated and terrorized, Jack wanted to scream for help. He now understood why prisoners talked. The worst of torments were often the most simple. The Chinese water torture was like the flies. Unhurried, unrelenting, inescapable. Mercifully, he drifted into a nightmare haze. All conception of time, even of life, left him. Then, with a thrill, he was jolted awake. The truck bed was convulsed as the ill-matched springs and missing cylinders rattled the chassis. The engine coughed and backfired, died and then, reluctantly, came to life.

The truck began to jolt its way toward…toward he knew not where.

PERCY

FADING IN AND OUT OF WAKEFULNESS, Jack was unsure whether the stifling heat and the cloying stench of the skins, the noxious fumes of the exhaust, or merely the lulling roll of the truck was drugging him. And, not knowing who it was perched on top of him, he feared, in his lucid periods, even to try to move or make a sound. He lost all sense of time. After what seemed an eternity, he awoke again. Then, as he could feel himself once more drifting into a black nothingness, his own private nirvana, he heard the motor change tone and the brakes engage with a greaseless high-pitched squeal. The swaying, pounding motion ceased. The throbbing motor fell silent. Still he did not, could not, move. The stop might be at a military checkpoint or a *chai-khana*, where the truckers stop to gossip, drink tea and get fuel. He waited, half smothered. Then, suddenly, the skins were ripped off his face. He gasped. The sudden flow of fresh air was like a bucket of cold water. Pale as it was, the fading evening light hit his eyes like a flash of lightning.

Disoriented and feeling sick and weak, he took a few moments to focus. Gradually, he sat up and looked around him. Rubbing his eyes and shaking his head, he came fully awake. With a shock he perceived that it must be just after sunset. Stunned, he realized that he had been buried in that vat of sheepskins for twelve hours at least.

Peering at him without expression were three Mongol faces. One, more grizzled than the others, he recognized as Qol Khan. The old man's narrow yellow eyes, compressed to slits, were examining him minutely, unsmilingly, from only a few inches away. Suddenly to Jack he seemed the giant green fly, remorseless, calculating, predatory. Despite the heat, Jack shuddered.

"You sleep long," said Qol Khan slowly in English. It was not a question, but, as a comment, it was entirely neutral. Merely a fact, said without regard to the hearer. Jack decided it was better not to respond. "We nearly there. One more hour. Maybe two. You get ready. I slow truck. Maybe cannot stop. You jump when I hit." He banged his fist on the truck panel. "Okay." Again, not really a question. A statement, almost an order. The only question was whether or not the dazed man had completely understood what he must, what he would do.

Jack nodded and mumbled, "Okay."

Qol Khan looked undecided. He obviously wanted Jack out of that truck as soon as possible. Apparently, he feared that Jack might fall back asleep. So he turned and said something to one of the Mongol boys. Without a word, the boy climbed in beside Jack. Qol Khan's face disappeared, the canvas flap dropped back into place, and the boy settled down a few feet from Jack.

Facing one another in the canvas-filtered gloom of the truck, each grabbed hold of one of the metal sides to steady himself.

Then the motor rumbled and whined. The gears engaged and the truck lurched forward again. After what seemed an eternity, the motor died. Jack heard a door open and slam, some voices yelling and then the motor ticked over again. It coughed and spluttered. Then throbbed more deeply. 'No wonder,' he thought, 'they don't want to stop to let me out. Might get stalled at the scene of the crime.' Slowly at first and then, gathering speed, the truck bounced forward.

Feeling more secure, Jack disengaged the rest of his body from his fetid fur cave. He started to slip across the bounding floor toward the canvas flap, to get some fresh air, but his silent companion motioned him back. He realized that his guard was right. He should not look out in case the truck were being followed or observed. It was still too light. So, absentmindedly, he sat picking tufts of blood-clotted fur off of his pants and jacket as the minutes went blankly past. Looking up and catching the eyes of his companion, he pointed at his clothes and shrugged. No response. "Well, what the hell," he said aloud. Not a flicker of emotion. So, in Turkic, he said, "What time is it?" Silence. "Friendly fellow aren't you?" The Mongol merely sat but his eyes never left Jack's face. "I'll bet if I don't jump quick enough, you will just knife me and throw me out, won't you?" It was really not a question, as it was said in English, but, to Jack's astonishment, the man slowly nodded his head.

Silently, the two men swayed with the truck, occasionally falling against the sides or tailgate when it hit a pothole. Once more, Jack essayed to peer out the back flap. It was now pitch black outside so he figured that there was no danger of being seen. But the Mongol boy must have misinterpreted his move. Jack wasn't sure whether it was because they hit another pothole or because of what he was doing, but suddenly the Mongol was on top of him, holding him down in the fur again. They wrestled a moment; then the boy disengaged himself and resumed his passive stare. "Okay. I'll just sit," said Jack. "Anyway, it is dark outside now."

Jack felt for his watch. Just as he was about to look at the dial, he heard a pounding knock on the side of the cab door. Throwing back the flap, just a second before his companion could move, he took a hurried look out onto the road and, feeling a hand thrust roughly against his back, jumped into the darkness.

As he had been taught in paratroop training, he rolled as he hit the road. It was well that he did since Qol Khan had hardly slowed the truck. Then, still carried by the momentum of his jump, he scrambled as quickly as possible into a small gully on the north side of the road. He waited, head low, until the truck had disappeared. If it were being followed, the tail car was either very far away or had stopped. Jack waited until he had counted a thousand.

Nothing had moved. He heard no sound. Satisfied, he crouched and dusted himself off, as well as the fur and blood would allow, and felt his legs and sides. His arms and legs felt like warm Jello. He was certainly bruised, but he felt no sharp pain. Again he looked around warily and was relieved to see no lights or trace of movement. Cautiously, to keep below the skyline, he raised up, stretched and shook his arms. After the long hours of immobility, he realized he would need to get the circulation going again; so he flexed, bent from side to side, and then sat down and rubbed his legs methodically. It was not time wasted as he would need a few moments to accustom his eyes to the night and to take his bearings. He looked up. The sky was clear. That would be a help, he thought to himself, since he had no compass. The thought of a compass reminded him of equipment so, as he would have done in a night-time parachute jump, he thrust his hands into his nearly empty pockets. "You really won't need anything," Smith had said. "Just in and out. Be gone by dawn and back in Kabul before you could brush your teeth..." But training proved the stronger guide. It was easier to check what he did not have: no compass, no canteen...no canteen. Then he realized how thirsty he was. He had drunk nothing since he left Nora, a lifetime ago, before dawn.

He played a little game with himself trying to keep his mind off of his thirst. As he peered into the black night, he reflected on the contrasts of the land. There was no subtlety in Afghanistan. Blinding sunlight alternated with the blackest of nights; freezing cold with sweltering heat; lush, wet river bottoms with absolutely nude rock and sand. "Just like the people," he shook his head and chuckled, "warm and kind or clinically cold and indifferent to suffering." He remembered having once seen a man apparently kill another in a street fight in Kabul and simply turn and walk away, not even interested enough to find out if the other man was dead or just unconscious. Yet, on another occasion, on one of his long walks in the mountains in the south, he had happened upon a Kuchi nomad encampment. There, he had been treated with ruinous, truly appalling generosity by a family which, he also knew, would pay a fearsome price of hunger for their display of hospitality.

As the minutes passed, his thirst seemed to grow. 'I was a damn fool,' he thought, 'not to just smuggle a canteen.' But, he reflected, Smith had specifically ordered him to take only the items on the curiously detailed checklist. The word 'attribution' had been always on Smith's tongue. He did not, he said, want Jack to have things that could be attributed to the Station, but that was obviously foolish, Jack had pointed out, because, ultimately, his body was the final attribution to the Station or, at least, to the Embassy. But Smith refused to discuss it. It was as though he had been embarrassed. He had just shaken his head and walked away. "Strange, damned peculiar, not at all like Smith," Jack had said to himself again and again as he mulled over his task.

"Just makes no sense." But there it was. No compass, no weapon to defend himself even against wild dogs, no canteen.

Finally his thirst overcame his caution. Slowly he inched his way out of the little gully to listen. Far off to the north — he almost unconsciously checked the North Star again — he could hear the braying of sheep dogs. Under no circumstances could he afford to get near them or even up wind from them. And, anyway, he could not afford to wander off in that direction. He couldn't be sure how far away the Soviet frontier was. But wherever it was, the Chinese frontier would be further and more to the East. Leading up to it was the long tongue of Afghan territory known as the Wakhan Corridor. He remembered reading that the British had drawn it into their maps to separate Russia from China and India in the days of the Great Game. He wasn't quite sure where he was, but he figured that the actual frontier was probably not near. He realized, however, that formal frontiers were not much respected up here. The Afghans shot at shadows in the night and both the Russians and the Chinese ran patrols to keep the area clear of tribesmen, smugglers and spies.

But, as he listened, Jack was more nervous about the dogs than the patrols. He felt a shudder as the hair on his neck rose. The primordial memory, an instinctive fear of the beasts of the night, that all men share was reinforced by the stories he had read and heard of the shepherds' dogs. Big shaggy brutes, always near starvation, they were originally bred to defend their flocks against men and wolves. But, as tribes moved, some got left behind or ran away to become wild. No longer afraid of men, they moved in packs and were known to overwhelm isolated travelers, devouring their bodies, their clothes, even their shoes.

Panning his head slowly, like a radio direction finder, away from the dogs, Jack thought he could hear water running. With a shock he realized the sound came from the direction in which the truck had gone. East. That was away from the direction he was supposed to go for his rendezvous, but, since he had plenty of time, hours in fact, and he was by now obsessed with thirst, he thought he might risk the walk. He hesitated, knowing that Smith would not have approved, but thirst was the stronger counsel. So, taking as precise a fix as he could on the starlit road and a peculiar hump in the mountains, and keeping to low ground, Jack walked slowly and carefully parallel to the road toward the source of the noise.

Several times he caught himself on the edge of unseen gully which had been scooped out by the spring melting of the snows or scoured by the raging winds of winter. His eyes played tricks on him. But, from his paratrooper training, he had expected these problems and he carefully counted his steps, stopped often to listen and kept checking on his markers.

When he had gone about 500 paces, Jack was surprised to see a shadowy shape that, as he crept closer, gradually morphed into a small cabin. At first, he assumed that he had just been thinking about the cabin and formed a mental image which he imposed upon a tree or a small hill. No, his eyes were right, he decided; it *was* a cabin. But it should not be there. It should be back behind him. Down the road toward Kunduz, perhaps a mile back. But there couldn't be two shepherds' huts so close together way out here. He sank down to the ground, peering cautiously behind him and listened. Then he raised upright just enough to see the thing in front of him. Yes, without doubt it was a cabin. "That stupid Mongol bastard," he said silently to himself. "Put me out too soon. Scared. Couldn't wait to get rid of me. Just like the flight masters with paratrooper strings…always making them jump too soon so they could go home."

With a shock, he realized that if he had not been so thirsty, he would probably have missed the rendezvous entirely. He would have either gone off in the wrong direction or have spotted it too late when the dawn had come. Again he cursed Smith and the poor planning of the mission. It was as though they had *wanted* him to fail.

That was a numbing thought, and he tried to dismiss it from his mind. But it hung over him like the miasma of the rotting sheepskins. 'Could it possibly be that…' he started to think, but then his training and cool logic took over. It was just too sinister to think otherwise. He looked at his watch. Ten PM. Plenty of time. He wasn't due to make the pick up until midnight. Probably the fellow he was to meet was not yet there. Or, if he was already there, he must be at least as apprehensive as Jack. It wouldn't do — in fact, would be extremely dangerous — to surprise him by going to the cabin early. Anyway, prudence born of evasion training suggested that it would be a good idea to know the lay of the land. Whether this was the right cabin or not, he reasoned, it would be a good idea to know about it, just in case anyone was there. The old paratrooper reasserted himself.

So, cautiously, he kept on walking in short and rapid but silent relays past the cabin toward the sound of the water. At that altitude and at night, the sound was deceptive. He was surprised that he had heard it so far off when suddenly he came upon a tiny stream. It glistened like silver in the starlight. As he looked down he was grateful for the kindness of starlight; in the daylight, he realized, it would probably be green, covered with scum and full of God-knows-what filth. But, deeply thirsty and clotted with blood and hair and dust, he was grateful for its cool wetness. Squatting down, Jack washed his face, the back of his neck and then doused his hair. Pausing like a deer at a water hole to look around before each drink, he then scooped up the running water in his cupped hands and rinsed out his mouth, spat out the water and then, after a long and careful look around his horizon, he drank voraciously.

The icy water hit his chipped tooth and stung. Then, as it ran down his throat, it felt like a blow on the chest, almost freezing his windpipe and empty stomach. He gasped and stood upright, suddenly constricted in the chest. Then, after stifling a cough, he drank again. He took a deep breath. As his lungs swelled, his whole body seemed to come alive. He rubbed his hands together and ran his right hand up his left arm. The skin tingled. He ran his fingers through his hair, wetting it down around his temples.

How marvelous it was just to be alive and out from that stinking truck. He was exhilarated to be on his own, out in the wilds, far from all his daily chores. Here, he reflected, his life had been reduced to simple pleasures and simple fears. After his intense thirst, a drink of dirty water from the ditch was better than champagne. After all those hours of suffocation in the truck, to breathe the clean mountain air was sweeter than perfume. Just to stay alive, no longer taken for granted, was a pleasure beyond reckoning. 'Perhaps,' he thought, remembering something he had read about Buddhism, 'that is the final secret. Having too much is to have nothing.' The thought must have given him extra energy because he suddenly felt supremely happy and at peace with himself. As he looked up, Jack marveled again at the awesome night sky. The stars seemed almost within reach. He drank in the clean air, feeling that he was emptying his lungs of the carbon monoxide and stench of the rotting fur.

Before his eyes, the image of Nora lying in the sleeping bag returned. He felt responsible for her. How silly of Smith to have sent her north. "Talk about attribution!" He muttered. Everyone for a hundred miles around would know about her being up there. But she was in no danger. Afghans were good about that at least. He played out her scenario. She would have awakened just about the time he reached the Mongol truck. The sun would have hit her early on the hilltop. Its first rays would have been like the beam of a searchlight, probing for her eyes under the flap of the bag. He imagined her first turning away, trying to stay asleep, then sitting up, with the bag falling from her shoulders. She would look around carefully, cautious girl that he knew her to be. Then she would have quickly slipped into her clothes. Just a few minutes later, he imagined, she would have got the Jeep started and moved off. By now, he thought, she would probably be back in Kabul having a hot bath and...

The thought of a hot bath and clean sheets gripped his imagination for a few moments. Little pleasures. He must enjoy them more. 'Live every day as though it were the last...' Here, he was alone, relying only upon his own skills; he had been right, it was the other side of loneliness. Primordial instincts surged through his mind, and they too brought their satisfactions.

How would Smith have reacted to this? First, of course Jack smiled, Smith would have no feeling for Jack's emotions. And the image of Smith squatting down to drink out of that ditch was almost too much. But more germane to the issue at hand, Smith would never have violated his instructions. He would have moved off in the wrong direction no matter how thirsty he was. But, Jack ruefully admitted, Smith would have soon realized his mistake and corrected it. He would just have just shrugged at Jack's anger at the way the Mongols had dropped him off too early. He could almost hear Smith now. "Well, Jack, that is why we picked you. You're a clever fellow. You are well trained and we expected you to use your wits. If I had wanted a robot, I would have ordered one from the supply room. Anyway, it is all over. Well done. Now, forget about the problems. Every mission has them."

'Perhaps, but not quite so pat or so easy,' Jack thought. Could the Mongols have *purposefully* dropped him off at the wrong spot? Obviously, they would have done anything to keep him from being caught in their truck, but by dropping him off at the wrong place, they made it even more likely that he would be spotted. Maybe they were just scared, he hoped. But, maybe...

The worry…paranoia? About games within games, deceptions within deceptions, moles within security, double agents, all the things he associated with the British service when he had been in training came back to haunt him. "Cousins", he said aloud.

"We owe them a lot," Smith had said. "They are the pioneers. After all, they had been batting in the big league for generations. The Great Game, up here in the mountains, was their game."

But, in his encounters with the British, he found that behind their gentlemanly pose, they could be even more cold, more clinical than his masters in Langley. "And, if I were going to be sold down the river by anyone…" He started. "Oh, shit," he said aloud. "What an old woman I've become."

He slapped his face, as though to be sure he was fully awake. He knew from experience that at a certain stage of the operation, any operation, the adrenaline of doubt takes over. He remembered one time when he had to get into a closely guarded building. Following instructions, he had no sooner got past the guards than something happened that was not in the script: he came face to face with an attack dog. Maybe that is why now he was so worried about the nomads' sheep dogs. Involuntarily he shivered.

His mind raced ahead. Those truckers had deliberately thrown him out early and set him in the wrong direction so that he would miss the hut. 'Goddamn them. That must be it,' he thought. 'Dirty bastards, the Brits. Their bosses. Up to their usual double game. Probably, at least, wanted to keep us from getting the credit. Maybe they have their man out here to get the documents —and, of course, he realized, it must be about documents -- so they could make a trade. Wouldn't be the first time! Or, just maybe it is worse.

We thought they got rid of the Philby connection. But their whole service must be lousy with Philbys. He was the third man. But they had had a fourth…maybe a fifth and sixth. Would the tenth be far behind?'

"Philby." Jack was obsessed by the Philby operation. That was the word Smith had used, 'obsessed.' Nora had agreed. Even Nora. "Well, probably they were right. Philby must have embarrassed them a lot to force them into such a drastic purge. Their service almost ceased operations for a while." Still, he felt uneasy. "At best the Brits were from another country. And they still resented 'us' as upstarts. As one fellow in MI6, perhaps a bit tipsy, put it to him, like the Greeks resented the Romans." One never knew.

The wise man — the man who came back — always assumed that the operation was blown before he left. And…well, what he had seen so far gave him little confidence that this one was not.

Anger and fear spent by the flow of his thoughts and the growing awareness of how tired his body really was, Jack cooled down. An easier explanation thrust forward in his logical mind: 'The poor sons of bitches just wanted to get rid of the incriminating evidence so badly, they dropped me too soon. And, hell, I was glad to hear that bang on the door too. Maybe I jumped too soon. Maybe it was really my fault.'

Luckily he had found the cabin. That was the bottom line; that was what counted. How silly, he had often thought it was, reading about other operations in the Agency's in-house monthly digest, that some little hitch, some tiny accident or change had thrown off months of planning and the hard work of dozens of people. One slip and the whole show was over. Almost always, the most complex came down on the shoulders of just one man. That was when failures occurred: "'Pilot error' they call it in aviation. Well, it's not going to fail because of this man," he mumbled.

Then he shivered and stood up. Instinctively, he determined that he had better not get cramped in the cold and wet. Pulling back his jacket sleeve to look at his watch, Jack was surprised to see how little time had passed. It was still far too early to go to the cabin, but he could not afford to let his tired body take charge.

'That would be a fine show, wouldn't it,' he mused. 'Curse the Brits, damn the Mongols and then blow the whole show by falling asleep. Imagine waking at dawn! — Sorry, sir, I just passed out, exhausted you know.' Might just as well walk across the border and join the Reds for all the difference any excuse would make to the bosses in Langley. Both would send him to Siberia. He laughed silently but took the precaution of splashing more of the cold water on his face and neck. Then he took another drink. Maybe, he thought, the last one for a long time.

Hunkering down again, he wiped his mouth on his sleeve. Then, unable to resist, he looked back at his watch. It must have stopped, he thought: the hands seemed hardly to have moved since he last checked the time. He had to sit. It was not wise to wander around and he could not afford to surprise the man in the cabin before he was expected. The only sound was the trickle of the water. Again he looked at his watch. 10:55. The watch must be slow. He held it up to his ear to hear the steady faint ticking. He stared at it, trying to see the hands move. The faint light played tricks on his eyes.

He counted to a hundred. He said the alphabet and then said it backwards. P-Q-R-S always got mixed up backwards. Then, with time tricked again, he looked back at the watch. It was almost 10:58. The watch was working. It was Time itself that seemed not to move. It was no use. He could stand it no more.

Silently, he got to his feet to retrace his steps toward the cabin. Carefully, putting each foot out and lightly testing the ground, he moved almost without noise through the sand and gravel and around boulders and occasional tufts of weed. Gradually, the hut took shape out of the gloom. Finally, about a hundred paces away, he squatted down, facing it. He waited. No sign of life. No movement. No flicker of light. Nothing. Not a sound except for the yearning whisper of the wind playing with sand and rock. No spark, no scratch, no scrape of foot or hand or hoof. He turned slowly right into the wind and listened intently, not breathing. Only the distant howling of sheepdogs now almost indistinct in the wind. To the left, nothing. He twisted back to listen behind. Again, he strained, not breathing, almost stopping his heart, to listen. Again, only the gentle wind.

Reassured, he squarely faced the cabin. His instructions now seemed far less clear than they had in Kabul on how he was to actually make the contact, how he was to meet this man, 'Percy'. At least, he was no longer was sure. Had the instructions actually ever been clear? Suddenly, that thought surprised him. Normally, in a mission like this, every breath he took would be spelled out, 'you will do this at __ time...then that at __ time...then you will say __ .' But, at this most crucial time of all, contact with the courier, the instructions seemed curiously vague and brief. Was he going soft in the head? Had he missed a page in the briefing? Impossible? But, sitting in front of the cabin, expecting to walk in on a probably terrified and certainly armed man, it seemed as though Smith really didn't expect him to make the contact. Must have missed something, he thought. Go back to square one, his training had taught him. He rehearsed the mission again as he had read and reread it: "Jump off the truck and go back down the road toward Kunduz." (Well, he knew that part and the mistake. 'Damn Mongols', he thought.) "Locate the cabin." (He had.) "Go there at midnight and get the papers from the fellow you will call Percy."

But *How*? That was the immediate problem before him. He could not remember any specific instructions. What came next was *after* the pickup. Then, as though that somehow happened without his getting a bullet between the eyes, as Smith had briefed him, he was to "Proceed down the road toward Kunduz to a wide spot in the road, approximately 5 miles, where, at dawn, you will see the same truck drawn up. Even if for any reason you have not got the papers or the mission was aborted go up to it, after seeing the blue border, and rejoin Qol Khan. Don't worry if you see another truck or car there as we may wish to rush you back sooner if the way is clear

How easy Smith had made it sound. But if he were Percy, he would be damned edgy right now. How would he know who was coming in that door? What did Percy know about him? And who the hell was Percy anyway? If Percy had any sense, he would not even be in the cabin. He would have the cabin staked out, and be 'lying up' somewhere outside – in fact, just about where he, Jack, was now crouched, watching for whoever might come.

Percy would live longer like that, Jack reflected. Would this fellow — Chinese? Probably Russian, but maybe Mongol, Uzbek or Kirghiz — be a seasoned agent or a raw recruit. A seasoned case officer would know the risks and might use an expendable agent. But such a man, would he panic? With horror, Jack suddenly realized that his instructions had not even told him what language to use! But that might make the difference between an outstretched hand and a bullet. If he used Turkic, Percy might not understand and think him an Afghan security officer. But, if he used English? What then?

Chances were that 'Percy' would be Chinese or Russian. But if so, why had Smith stressed Jack's knowledge of Turkic. Jack knew not a word of Chinese and very little Russian. Anyway, the only logical reason for this spot was to be near the junction of Russia and China so the documents, whatever they were and wherever they came from, could be brought over the frontier. And, for the same reasons that Smith would not entrust the mission to a local, 'Percy' was unlikely to be from one of the borderland minorities. No, he probably would be Russian or Han Chinese. But why the hell hadn't they told him? It might have kept him from being shot at...or shot.

Another thought, another worry. Percy might not even be there. If 'they' had caught him and decided to find out who was at the end of the fishing line, that man would be primed to kill or at least incapacitate the courier. Jack. Smith would not let him carry any sort of weapon; so Jack could not defend himself. Even if it was Percy, he would be terrified. So Jack knew that he had better move cautiously, but what would be 'cautious' in these circumstances.

If he had any sense, Percy would be taking his own precautions. He would certainly know that the papers he had smuggled out were worth the lives of a thousand men. From what Smith had told Jack, they would blow the whole Chinese security service apart. As Smith put it, "those Chicom bastards will be purging one another until Hell won't have any more room... this would make the Philby affair look like a morning coffee break compared to a war." But was Smith telling him the truth. Not likely. Because if Jack got caught, he would be made to talk. So it was not likely that the papers were what Smith told him. Anyway, he was just a messenger boy. Whatever they were, he would not be able to read them or, even if he could read them, he could not understand what they meant. He didn't plan to try. What was that phrase, 'an enigma inside of a paradox,' or something like that.

Smith hadn't told him much. He expected that. Like everyone else, he lived by levels of clearance and in 'their' eyes, he had no need to know. So his attempt to understand met just a rebuff. 'Curious,' Jack had thought. 'Why would whoever wanted the Agency to get the papers go to the trouble -- and danger -- of putting them way the hell out here? Surely it would have been easier to hide them, if that was necessary, in Kabul or somewhere nearby. And even if Percy, whoever he might be, wanted to bargain and get a better price for them, he would be in a better position to bargain from some place where he could break off negotiations and get to a safe place. Out here, he would have no chance to hide. He would be a sitting duck! Either he was a fool or there was something Jack was not told.

It had seemed so illogical to him. But, when he questioned Smith, Smith frowned and came down very hard. "No, Jack. This is not your business. The Agency has a complete take on the process. Our colleagues know what they are doing. But, just to satisfy you, let me say that this is the first real break we have ever had there. If we can make the contact, it opens up the whole issue to us. To blow them...well, let's just let that drop. Anyway, it is not my decision to make. The folks at Langley want to leave their options open."

Jack had been puzzled. He realized that Smith had evaded his question – why way out here? -- But obviously Smith wasn't going to tell him any more. Presumably, or at least that was the best interpretation Jack could put on it, this 'Percy' had set his conditions, stupid though they seemed to Jack. That seemed to Jack to be the only reasonable interpretation he could put on the mission and on Smith's remark.

Whatever he had been told – could anyone have briefed him about Jack? How could they? Percy could hardly have been in contact with the Agency before or he would have made his deal already. So he probably knew only that someone would meet him to receive the papers or whatever he was bringing. But why would Percy hand them over? If he was selling them, he would be a fool not to get cash in advance. Of course, some deal may have been made to pay through a Swiss bank. But, Jack rationalized, if he were Percy he would want proof that the money was there. And Jack could not offer any proof. In fact, Jack really could not offer Percy anything. The only thing he could offer was the sight of his passport. Percy would certainly be suspicious of Jack. Even if he did not mistake him for a security officer – Russian, Chinese or Afghan, what difference would it make to him — he might well reflect that Jack himself could be a double agent. After all, that is what Percy was. So, the idea could not be far from his thoughts. Or, worse, if Jack had been caught and replaced by an Afghan, meeting him would be a one-way trip to the dungeons of Kabul for him. That is, unless the Afghans thought it better to trade him back to his own service. Then the really exquisite torture would begin. So, however nervous Jack was, it must be nothing compared to what Percy was feeling. Walking into that cabin would be just about as safe as crawling into a rattlesnake hole.

With this jumble of thoughts racing through his mind, he realized that the tension could only get worse the longer he sat and speculated. Better move on up.

Very slowly, like the hands on his watch, Jack moved, freezing every few paces to listen and search the limited horizon. His eyes ached from straining into the abyss of shadow. Tiny streams of sweat poured down the back of his neck. As the cool air passed over him, his body felt alternate surges of fever and a clammy cold. He now feared, more than anything, that he would sneeze. Luckily, he had remembered to bring along a dark handkerchief and with this, he dried his neck and face and then tied it over his nose and mouth like a highwayman.

Finally, after what seemed an eternity of short stages, he arrived at the blank, windowless wall of the cabin. Crouched down, he reached out his fingers and touched the rough surface. The cold stone was drenched with dew. Involuntarily, he jerked his hand back as though he had touched something dead and rotting.

Then, longer than at any of his stops, he paused to listen. His very heart stopped. Every fiber of his body became an ear, but only the wind and the ever-rustling sands rewarded his effort. Easing upright, he inched his way along the wall, ready to drop at the slightest sound or movement. One pace... two paces...three. Finally, his probing fingers found the door. Flattening himself against the wall, he whispered. "Percy" He waited. "Percy." A bit louder...so loud a whisper that his own voice made him jump. "Percy...are you in there?" Then, in Eastern Turkish, "Percy...are you here?" Nothing. Even the wind seemed to fall. It was dead quiet.

Jack bent more than moved slowly toward the door, knowing that in doing so, he would have to silhouette himself against the sky. Just before he turned into the doorway, he dropped to his knees. Absolutely silently, he pulled down the handkerchief, to make himself look less like a felon, and then, with his left hand, he reached into his jacket and pulled out a small flashlight. Steadying himself on the wall with his right hand, he pushed his left arm up the jam as high over his head as he could reach. The light from the flashlight, he figured, would attract any shot that might come from within. He tensed his muscles as for the start of a race and switched on the light.

The room jumped into blinding relief. For a moment, he could see nothing. Then, as his eyes adjusted, he glimpsed bare, rock walls supporting sagging wooden roof poles. Immediately switching off the light for fear of attracting attention, he rose to a half crouch and jumped inside the door to couch again. Again he risked the light.

Then he saw.

Almost at his feet, a man lay face down in a pool of blood. As shocked as he was, Jack ignored him and shined the light hurriedly over the rest of the room. Facing him, in the direction of the nearer man, slumped, nearly sitting against the wall, was another man.

"Jesus Christ!" Jack almost shouted despite his fear.

Quickly switching off the light again, he stepped back against the wall to listen at the door. He slowly counted 100. Then he took a small handful of sand and threw it to the end of the room. It rattled like shot against the stones. Again he counted and listened. There was no sound and no movement.

At least momentarily reassured, Jack switched on the light again, bent over the nearer man and lifted his arm. It was limp and, when he released it, it fell back into the dust. Just beyond the man's grasp lay a pistol. The man had not been dead long enough for his body to stiffen. Jack sprang across the room in a single bound. He turned halfway to the side so that the door was not behind him and reached out for the second man. Slowly, he lifted the man's chin. His neck was still warm. But, he too was dead. Jack stepped back to assess his body. It was contorted, slammed by a heavy blow of some sort, perhaps a shot, which had knocked him into a half sitting position against the wall. The way his head had fallen on his chest showed that he must have died slowly.

His hand still clutched an automatic pistol. Jack pried his fingers loose and recognized the gun as a 7. 65 mm Czech automatic. He checked the magazine. Only one shot had been fired.

The gun felt reassuringly solid in his hand. Percy, if this man was Percy, would make up for the failure of Smith.

Then, turning warily again toward the door, Jack reached into the man's jacket. He undid the button on the shirt and with his left hand, now free of the flashlight, he groped for the expected packet of papers. With his eyes on the door and steadying the automatic on his knee, he almost put his hand through a huge, gaping hole in the man's chest. He jerked his arm back. The blood was still sticky. He wiped his hand on the wall. It was all he could do to keep on searching. But he knew he must. There it was — a small plastic case fixed like a shoulder holster to the man's body. It was Percy. Clumsily, he tried to undo the holster. His hand, coated with blood and dust, slipped. At best, it would have been hard but with his mind on that door, he just couldn't manage the catch on the harness. He yanked. It wouldn't budge. He got up and quickly tiptoed back to the door, bent over to be near the sill and peered out, listening.

Temporarily reassured, he returned to the fallen man and putting the automatic in his pocket, he pulled out his pocketknife. Pausing again to listen, he opened the blade and began to cut the straps. His hand shook and, clumsily, he nicked the skin of the dead colleague, 'Percy.' Stupidly, he realized, he mumbled "sorry." The sticky, wet package fell into his hand as the now bloody knife slipped from his grip. Obviously, 'Percy' had bled to death. And very recently. He owed his life to Percy, he realized, since the other man would surely have shot him. 'He had slumped against the wall to wait for me,' thought Jack. "Poor bastard." He said, quite aloud. "Well, Percy, whoever you are, I owe you one. I promise get your papers where you wanted them to go…"

Better get out of there fast before he joined them. First, he would wipe off the blood. He took Percy's torn sleeve in his hand and tried to wipe off the plastic case, but it was no use. The blood had thickened enough that wiping just made a worse mess. With the physical strain and the emotional anxiety, the muscles in his leg were getting cramped, and he stood up to relieve them. As he did, he caught the reflection of headlights outside the cabin. He reached for his knife on the floor, but it was gone in the dust. No time to fool with it. In a bound, he was out the door, crouched over, and running hard...along the only certain way he knew, toward the little stream.

The truck motor wheezed louder and louder as the headlights swept down the road. Watching them and the cabin in one sweep of his eyes, Jack fell flat on the ground. As it drew abreast of the cabin, the truck slowed. Its gears screamed in protest, but it did not stop. It rolled on down the road toward Kunduz. Gradually, its headlights receded and then disappeared. Again utter darkness fell. Jack was alone.

LITTLE GAMES

WHEN THE DOOR ON old propeller-driven Ariana Airways DC3 opened and Nora looked down the ramp, she was astonished to see Malcolm standing there. Her jaunt to Kunduz was supposed to be secret, and although she and Malcolm had dated a few times, she had certainly not told him about it or how she would return. So her greeting was perfunctory and cool. "Why Malcolm, how sweet of you to come to meet me." She said, but her face betrayed her: what she really meant was how had he known of her plans?

He just smiled made some equally bland reply.

It was not until they got into his car that she asked what she really wanted to know. But first she checked. "Is your car clean?"

"Well, I have it washed from time to time…"

Nora wasn't amused. "Silly, I mean has it been checked for bugs…for listening devices?"

"Ah, that. Oh, yes, even on our side of the embassy, we take care of little problems like that?"

"Then, tell me," she demanded, "How did you know I was coming?"

What he replied horrified her. "I listen to a lot of people, and your 'camping trip' up by the Russian frontier did not exactly go unnoticed."

Lost in the thought of what that might mean for Jack, Nora was momentarily speechless. She shook her head as though trying to take his remark in and just gazed out of the window. Then in a rather lame attempt to change the subject, unwilling to say more, confused and trying not to be worried, she

85

tried to hide in a silly remark. "What an incredible city. Not beautiful by a long shot but full of jumbled sights and smells. Stark and dry, when you first look at it, but so full of color and contrast just beneath the surface..."

"'Teeming,' I believe is the accepted cliché for the Oriental city," Malcolm replied dryly, understanding what she was doing.

"I'm sorry. I was just far away, I guess."

"I understand. I won't pry. I really don't want to know any more about...about that. So let's..."

Just at that moment, his eye fell on a group of young American hippies walking down the street. He used the sight to help Nora recover her balance. "Oh, here come a group of the later-day Thoreaus," he laughed, "out looking for the latest versions of authentic antique flintlocks and daggers."

Grateful for the chance to bury her worries, she plunged into the gambit Malcolm had offered. But in her mind, she probed the guess that Malcolm's circle, whom she thought of as the bored and gossipy diplomats, speculation about Jack and her would be on every agenda. Jack's his real profession – and hers – were of course common knowledge. "Well, for them," she continued, pointing at the westerners, "even the fakes are exciting. I guess that is better than just going to supermarkets in Dayton or Dallas. They're just young rebels."

"I don't mind the rebellion, even a rebellion without a cause, but it annoys me that they have so little imagination." Glancing ahead, Malcolm tapped his driver on the shoulder to get him to slow down to avoid a peddler's cart.

"Well, it took some imagination to find their ways up here. Why do you think they came to Afghanistan, anyway?" Nora went on. She of course knew the answer he would give, but both were playing a game to avoid topics they didn't want to discuss.

"I think they like Afghanistan because, in a funny way, they can conform."

"Conform? That's a novel interpretation, *Doctor* Malcolm!"

"Well, try this on, then. Here in Afghanistan, there are twenty-six minorities. So the 'world travelers,' as I believe the current name is, can dress up in their fancy costumes, like overgrown children, look as bizarre as they want, shack-up with one another or all together, and still be, in Afghan terms, conventional."

"Wow! Quite a definition of 'conventional.' How do you get conventional out of that?"

"It's all in the line-up of the minorities. They just fall in line, somewhere between the Uzbeks and the Tajiks. To the Afghans, they have just become another minority. And, since each group dresses differently from the others, the hippies are just another group with their own customs and conventions…"

"Oh, come, how do you…"

"I would respect the really odd ones, if there were any. I mean, odd ones like the nineteenth century 'world' travelers. People like Richard Burton or Lady Hester Stanhope. Victorian odd balls. But I have yet to meet or even to hear of one of these intrepid explorers who has bothered to learn anything about the country. Or really about any other country for that matter. All the kids I have seen, or heard about from the consul, are just a lazy bunch of bums living off their parents because they can't hack it anywhere else. They just come out here and jump into make-believe …"

"Well, the game they're playing is at least not hurting anyone. I guess they are the most peaceful people in this country. And remember you couldn't say that about many of you Victorian 'odd balls.' A lot of them were certainly up to no good."

Unintentionally, she had allowed her secret worry to surface again. Which kind of oddball was *she*? She frowned. Malcolm's ploy had not worked. That conversation was leading in the wrong direction. Without much hope, she clumsily set out the cover story, knowing that Malcolm was far too intelligent to be drawn in. "It was so beautiful up in the mountains. We wanted to visit one of those quaint little villages, still unspoiled by modernization..." Then she fumbled but would not give up. "Jack and I don't have much in common but we both love mountain climbing, so when he asked me, I thought it would be fun. Sure, I admit it is in a rather dangerous area, but then we had an embassy car and...and of course we didn't stay long." Again a pause. As Malcolm realized, she was having a hard time with her story. "In fact we had a spat so I came home."

He first gave her no break, "In the car?"

"Yes, I drove the car into Kunduz. I left him out in the wilderness... He wanted to go on climbing so I don't know how Jack came home. We weren't speaking by then..."

Malcolm didn't reply. He just raised his eyebrows. It was too silly a story to even contemplate.

"Anyway," she lamely went on, "he's due to be transferred at the end of the month so it doesn't make any difference. Everyone will have to find something else to gossip about..."

Just at that moment, the car was forced to jerk to a stop by a pack of heavily laden donkeys and off to the side, in a vacant lot between buildings, Nora saw just what she was looking for, an escape from the conversation. It was a miniature carnival, a tiny street fair. Eagerly seizing on the distraction, Nora gestured toward it and said, "Oh, Malcolm, look, a street fair. What fun! Let's stop for a minute and watch."

Malcolm knew exactly what she was about but he too wanted to drop the dangerous conversation. So he leaned forward and tapped the Afghan driver on the shoulder and in a now official tone said, "Driver, stop at the end of this block and wait for us, if you will please."

The Afghan driver peered into the mirror for a moment, surprised at the new order since this was a poor area of the city which, as far as he knew, Embassy officers never visited, but when he saw Malcolm's nod in confirmation, he pulled over and stopped. Switching off the motor, he was about to get out to open Nora's door, but, not wanting to advertise further that they were foreign diplomats, she jumped out before he could. Then, pretending to be more excited than she really felt, she almost yelled back through the car window, "Oh hurry, Malcolm, what fun. I wish I had my camera. Please tell your driver not to get out. It makes me…us…look so foreign to be seen with him in his fancy uniform."

Malcolm put his hand on the driver's shoulder as, confused by Nora's breaking of the routine he had been taught, he was about to open his door.

"Don't bother. We'll just wander off by ourselves. Just wait here for us, please."

They turned into a small alley that opened off the main road. There, a few paces ahead of them, an old man who appeared to be a Gypsy had set up a crude, homemade merry-go-round. As they walked closer, they could see that it was fashioned from four rough wooden poles mounted on the trunk of a dead poplar tree. The beams were tied together to form an "X" and hanging by chains from the four ends were carved and stuffed replicas, not much more than little wooden seats ornamented with doll heads, representing the horses of the characteristic Afghan *buzkashi*. And riding on each doll was a child, playing mounted warrior, the *chapandaz*. Their padded jackets were torn and stained in the same way they had seen on the real *chapandazs*, and the little boys affected cast-off *karakul* fur caps just like real *chapandazs*; as they furiously lashed their mounts toward the distant goal, the wheel slowly creaked round and round.

"Malcolm, it just like the real *buzkashi* you took me to last week, remember?" whispered Nora. "I like this one better."

"Well, it certainly is a lot less dangerous. I'll give you that." Malcolm laughed. "They were killers. Just like Genghis Khan's Mongols, only they were armed with whips instead of swords. And now we see even the little kids are hard at work learning how..."

"Oh, don't exaggerate. They're just having a good time."

"Well, I promise you. You'll see the effects. When they're grown up, they won't be much fun to run into...especially out in the mountains."

Nora frowned and turned away. One more trail had led back to Jack somewhere out in the mountains. To cover up, she pointed to the unsmiling old man, bent with age and with a stoic, bored look on his cavernous face. "Why, he's just like the governor we saw running the *buzkashi*," she laughed.

"I'm glad the governor didn't hear that. In the old days, he would've had you boiled in oil and lopped off this old man's head to boot. Now, we would have a real stink of a diplomatic incident, offending Afghan pride and self-respect. A gypsy no less!" Malcolm laughed.

As they watched, the gypsy ducked under the nearest beam and gave it a push, sending the creaking wheel spinning. The young 'horsemen' flailed away with the rags they pretended were whips and squealed with delight. As each overhead beam came into reach, the old man ducked slightly and gave it another push, sending the young horsemen lunging round and round.

"They sure start training'em early, don't they," laughed Malcolm.

"Oh, look at the face of that Gypsy, Malcolm," Nora pointed. "The whole history of his people is written there. Gosh! I'm sure he has seen more than I would care to know about."

"Such a romantic, you are." Malcolm scoffed. "The poor old bastard has probably just got indigestion from eating too much *pilaw.*"

Nora gave him a dirty look, but then rushed over to the other side of the small courtyard where a throng of children stood, bright eyed, fidgeting and impatiently waiting to become *chapandazs* themselves. Malcolm followed, making a show of sniffing the air and gesturing toward his nose, said, "Whew... when I come down to the bazaar, I sometimes wonder what it would be like if we could still really smell, I mean like dogs or leopards can. What do you suppose we are getting now, besides the obvious, of course"?

Shrugging her shoulders, Nora replied, "It's so rich and wonderful, isn't it, Malcolm? So..."

"Not exactly the words *I* would have picked!" He interjected.

"...pungent. Well, for a start, there's cardamom. Someone must be cooking rice or making tea."

Malcolm pretended to hold his nose, laughing. "Then there's sweat. These poor devils never take off their clothes. They just let them rot off. And these little urchins," he gestured toward the would-be *chapandazs*, "well, they aren't old enough yet to qualify for their second set."

Ignoring his comment, Nora wet her finger and stuck it up in the air, then faced upwind. "Ah, someone is burning incense. I love incense. Don't you? But that must be an Indian. I didn't think Afghans..."

"Thank God for that public minded soul, Indian though he may be! It helps a bit with the urine."

"Malcolm, be positive! What a prig you turned out to be."

"Well, I do rather like the smell of leather. Do you see the tanner's shop anywhere?"

"Leather it is you like, eh? Well, you should like that, my refined diplomat. After all, the French perfume companies sell a synthetic imitation called 'Russian leather' for about fifty bucks a half ounce. Of course, you would like the synthetic better. It's more refined…but you're right. It must be somewhere nearby. I can almost taste it. Let's go see."

"You mean, my intrepid friend, let's go smell!"

A few steps brought them to a small bend in the alley. Sure enough, plastered against a whitewashed wall were dozens of freshly tanned skins. Some were quite small, perhaps rabbit, while others appeared to be whole camels. Most were still wet, sweating out their salts and oils. Just beyond, perched in a dark cubbyhole, sat an old Uzbek cobbler, beating and sewing the thin leather strips into the supple knee boots worn by the *chapandazs*.

"Gosh, imagine how much some "Cossack" dancer in Paris nightclubs would pay for a pair of those."

"You lost me," Malcolm replied dryly. "I think it would be lots of fun to wrap yourself in one of those skins. Look at the flies. The cobbler doesn't need to scrape them. The flies will do the job for him. We'd better beat a retreat before they turn on us! They're real carnivores!"

They had run into a blind end to the alley so doubling back, they noticed that the noise of the merry-go-round *buzkashi* had stopped. The street was dead quiet. Just behind Nora, Malcolm gave a start and cried out, "Hey, stop that!" He whirled around, suspecting a pickpocket, only to find himself face-to-face with the weathered, almost tanned old Gypsy who had gently touched his arm.

"*Bifarma*," bowed the old man with elaborate courtesy, pointing his scarecrow-like arm toward the now empty merry-go-round.

"Oh, Malcolm! He's inviting us to ride," Nora blurted with delight.

"We must. What fun! I haven't been on a merry-go-round since I was a child."

At once the crowd of small boys began to clap, just like the audience at the real *buzkashi*. On a whim, Nora reached into the group and grabbed the hand of a short, thin little boy, one who looked to be only about six or seven years old. He was decked out in a tattered brown gown that dragged on the ground. In terror, fearing that she would have him beaten or arrested, the boy tried to jerk away, wriggling like a fish on a line. Nora was shocked to see the panic in his eyes, but could not say anything to reassure him. She didn't even know what language he spoke, but she was afraid that if she let him go there would be a small riot as all the children fled.

Then she thought with real fright, even the local newspaper might pick up the story, "American diplomats attack Afghan children." 'Just what I needed,' she thought, 'to finish my secret reentry into Kabul! That was all Jack – oh, my God, Jack,' her face darkened. 'All Jack needed.'

Suddenly brought out of these thoughts, she realized that the little boy was howling like a trapped animal, but he was too small to break loose. The boy squirmed and pulled, but she held firm. Once she had begun, she knew she had to go on. There was no other way to avoid an ugly scene. Just in time, and on a whim, she squatted to his level, and whispered the same word as the old Gypsy, *"bifarma"* and pointing to the merry-go-round.

At last he understood and, relieved and delighted, he ran over to a garish lavender-colored wooden horse and leapt proudly upon its back. He had broken the ice so when Nora turned back and seized another boy from among the now many volunteers, he rushed to jump aboard. But as the contraption swayed he plunged right over the top, a ball of turban, robe and sandals, into the dust, as the other children went to paroxysms of giggles and taunts. The now shamefaced *"chapandaz,"* his dignity in shreds, just managed to clamber upon the swaying horse.

"Now your turn," she yelled at Malcolm and grabbed his hand, drawing him toward one of the two remaining dolls.

Trapped, Malcolm tried to rise to the occasion. Playing the game for the children, he made a great show of terror as the children jeered, clapped and squealed. Never had they dreamed of seeing a Western man playing at their game with them. But, more than a bit worried, he stage-whispered to Nora, "I'll get even with you! What if the ambassador hears about his pride-and-joy riding merry-go-rounds and playing the *chapandaz?* Especially, being set up by the likes of you!"

But, almost engulfed by the children, he let himself be dragged and pushed toward the third horse. Then, as he swung a leg over the doll, the whole contraption swayed ominously on the poplar pole. The two terrified boys shot up in the air as Malcolm thudded to the ground.

As the worried Gypsy rushed forward to save his contraption, Nora mounted the fourth horse. It wasn't easy, wearing a skirt, but she managed to throw a leg over the seat and flailed away at the "horse" with her imaginary whip. "See, Malcolm, I have become a Victorian lady, riding sidesaddle… just like Lady Hester Stanhope or Gertrude Bell." Then, bending out of the saddle, she pretended to pick up the body of the dead calf.

As the urchins screamed their approval, the Gypsy gave a reluctant push. For him, it was not a game. For him, the merry-go-round was the source of his daily bread. To his dismay, the poles groaned under the strain of the unequal weights as the new foursome lurched forward.

But, clapping madly, the children paid no attention to him. They surged forward and then pretended to run away in terror as Nora sped toward them. Magically, for a few moments, it *was buzkashi.*

The spell lasted only a few minutes. Wisely, Nora decided to stop before they broke the merry-go-round. So she signaled to the Gypsy and, as the merry-go-round slowed, she jumped off and gravely bowed to the Gypsy, like the winning *chapandaz* to the governor. Then she turned and bowed to the spectators. Gravely, loving the charade, the children bowed to her. They were transfixed, expectant; for a moment she was not a foreigner or a woman, but the hero of the alley, the winning *chapandaz*.

So far it had been fun, but she was unsure what to do next. The air was electric and she realized that they couldn't just walk away. The children would follow them, shouting and screaming. That would surely bring out the police. Then the poor children would probably be beaten and word would spread even to the Foreign Office. The Ambassador would be called in and Malcolm would be in serious trouble.

Fortunately, the commotion had attracted a gaily clad Tajik vendor of sweetmeats. Nora almost grabbed him as she had the little boy and in her best kitchen Dari said, "sweets for all the *chapandazs!*"

She was playing out in miniature the climax to the *buzkashi* where the winning *chapandaz* treats his fellows with his winnings. But, for the children, it was no longer a game. The spell was broken and, no longer *chapandazs*, no longer spectators at *buzkashi*, they were once again hungry, poor, street-wise urchins. Reality took over. In a second, they had surged forward to the gaily painted cart, pushing and shoving one another like hungry little wolves over a fresh kill. Scuffles broke out, and a small boy was thrown against the tin tray of cakes on the top of the cart. With a crash, it fell to the ground and the cakes were scattered into the dust. In the scramble, the merry-go-round and the *buzkashi* were forgotten. Honey cakes, the tray itself and the children rolled together in the mad jumble.

The furious Tajik vendor began to scream and beat the children back from his precious cart. He had no illusions: the cart was the source of his livelihood while the children were just so many hungry urchins. Then, as Nora watched in horror, a policeman suddenly appeared from nowhere and began to lay into the children with a stinging bamboo pole, sending them screaming and crying, dashing for cover like rabbits, In a few second, the little alley was empty except for the five adults, the pathetic horse dolls and the now ruined sweetmeats.

As Nora stood speechless, the policeman, dropping his now useless bam- boo, saluted Malcolm, bowed to Nora and mumbled in Dari, "I apologize for this rudeness. My people have been impolite. I shall punish these dirty children, you may be sure. *Hamdu'lila*, all is now safe. Shall I conduct you to your official car?" He had obviously seen the diplomatic license plates and was frightened at the report this powerful foreigner would make to the senior officials. Perhaps his name would be mentioned. "I seek refuge in God," he muttered, but *Hamdu'lila*, they were safe, he thought to himself; he would get those filthy brats later.

Sadly, Nora took out her purse, extracted a role of bills and divided them between the Gypsy and the Tajik. Shaking her head, she sighed to Malcolm, "Does everything in this country have to turn to violence? Gosh, I know how those NGO people must feel when their valiant aid efforts go astray."

Malcolm was no help. He just shrugged and, taking her arm, he pushed rather than guided her down the alley toward the car. As they passed the shop vendors, and seeing the policeman, they pretended to have seen or heard nothing. None of them even looked up. They knew that the police would come and questions would be asked and they would be made to answer. For them, it had been a bad day.

As they got in the car, Nora was close to tears. "Gosh, Malcolm, I am so ashamed. I really scored on that one, didn't I? Americans really know how to blow ourselves out of the water, don't we? It was sort of like AID in miniature, great at the beginning...and then..."

Reaching over to pat her arm, Malcolm didn't try to answer, but just said, "maybe we could use a good stiff drink. Your place or mine?"

The driver answered for them. In a few minutes, the car pulled up in front of Nora's house.

Outside the house, the street was littered with the droppings of animals and the refuse of people, scraps of cloth, bits of newspaper, an occasional rusting tin can, pieces of bone and even a rotting sheep skin, all picked over by stray cats and street dogs. No one cleaned up or took away anything; for a garbage service the city relied on the wind-borne dust which gradually buried the older trash, but, in the winter rains, the layers of dust and trash turned each street into a quagmire.

Afghan peddlers, wending their wary ways along such streets, seldom noticed but if asked might remark, with a wink, that the streets were made deliberately ugly to baffle the tax collectors. Seeing signs of dire poverty outside each gate, as at Nora's house, they would pass by, thinking it not worth entering the obvious hovel and so left the inhabitants in peace.

Protected by high mud-brick walls, the inhabitants of each fortress-like house were not concerned with the dangerous, dirty world outside. But inside, ranged around a fountain, cascades of jasmine and roses blended with the pungent smell of charcoal smoke to create a world apart. As Malcolm had put it when Nora first arrived in Kabul and he was acting as her self-appointed guide, the street and garden were like Afghan women: outside, the women shrouded themselves in formless black sacks with only tiny eye-holes, bent on making themselves as unattractive, indistinguishable, even inhuman as the street was in appearing poor, unkempt, a refuse heap; but, under their *burqas*, women wore vivid reds, greens, and yellows, made even more brilliant with sequins and decked with jewelry. Deep slits and risqué cuts exposed and hinted at sexual charms and musky perfume was liberally applied to clothes and body so that it issued in virtual clouds. A man's garden was his wife and he treated both garden and woman with the same protectiveness, the same privacy, the same sensual delight.

Finally showing some concern as he realized how upset about Jack Nora really was, Malcolm tried to divert her thoughts. He looked around and almost like the *chapandazs* silently clapped his hands and bowed, "Nora, this is a treasure, a real palace...not just a house. You could have a concert in this garden!"

"Here I'm just an aging dowager," she replied. "I lucked into it, but I feel like the Afghans in the story about avoiding the tax collectors. My tax collectors are the Embassy officers. If I really fixed the house up, someone higher than me on the pecking order would outrank me and take it over. So, we just fade away slowly together, the house and I."

"Don't worry, I won't denounce you," he said with pretended seriousness. "But what about that drink?"

Just at that moment, both Nora and Malcolm noticed a figure silently watching them from the doorway to the living room. Momentarily startled, Nora recognized Jack's man Abdul. He had let himself in through a window or else he had a key, because the door had been locked when Malcolm and she arrived.

"Why, Abdul," she said as evenly as her surprise let her, "what are you doing here?"

He bowed with elaborate courtesy. Then straightening up, he said what she knew was not true, "Jack Beg told me to come to you while he was away for you to tell me when to expect him. And, to help you until he returns." With that, he bowed again.

"Thanks, Abdul. That was very kind of you, but I really don't need any help now, and I expect that Mr. Farnsworth will be back tomorrow. He just stopped off in Kunduz to see some friends while I came back early. We were up there camping and buying rugs as you know."

Silently, Abdul looked appraisingly at her face. His showed no emotion. Then, without another word, he turned and went out of the room.

When he was well out of sight and, perhaps, out of hearing, Malcolm said, "what was that all about?"

"Just a minute," Nora replied. "I want to be sure he has left." With that she walked over to an inner door, peered inside, opened a closet and went into the bathroom. Returning through the kitchen, and looking out into the garden, she came back to the living room where Malcolm was pretending to busy himself looking at her collection of rugs.

"Old Abdul is Jack's servant," Nora began. "Or, actually, not really his servant. Abdul seems to run a sort of agency supplying servants to diplomats and spooks. Since I don't use his service, I rarely see him, but Jack tells me that he often comes around, unannounced like just now, to check on the people he has furnished. I find him a most peculiar fellow. I am really not quite sure what to think about him. Jack says that he is just a Pathan servant, or former servant, who has set himself up in business. Frankly, that story seems a bit far-fetched to me. I feel uneasy when he is around. And strange that he should come here. And I don't know how he got in. He is so quiet, appearing and disappearing like a cat. There is something about him… but let's get that drink."

Walking around the living room, Malcolm's eye was drawn into a small alcove made up like the traditional guest room of a villager, complete with charcoal brazier, brass samovar and piles of *kelim*s made into cushions. On the facing wall was a collection of Turcoman weapons, wicked looking long pointed daggers with ivory and bone handles, a delicately curved horseman's bow and a flintlock musket. Following his eye, Nora picked up the musket and handed it to Malcolm. "Here is an antique 'counter-insurgency device.'"

Reading on the firing plate "Amory 1779," he said, "Ah, yes, but we don't regard that particular war as an insurgency. It was a glorious revolution to achieve American liberty."

"As I remember, he British felt rather differently about it," Nora chided. "Anyway I guess the musket saw service in America and then ended up out here where some Afghan took it off David Niven or Errol Flynn in *Gunga Din* or was it *The Bengal Lancers?* But, let me get that drink. Whiskey, okay?"

"Great! Embassy issue. But I'll follow you. Don't leave me here." As he followed her into the kitchen and watched her get down two glasses, he continued, "I want to hear more about this fellow Abdul. Seems odd him showing up just as you come back, doesn't it?"

His remark stopped Nora in the middle of pouring the whiskeys. Malcolm noticed that her hand was shaking. Handling Malcolm his glass, she managed a perfunctory, "Cheers." Then she slowly shook her head and looked carefully at Malcolm. "Yes, it does seem odd, very odd. As you say, you heard rumors. Maybe you should tell me about them."

"Nothing very specific." He replied. "Just that you and Farnsworth were going off on an unlikely trip, to the north, where foreigners, particularly diplomats or…well, no one usually goes…There were a lot of guesses and some wild remarks, but no one offered any enlightenment. Just thought it peculiar. And I have to say that I found the explanation you two put out unusually, indeed surprisingly, lame, 'buying a rug,' for Christ's sake. When the whole market is full of them right here. But please don't enlighten me. I would rather be left in the dark. Say, are you sure Old Abdul has really left."

"Now you've got the willies too," Nora said with a poor excuse at humor. "But, I looked everywhere he might be. Of course, he could be outside the wall, but then he couldn't see or hear us. I'm pretty sure he has left. At least I think so. He glides in and out like a shadow at Jack's house. But I don't remember him ever coming over here. How he got in, I don't know. The door was locked and the windows all bolted. Very strange." She involuntarily shuddered. "But, you will think it even more strange when I tell you that Jack had found out that he is not only good in English, but in addition to his native Pashto, he speaks perfect Dari and Turkic, which Jack knows, and also, apparently, even Mongol. Maybe Russian too."

"Quite something for a servant," Malcolm nodded.

"And, out of the blue one day," Nora went on, "he told Jack a story that made a big impression on Jack and, I must say, on me too."

"Let's have it."

"Well, Jack said that one day last winter he was sitting in his living room, huddled by the fire. It was one of those damp days when you can never seem to get warm. He was reading and reached out for his drink when, looking up, he saw Abdul, dressed in a Western style suit, one of those shiny synthetic silk suits officials wear rather than the white cotton outfit he always wore, staring down at him. Jack said he hadn't even heard Old Abdul come in. Didn't even expect him. It was the cook's day off – Jack's cook was one of Abdul's men. Jack said he had paid the cook's wages direct to him as he usually did. And Abdul had no reason to drop in.

"Well, Jack thought it was strange, but he was used to Abdul doing his own thing so he just asked if Abdul wanted something. Abdul didn't reply, Jack said. He just stood there for a minute or so looking at him with a blank expression on his face and then said, 'Jack Beg.' That's what he always calls Jack. Funny, even I could recognize him anywhere, even blindfolded, by the way he says those two words.

"Jack thought he was going to ask for a raise for the services of the cook. Oddly, he never had asked for one and never seemed interested in the things servants usually want, you know, a trip back to the village or something from the PX. Then, he told this incredible story. I remember every word even though I wasn't there."

"Sure sounds strange, I admit. What was the story?"

"I can almost mimic his voice:

"'Jack Beg, a man of my people went out into the world to seek riches.

He walked until he came to the trunk road. Then he sat. The sun broke over the hills to the East. The valley was flooded with light. The day grew hot. But the man sought no shade and went to no teahouse, fearing to miss the bus. At last, as the sun dropped, he saw distant cloud of dust and heard the bus. He rose. He held up his hand as he had seen men do.

"'But the bus rushed passed him, covering him with dust. He turned and walked back to the village. There he got his rifle and returned to the trunk road. He waited there three days for the bus to return from Peshawer. When it was nearly upon him, he raised his rifle and shot the driver, right between the eyes. He turned and walked back to the village. The world was not good to him.'

"And without another word, Abdul turned and walked out of the house. Not another word, no goodbye, no explanation, nothing.

"Jack admitted that he didn't have a clue what it all meant. He said that if it were a request for a raise, it sure took the cake! So what do you think?"

Malcolm rubbed his chin and stared off toward the display of weapons on the wall for a moment. Then he asked, "How long has Old Abdul been working for you all?"

"I guess you mean by 'you all' the station. Well, I understand that he has been passed down from one person to the next for…well, I don't really know…but, certainly for a very long time."

"What do the security people say about him?"

"As far as they can tell, he is just a simple Pathan servant or maybe more accurately, a businessman."

"Well, on the surface, without ever having exchanged a word with him, I've got to tell you, I find that very unlikely. Who else has he worked for besides Americans?"

"Oh, that's an interesting idea: I heard that he used to work at the British embassy…I guess that's where he learned his English."

"Well, that's probably not important. We're all too paranoid about the British, still living, and your fellows in particular, under the shadow of the 'Great Game.' But if Farnsworth was so concerned, why didn't he just fire him and find himself another Pathan. Servants, especially cooks, are a dime a dozen I hear."

"I asked Jack the same question. His answer was that he really likes Abdul and believes that, in his own way admittedly, Abdul really likes him too. And they're used to each other. As an old bachelor you should know all about that. Anyway, I understand that Abdul has a monopoly of sorts on the servants who work for Americans."

"Okay, obviously that's Farnsworth's call, but to answer your earlier question in one word, it seems to me that maybe Abdul was giving Jack a warning. Of course, he couldn't come right out and warn him in so many words, but maybe he was trying to do it indirectly with that story. I can't see any other explanation.

"How about another drink?"

THE SECOND RENDEZOUS

AS JACK LAY ON THE COLD GROUND, he listened to the dull thump of the truck's aged diesel engine long after it had disappeared into the darkness. After a few minutes, when he could no longer hear it, he rose to a crouch and carefully looked around him. The starlight reflected off the road, making it a ribbon of white, but it distorted rather than illuminated the surrounding landscape. The perspective was thrown out of focus: the mountains came close while the familiar shapes of bushes and trees turned into houses, trucks and people. It was disorienting, but from his training in night operations, he expected such distortions. Shapes meant nothing. He watched only for movement. Slowly he pivoted his head and strained his eyes and ears, but he could detect nothing alive. Except his own rebellious body.

Even after the excitement of the last few minutes subsided, he found that his hands were trembling. The back of his neck felt cold and clammy. Involuntarily he shivered. His legs were like rubber. He suddenly felt exhausted. In this feeling, he recognized the first signs of shock and knew that he must be very careful or he would lose that edge of alertness and balance upon which his life now depended. A wrong move and he might not live to see the dawn.

First, he needed to assess what he had actually seen. That should help him to reconstruct what had happened before he reached the cabin. "Rule number one," he whispered to himself. "Be realistic." He knew he must first make a conscious effort to separate the facts as he now found them from what he had been told to expect. That was not much more than the name of the operation, a code word. Nothing was ever called by its own name. The intelligence and military people loved to think up some fancy name. This one was named "Dirhem" a small coin. He had been amused when he heard it. Now he was no longer amused. Why had no one told him more than the name or at least more than just the barest details?

'Obviously, somewhere, somehow, Dirhem had gone wrong. But wrong from *what*? What was right?' He puzzled through all the scenarios he could imagine but could find no logical way to get an answer. Yet, that was the critical assessment. He would have to make a judgment on the breakdown of the plan in order to decide what to do now.

From his training and experience, he realized that even though he could not find a firm answer, the act of making the assessment would calm him and help him to keep his balance. So what, he asked himself, did he know for sure? The answer was 'very little.' Only that someone had followed the courier he was supposed to meet and that they had killed one another. He was in and out of the cabin so fast, he had hardly had time to learn more even if there had been some way to do so. And, of course, both men were already dead and could tell him nothing, even if they — or one of them, presumably "Percy," whoever he had been — wished to.

The critical point was whether they were the only people involved... at least in this neighborhood. He assumed, although on this point his instructions offered no guidance, that the courier had been acting alone. It was unlikely that he would have had anyone to help him.

'But, what about the other man, the man who must have been tracking 'Percy? Was he too alone? Not likely. That would not be the intelligent way to follow a man. No professional would try to follow a man alone. It just didn't work. Normally, if that word had any meaning any more', he thought, 'if he were in charge of a surveillance, Jack would use at least three, or maybe even five other people to help him track his quarry. Otherwise, the quarry would evade his pursuer while he slept or went to the toilet. Percy's hunters would have to have been stupid to rely on only one man'. And Jack had had the message drummed into him in all his training that survivors did not assume that their adversaries were stupid. 'No, the now-dead hunter must have been one of a pack'. And as far as he knew, *they* were not dead. But, perhaps they had spread out to follow other leads. However many there were altogether, *here* perhaps the hunter was all alone. That gave some solace. And God knows, he thought, he needed that!

But he speedily dismissed this idea as just wishful thinking. Something he could not afford. The obvious fact was that there wasn't any place on either side of this road they would have to search. Just bare mountains. No place to hide. No one to hide with. The road was life...No reason to leave it. But, in order not to frighten his quarry, the pursuer, he figured, probably was acting alone as a 'point man', with his support team not far behind. That made sense. That is the way, he thought, he would have followed a man, close but not too close, supported by a team, but not always with them.

Perhaps, but only perhaps, the pursuer — whoever he was, Afghan, Russian, Chinese — had not been able to inform his support team or headquarters exactly where he was or what he found. Be that as it may, how could he have known about Jack even if he had known about, or had even identified, 'Percy.'

Of course, even that already disturbing enough interpretation, he realized, left the really frightening question unanswered – how had he or they known about the cabin? And quick enough to get there and kill Percy before Jack could arrive. The timing was astonishing. And, after all, how many candidates could there be up here for the hit man and his support? Going back to his idea of how he could have followed Percy, Jack guessed they were at least two or three.

Percy, apparently, had not been able to alert his team. If he had not, and apparently he and Percy shot it out on sight, then Jack was at least temporarily safe.

No, that also was wishful thinking. How many candidates could there be up here for the murderer? He had to assume that whether this fellow had time or the means to tell his team, they would make the connection all by themselves if they caught an American nearby. It wouldn't take any brilliant insight to put Jack and Percy together if you already knew about Percy.

'Obviously, the mission had been penetrated'. He tried to push that question out of his mind. It didn't bear asking. But it kept nagging at him. And with good reason.

Even before he left Kabul, Jack had picked up little whiffs of gossip – Kabul diplomats and politicians lived on gossip -- about some sort of undercover action. Nothing specified, of course, but enough to make everyone pay attention. But, who could know? Maybe it was enough to get whoever it was that was involved nervous. That might have been the spark that set off the action, indeed fired the shot.

In that black and desolate night, the idea that he or at least some sort of mission in which he was involved was the focus of attention, even if it were not accurate, was chilling thought, a thought that turned each boulder into a crouching assassin, each bush, into a parked car ready to fix him in its headlights like a rabbit as armed men rushed out to seize him.

No solace there: a cool and realistic assessment gave grounds only for terror.

'But, there it was.' Jack could see no escape from that assessment. 'Somewhere, and not far away, he had to conclude the hounds were already searching for him and that if they found him they would kill him. Kill him if he were lucky. There was much that was worse than death.

'And what about the mission. That had to be his main concern now. Everything he had been taught made him put that first. The papers, whatever they were, were with him. Everything depended upon him now.'

Jack thought back over what he had seen. With a shock he realized that if he had to describe 'Percy' now, he could not. He had seen little more of him than a Chinese- or Mongol-looking face. Or was that just the effect of the flashlight and his imagination? Maybe he was an American...or an Englishman. That was a confusing thought, but it did not lead anywhere, at least anywhere where he might be safer.

The 'hunter' left an even vaguer impression. Jack had no idea who or what he could have been. But, whoever or whatever he was, he obviously had ambushed Percy. With a shock, he suddenly thought, 'Probably whoever the pursuer was, Percy thought he was me, arriving early. Damn good thing I didn't arrive any sooner. It could not have happened long before I arrived since the bodies of both men were still warm. The other fellow must have shot first, but Percy had lived long enough to shoot back. Otherwise, I would now probably look like Percy with half my chest blown away.'

Jack knew that there were no more 'Percys' to shoot *for* him. This side of the Hindu Kush, except for a ragbag group of truckers, on whom he could certainly not rely for any support he was absolutely alone. His only chance was to put as much distance between himself and the cabin as he could in the darkness that remained. To stay where he was to await the dawn was to await the pursuers. He was now the hare to someone else's hounds. But how to run and where to go to ground? Well, the answer to that question, at least, was reassuringly obvious: on that point, Smith has been absolutely clear -- he must get to the second rendezvous with the truck. That was his lifeline.

'But was that lifeline still secure?' He wondered.

If they had penetrated the mission enough to know about the cabin and the documents, the hit man's team would not have to be very smart to focus on how he could get away. Maybe they already knew about Qol Khan. 'Of course,' he thought.

'That's where the others are, on the track of my transport.' He reflected that he would have done the same. At the very minimum, they would suspect a connection between Percy, Qol Khan and Jack — or someone near the cabin. Even if they had never heard of Qol Khan, they would likely want to 'talk' with him. At the minimum, they would be watching him.

'Perhaps,' he thought, 'there is some alternative escape route.' But, soberly, he realized that that thought was a luxury far beyond his means. Unlike the hare, who could run in any direction, Jack had only one direction, and only one road, he could follow. Qol Khan's truck was his only hope.

The truck should be about four miles down the road toward Kunduz. After it dropped him, it had probably gone on and then turned back – that must have been the truck he heard pass the cabin, heading toward Kunduz — and then stopped there for the night, just as it had at the first rendezvous. And, assuming the crew was alive, they would expect him at dawn. He looked at his watch. First light was a long time away, but Jack wanted to put as much ground between him and the cabin as he could — and quickly.

To make time in the dark, he would have to stick to the road. It was too risky to try to cut across country, too easy to fall into a ditch or trip over a stone and sprain or break an ankle. That hardly bore thinking about. Without food or water, he could not just hide until his leg healed. He would die of thirst if he tried that. He remembered vividly what the survival manuals he had read in his training course had said: a healthy, young, well-trained man could survive for two, maybe three days, not more. No, if he tried to go across country in the dark and fell down, he would have to bury the papers, crawl to the road and try to hitch a ride. But that ride would be straight to the nearest police post, unless he were picked up by whoever was tracking 'Percy'. That would not be pleasant as 'they' tried to make him tell where he had buried the documents. "Once more...American spy...where are the papers..." He could almost hear his own screams now...but, no one else would hear them. Ever. No, keep to the road and get to that truck quick!'

And, anyway, on that point, at least, the instructions had been crystal clear...even, as he thought about it now, almost too clear. They told him that he should join that truck no matter what had happened, even if he saw other cars or trucks around. Even, in fact, if he failed to find the cabin. Despite the faulty instructions he had found it. But, of course, Smith could not have guessed what he had found *in* the cabin; so he had outrun his instructions. He must now be doubly cautious. As cautious as the hare when he has heard the braying of the hounds.

So, keeping to the shoulder of the road, glancing back every few strides, and ready to jump into a ditch or run to ground at the first sound of a motor or flash of headlights, he set out westward. He figured he had about four hours, maybe five, before first light, and he planned to use the time to as much advantage as possible.

With luck, he would reach the rendezvous point very early, perhaps in just an hour or an hour and a half. No one would expect him so soon and he could, if he were careful, and lucky, find a place to 'lie up' as before so that he could observe the truck carefully. Just in case someone had beat him there and had begun to set a trap.

Treading cautiously but stretching his legs, he half-walked and half-jogged a hundred paces a time, stopping to look around long and carefully and then jogging another hundred paces. He could have gone faster, but every few paces, he paused to look over his shoulder. The stars gave his now-accustomed eyes enough light to enable him to avoid the pot holes and the piles of stones the truckers had set up to help them change tires. That thought reminded him of the piles of rotting, stinking skins in 'his' truck. Now he could hardly wait to dive back into them!

Around him the night was dead quiet. The wind had dropped and the air seemed a velvet curtain. He hoped that curtain was absorbing the pounding of his boots and the panting of his lungs. At least, he took solace, up here so close to the Russian border, only a mad man would be about at night. Even in daylight, there was scant chance of an encounter. With so little on these bare hills — which in the daylight looked like they had been sandpapered smooth — to feed animals and with the ever-present danger of encountering a frightened, trigger happy army patrol, herdsmen found the area unprofitable – and unhealthy. Even smugglers, by the nature of their work, moved across it quickly. To get caught there with contraband, particularly weapons, was distinctly unhealthy. He was unlikely to meet anyone, but, of course, that would make him, 'the hare', even more obvious to the hounds.

Again he dropped off the road and squatted down to listen. After a few moments, his heart slowed down and he strained every nerve to find a sound. He heard nothing. Then he scanned the silhouette of the nearer horizon, but no human thing broke the jagged lines of nature. To get a better view, he picked his way carefully up a small hill and stopped just below the top so that he would meld into the shadow. From there, he could see in both directions down the road. He searched from near at hand to as far as he could see to the East, the direction he had come from, and then to the West. Nothing moved and nothing looked like a truck or car parked anywhere within his range.

Silently, he picked his way down the hill, careful not to disturb the rocks or gravel. Back on the road, he set off again. The good, honest work of jogging and walking fast made his body tingle. Now his sweat came neither from fear nor from the acrid heat of the rotting skins. He felt clean and strong. To his surprise, once more he found that he felt a sort of contentment even after the terrifying events of the night. "While there's life, there's hope," he intoned loudly the reassuring cliché. He hadn't meant to speak out loud and almost panicked when he caught or imagined an echo off the rocks.

After what he guessed was an hour, he stopped again to look around. As he got closer, he saw a large rock off to the side of the road. He laughed to himself, thinking how easy it would have been, had he seen it a bit further off, to imagine it to be a parked car or Jeep. Relieved, he climbed on top of it and sat down. From there, he had a slightly longer view of the road. So he felt safe in taking the time to calculate: How far had he come?

The instructions had said the truck would be four miles away. But that might be as inaccurate as everything else had been. Perhaps 'four' meant three or six.

Under no circumstances could he afford to overshoot the truck stop or to just blunder into it. He tried to figure out the possibilities. Counting his hundred-pace walks and jogs, he guessed he had come about three miles from the cabin.

Maybe 'four' miles, he thought, was not a distance estimate but a time estimate. 'Try it their way,' he decided. He was supposed to meet Percy at midnight. If the plan had gone right, he would have needed, say, half an hour to an hour to identify him, receive the documents and get away. Call it 1:00 A. M. In this season, dawn came early. First light was about 4:00 A. M. but, before first light, he would need to get hidden to get ready to identify the truck. That would take at least half an hour. Prudence would suggest an hour. So probably the planners had thought in terms of between two and three hours of walking time. Allowing for the dark night and not expecting him to be in such a hurry, they might have thought of somewhere between four and nine miles. He looked at his watch. It was 2:05 A. M. Good thing he had a watch — he would never have been within an hour of guessing the right time.

He was just about to set off again when a new thought leapt unbidden into his mind. Could Qol Khan be involved in Percy's murder? He sat back down to think that through. To what end could Qol Khan have taken that risk? He tried to put himself in Qol Khan's place. Well, if he knew of the documents, and he must have thought there was some terribly important reason for Jack to be sent up here, he could probably make a deal, dangerous as it might be, to sell them. In his terms, they would be worth a kingdom... but more likely his kingdom would turn out to be a shallow grave. After all, he would be in no position to bargain. If the would-be buyer was Afghan security, they would just take the documents. If he tried to hide them, they would torture him to make him say where he put them. And he was unlikely to be touch with the Russians or the Chinese. He would be almost as afraid of them as of the Afghan security service. The British? Well, that might be possible. After all, he guessed, he must have or have had a relationship with the British since they must have arranged to have him take Jack to the cabin. He believed he would have known if Qol Khan had any relationship with the Agency and almost certainly he had none with Smith. A deal with the British might have been possible, but unlikely. Anyway, he probably would not have known much about whatever the papers contained. And if he wanted to "sell" Jack, it would have been so much easier for him to turn Jack in when he had him in the truck. Finally, since it appeared that the British had sent Qol Khan to help him, they would presumably have been able to control him. Moreover, he did not really have time to do much of anything after dropping Jack, Jack would have heard the truck stop and certainly would have heard a shot. Whatever happened in the cabin must have happened before Qol Khan arrived in the area.

But, of course, Qol Khan could have known of the ambush in advance. Unlikely, though, because if he had known anyone was going to be killed, he could not have been dragged there by a team of horses. It was worth his life just to be in the neighborhood.

Jack decided he could dismiss the idea that Qol Khan was more than a taxi driver. But, like everything else, "dismissing the idea" was not firm. Doubt still clouded Jack's mind, and he decided that the wise thing was to be well off the road when dawn came. Since the flat land beside the road offered almost no cover, he must find a hill or gully. "That," he said quite aloud to himself, "is one part of this operation that poses absolutely no problem. Damn near every foot of Afghanistan is either a hill or a gully." So, taking his time, he selected one hill somewhat larger than the rest and cut off the road toward it, picking his way through the shadows with ponderous care.

It was well that he started early because the hill was protected by several deep and steep gullies he had not observed from the road. Going down one, he slid and slipped, and finally fell, scraping his arms and hands on piles of loose and shifting stones left behind by the melting snows of spring.

The miniature landslide he set off made a tremendous racket. The noise, more than the fall, frightened and shook him. He dusted himself off, feeling lucky that he had not twisted an ankle. He would be even more careful, he promised himself. And, after about twenty minutes more of uncomfortable scrambling in the dark, he found the top of 'his' hill and dropped, now quite tired again, into a small crater, a sort of natural foxhole.

Immobile and lying in the declivity, Jack felt the sweat on his back turn cold. He buttoned up the collar of his jacket and reaching down, he untied the laces and slipped off his boots. He felt like he had grown into those boots. Then he pulled off the wool socks and spread them out to dry, How simple, he laughed silently to himself, were the really great pleasures in life, just to be alive, to be dry and warm. He lay resting, but afraid that he might fall asleep, for perhaps half an hour. Then he carefully slipped his feet back into his now-dry socks and laced up his boots the better to be ready to move quickly if he had to.

So far he had not had a chance to examine Percy's pistol. He reached into his pocket and pulled it out. Taking out his handkerchief, he wiped off the dust, eased out the clip, cocked the hammer, gently slid back the slide and took out the bullet. Then he worked the slide back and forth and wiped it again. Satisfied, he reloaded it, fixed the safety and slid it back into his pocket. Then, he checked to make sure that the papers were still under his shirt. Reassured, he tried to find a comfortable position to await the dawn. More exhausted than he had realized, he did what he most feared. He dozed off.

With a start, he awoke as the brilliant and already hot rays of the sun hit his eyes. He half jumped to his feet and then, remembering why he had left the road, slumped down again. Cautiously, he edged to the rim of his vantage point. To his astonishment, he saw that there was no road below. He glanced up at the sun. Stupidly, he realized, he had got turned around in the scramble up the hill in the dark and had gone much further from the road than he had intended.

Between the road and his vantage point was another hill. He could see the road going in behind it and then coming out again, but it had looped there, and he was perhaps a mile from it. On the parts of the road he could see, not a sparrow could have moved anywhere for miles around without his seeing it.

But what lay behind the hill, he could not know.

What he did know for sure was that old Qol Khan would not wait long after sunrise. He would have been even more apprehensive than Jack; so Jack had little time to reach his rendezvous with that truck. Now able to see clearly in the early morning sunlight, he worked his way rapidly down the hillside, being very careful not to set off another rockslide, then across a small gully, probably the same one that had seemed so much like Grand Canyon the night before, and up the side of the hill that overlooked the road. As he went, he followed his now established routine, walking a few steps, pausing to look and then moving ahead. Still no dust, no sign of movement. In a few minutes, he was at the top of the hill. There, he crouched down and picked up a handful of dust. He rubbed it on his face to dull any reflection of his white skin in the now intense sunlight and tied the black handkerchief over his forehead and hair. Then he pressed his head slowly up to the edge so that he could see over without exposing himself.

Very slowly, as he inched up, the valley below came into view.

What he saw hit him like a body blow.

A truck was stopped, apparently pushed off the road by two dust covered Russian-built Jeeps. Milling about were several men, men whose dun-colored uniforms identified them as Afghan soldiers or security police. Stunned, he dropped back below the rim of the hill and crawled over to a clump of dry grass where he could look with less chance of being seen. Again, he edged up to the rim and looked down. It was Qol Khan's truck all right. No mistaking that blue band in the bright sunlight. Soldiers were all around it, swarming like angry ants on a nest. At first, he could not tell what they were doing. He cursed his lack of field glasses.

But soon enough he realized what they were doing.

One man detached himself from the others and walked over to what appeared to be a sack, crumpled on the ground beside the truck. No, he suddenly saw, it was a man. No mistaking that castoff army coat. Qol Khan! It was Qol Khan stretched out beside the truck. The soldier stopped, perhaps said something — Jack could not hear — and then savagely kicked it...him. As Jack watched, horrified, the soldier...no, he could now see that it was an officer, looking just like the one with whom he and Nora had taken tea on the pass, took out a revolver, cocked the hammer and, bending over, aimed point blank at the face of the prostrate man.

Before he heard the shot, Jack saw the head of the man jerk backward and fly apart. The officer jumped to avoid the explosion of blood and bone. Then came the noise. The shot echoed from the opposite hill so that it sounded like the crack of a whip. So near was the sound as to make Jack more of a participant than a spectator. Jack went limp and involuntarily slid back from the edge of the hill. He shook his head, trying to clear it of the awful sight and then, after a nearly paralyzed few seconds, forced himself to climb back into position. He was just in time to see the officer replacing his pistol in its holster. Meticulously, he wiped off his shoe on the leg of the body and turned toward one of the two Jeeps, shouting something at the other men.

Dazed, Jack just stared blankly at the scene below. His instructions had specifically told him to walk up and identify himself if he saw other cars around Qol Khan's truck. "We might want to get you back to Kabul sooner," Smith had said. But, obviously, he could not have anticipated this... *this carnage.* If he had walked in here, as he was supposed to, at dawn, those soldiers would have seized him. Perhaps they would not have intended to kill him, but they could hardly have let him go, never-mind his diplomatic status, if he had witnessed what they had done. Even if they had decided to let him go, they certainly would first have searched him and taken Percy's papers. Then, everything that Percy had died for would have been lost. The Afghans, corrupt as they were, would certainly have sold the papers to the highest bidder. Maybe to the Russians, maybe to the Chinese. Both had big missions in Kabul. If Smith had told him the truth, then dozens, maybe hundreds, of Chinese would certainly have...He faltered...have lost their chance to do whatever they were trying to do...funny, he didn't even have a clue what that might be. But, whatever it was, it was regarded as very important by Washington. So, without meaning to, he would have given the Russians or the Chinese, someone -- he couldn't be sure who that might be -- a coup worthy of a...a Philby. In fact, worse than a Philby.

The instructions could not have foreseen this...this massacre. He had to react. But how? "Listen," one of his bosses had said to him when he was in training, "if we had wanted a machine, we would have got I. B. M. to build one. If we send a man, we expect him to think." Whatever else it did, that shot had certainly made him think. The soldiers must have found the bodies in the cabin. That was it. They found the bodies and thought Qol Khan was a smuggler. Probably assumed he had killed them. 'Well,' he thought, 'I cannot help Qol Khan now...no one can.'

Unconsciously, he felt for his pistol. Suddenly the thought struck him that if they or their bosses had the means to do a ballistics analysis, they could convince even an American jury that he had killed at least one of those men. But even putting aside the worst cases, and there were many possibilities, it would be very hard to explain why an American with the title of U. S. vice consul was up here, in the forbidden zone, a few miles from the Soviet border and just four or five miles from where a double murder had taken place, with incriminating papers, probably with a bit of blood on them, and...'Oh my God,' he shuddered, 'the pocket knife I dropped in the cabin. Evidence for any court, anywhere...But, who needed a court? That Afghan officer used a more direct method.'

No matter what his instructions had ordered, he could not even contemplate going down onto that slaughtering ground. Slithering rather than crawling back to the lip of the hill, he watched the remaining men mill about, apparently searching and getting ready to leave. In the midst of their hurried preparations, he heard an unworldly scream. It was more a howl than anything human. Jack froze. The hair on the back of his neck stiffened. His whole body sagged. He desperately wanted to pull back, but he knew that if he moved at all, his legs would take control and he would just run and run and run. He couldn't – he dared not — move.

The scream lingered and finally died in a gurgle. As he watched, two men whom he had not seen before emerged from behind the truck. One was wiping what looked like a knife on a piece of cloth, the head covering of one of the Mongol boys.

Without the time, or even the will, to turn aside, Jack vomited. Gagging, he clamed his hand over his mouth, just in time to stifle his own scream.

Drained and numb, he fell back from the rim, sinking against the earth to wait. Wait for what, he knew not. Gradually, after what was probably only a minute or two, he recovered and tried to figure out what was happening. The Jeeps, he realized, would have made his two-hour trek in a few minutes. It was so near a miss that they…'My God,' he suddenly thought. 'How could they have known about the murder or the truck so soon? They would hardly be out here on a routine patrol. And they couldn't have just stumbled on that cabin in the middle of the night. Christ, there must be thousands of cabins like that one in Afghanistan. It couldn't be an accident that they picked this one…this night! The only logical explanation is that they were tipped off. The mission must be blown.'

Then he lost control and a horrible dead feeling rose from his bowel. Flies, smelling his fear, buzzed around his limp body. Fearing even to swat at them, he squeezed his eyes closed. Did he carry them with him, he wondered, or did the smell of the dead sleep hang onto his clothes? Whatever it was, he was the center of their attention again. They came in a great swirling cloud. In his shock, they assumed the proportions of vultures. Would they lead the Afghan devils to him, he worried. After nerve-racking, endless minutes, he heard one of the Jeeps start up with that characteristic high whine of the Russian Jeep's air-cooled engine. Then the other started and with several backfires, like shots from the officer's pistol, they swerved onto the road and, with tires screeching, raced off down the road toward Kunduz.

Without even daring to turn his head, Jack watched them go. In just a few moments all that was left was the faint scent of exhaust fumes and a receding dust plume, down the road to the southwest. Toward his only hope.

Cautiously, again, he crept to the edge of the hill. Peering down at the truck, he searched for movement. Had they left a guard behind? As an experienced intelligence officer he certainly would have, but would they? Was the lure of tea too strong? Anyway, what for? To guard the dead? One look at that scene and any passing truck driver would step on the accelerator. Even if Qol Khan's truck were full of gold bars, he would want to put all Afghanistan between it and himself. Still, better take nothing for granted. He waited and watched. Trying not to move a single muscle, he stared so hard his eyes ached as he swept layer after brilliant layer of the sun-blasted scene before him.

Was there any place a guard might have hidden? If so, it would probably be a shaded place — a gully or the shade behind a rock. The merciless sun picked out for him every tuft of grass. There was no shade. No place to "lie up." The whole landscape was stripped bare, flayed like a dead sheep. So, after what seemed hours but was only a few minutes, he began to inch his way forward for a last look down the highway. If he saw nothing, he told himself, he would have at least 15 minutes before anyone could come upon him.

As he looked, nothing in the whole immense landscape appeared alive. Miraculously, even the flies had departed. Not a breeze rustled. Not a fleck of dust stirred. The world was his alone.

Half rising, Jack moved down hill by short stages toward the truck. He looked carefully at his watch. Each stop was punctuated by a hurried search of the landscape. Then on again. After two minutes of his 'safe' fifteen, he was within fifty paces of the truck and it was useless to try to hide any longer. There was absolutely no cover against the bare, chalky white hill, and any living person in that truck could have counted the freckles on his nose. He tensed himself and sprinted toward the truck, throwing himself down beside the motor, the 7. 65 mm automatic in his hand.

Half expecting a shot or at least a shout from under the dark body of the truck, he peered in. There, not more than a body's length from his face, his glare-blinded eyes made out a form. At first he could not discern exactly what it was. Then he wished he had not. Head thrown back with bulging eyes glassily staring and lifeless mouth open in a silent scream, lay the young Mongol with whom he had wrestled in the back of the truck...in what seemed a lifetime ago.

Crawling toward the body, Jack quickly saw why he had heard that agonized howl. The boy's arms had been twisted and bound behind his back with wire. His clothes had been ripped apart to expose his belly and genitals. Both had been gashed and mutilated. The layers of skin had been peeled back as one might peel a tomato. Then he had been dissected like a cadaver to expose the muscles and the intestines. That was why the soldiers had wiped off their knives. It was torture of the old school. Like it might have been done in a Bukhara dungeon a century ago...Done by sheep men, used to slaughter, used to flaying the body of the dead animal. Already the flies had begun to gather. No wonder they had abandoned Jack. Here was a new feast. Without even getting up, he vomited again. But he had little in his stomach so it was a wracking, dry vomit that would have hurt if he had the leisure even to think of it.

Then he shuddered and shook his head, wiping the cold sweat off his clammy forehead with his left sleeve, trying to get hold of himself. It was no use. A spasm shook his whole body. He retched again, dryly, emptily. He became aware that his right arm ached above all the other anguish that reached his brain. Looking down, he saw that his hand was white and bloodless from squeezing the pistol so hard.

Looking at his watch, he saw that he had used less than a minute. Four were gone. Eleven remained. Crawling along the side of the truck, he saw the other two bodies. Faces and bodies were more or less whole. He recognized them as the men he had seen squatting around the fire drinking tea.

Then, rising to a crouch, he peered into the cab of the truck through the open door. It was empty. He dropped down and, creeping now on his feet for speed, he worked his way along the body of the truck. As he rounded the front, he saw a body which had been, must have been, Qol Khan. At first he could not be sure. The face was smashed like a ripe melon hurled against a wall. But there was no mistaking the clothes. He remembered them well from the first encounter.

Like the young boy, Qol Khan had his arms twisted behind his back, held in contortion with strands of wire that had cut to the bone of his wrists as he had writhed in agony and tried to break loose. Again, they had been at his belly. The clothes had been ripped roughly aside to expose the sensitive parts. He had been slashed and partly disemboweled.

Obviously, he realized, the cruelty had not been aimless. It had been torture. For information. Qol Khan must have known something of immense value to those who had driven away in the Russian Jeeps. "Whatever he knew," Jack found himself saying aloud, "he must have told them. No living creature could have kept his tongue when they went to work on him. Death would have been a mercy. They…he…would have told them anything, everything for release. And it must have been about me. Beyond any doubt, they would now know, at the least, that some European man was at large up here."

He looked again at his watch. Seven minutes were gone. Eight more or less safe minutes remained by his estimate of how long it would take for a truck or jeep to get down that road.

Quickly now, he crept along the side of the truck. Like a third eye, he pointed his pistol into the back of the truck. The stinking coffin of skins, as he had thought of it, now looked almost inviting in comparison to the dusty, bloody killing ground around the truck. Scanning the dark interior, he saw it just as he had remembered. No one, not even one of those fiends, he felt sure, would choose to hide in there. But, taking no chances, he probed with a shovel he found attached to the back panel and then, climbing in, jumped and kicked mindlessly at the pile of skins. They were as devoid of life as the rest of that valley.

Hurriedly, he again consulted his watch. Only four safe minutes remained. Then someone, perhaps they, might come upon him. "Use one minute to think," he told himself quite out loud. "The friendly British-controlled crew is dead. Whatever it had told…wait," he called out in alarm. "One man is missing!" He jumped down from the truck and counted. Yes, one man was missing. "He must have been taken away in the Jeeps for further interrogation…or, perhaps, he was a mole, somehow put in the truck by the hunters, the men in soldiers' uniforms, whoever they were, and now was going off with them," again quite out loud to himself. He didn't have time to think that one through. "But they really didn't need a mole…God! That man would have been lucky to be a mole. If he wasn't, he would pray that he had been. And, it amounted to the same: that man would talk or would be made to talk."

Since two of the men had been simply killed, not tortured to death, the hunters must have found out whatever it was they wanted to know or what they thought was the whole story before they even got to those men. The "whole story" — at least the one the truckers knew — was Jack.

They would know that he was on foot and so at their mercy. They could take their time. He was in the trap already. He would starve if he tried to strike out across the mountains. Even if there was food and water in the truck, he couldn't carry more than a couple of days' rations.

And where could he go anyway? Between him and Kunduz was at least 300 kilometers as the birds fly. But he couldn't go in a straight line. The land was rough and cut by gullies and hills and mountains. Even if he could make 50 kilometers a day — which he could not do and stay hidden — it would take him nearly a week. He would die of thirst long before he got half way. Not a chance on foot.

Probably that was why the men in the Jeeps drove away. They could afford to. They knew he would have to come to them, begging for water.

Trying to think what options he might have, he quickly dismissed the only other one he could think of. What about burying the papers and just walking into the nearest town, waving his passport?

That led to the same sort of death Qol Khan had suffered, he thought bitterly.

Even if he could get the slaughter scene out of his mind and try to make his way toward Kabul, that gambit was clearly impossible. The nearest town was about 100 kilometers away. And, even if somehow he could cover that distance on foot, 'they' – the officers who awaited him and now probably a more senior command with more resources and more authority -- would want to know where he buried the papers. Helped like they had helped his Afghan friends, it wouldn't take him long to remember.

And, after they worked him over to get him to talk, they could not afford to let him live. Alive, he would be too dangerous. Official protests, maybe a threat to cut off the development aid, complaints about diplomatic immunity. Far too risky. Far too embarrassing. No, they would have to have him run over by a truck or something. He could guess the report to the

American Embassy:

'We regret to have to inform you that your vice consul, who as you admit, in violation of your instructions, was in the forbidden zone on a camping trip, got drunk and stumbled out onto highway where he was struck by an oncoming truck. By the time we found it, the body was so decomposed that, in the interests of public health, we arranged to have it burned.'

'And, under the circumstances', he thought, 'the embassy would not even protest. Fat lot of good it would do him even if they did -- after the fact. Diplomatic immunity was a mighty thin shield if no one knew where you were.'

Worse, the venal Afghans might arrange to sell him to the Chinese or the Russians or whoever was involved. 'How much for a middle aged, experienced American spy? One who knows all about those fascinating papers of yours.'

Should be worth quite a bit, he guessed. Then he would really be able to appreciate the accounts of those British agents in the Great Game who ended up in the Bukhara dungeons. Pretty basic research they conducted there. No matter what Smith had said, he would do his damnedest to stay as far from those devils as he possibly could.

He looked again at his watch. Only two minutes remained. Thirsty as always, he looked in the cab for a water bottle. He would need it anyway, no matter what he decided to do. Reaching over the seat, he began to pull on the sleeve of what years before must have been an olive colored but now much patched and filthy great coat that probably covered the bottle.

The coat stuck on some hook or catch. He pulled but it wouldn't give. To get at it, he crawled up into the cab behind the wheel. There it was, the gaudy thermos for which the Koreans were known in the bazaars.

Then, suddenly he realized that he had his hands on the best, perhaps the only, solution. *The truck.*

He must drive. The roads would be watched, of course, but probably *they* would not yet be ready for him. If he could move quickly...with luck no one would notice the blue band or identify this truck with Qol Khan.

There must be enough trucks on this road that no one would watch too closely. At least not yet. At least until he got near a town. Hope, he realized, had warped his sense of reality. But, nothing for it, the alternative was to die. If lucky, to die of thirst. If unlucky...

His mind made up, Jack turned the switch and pumped the fuel pedal. Fumbling with bare wires and pins, he got no response. The 'safe' fifteen minutes were gone. He tried once more. Sweat ran down his face and neck. He was frantic. Just as he was about to panic and race back to the hill, the motor gave a cough and backfired. Jack jumped as though *he* had been shot. The motor died. Once more he tried. Another cough and an earsplitting backfire. Aghast at the noise, Jack reached for the door handle. But the motor turned over. It had caught. He pushed down on the limp clutch pedal and slammed the gearshift forward. With a rusty whine, the truck began to roll...To roll forward toward Kunduz over the inert and useless legs of Qol Khan.

THE SAVAGE PACK

WITH HIS FACE WRAPPED IN THE headcloth of the dead driver and his European clothes hidden under an olive drab great coat, Jack slumped down behind the wheel. The road he followed was hardly more than a trail and was deeply pitted with potholes. Worse, it was frequently littered with the stones used by the truckers to jack up the axles of their broken-down vehicles. Keeping the truck moving but not breaking an axle or gutting the transmission took all his attention. He was grateful for the task as it kept his mind off of still worse worries about which he could do nothing.

As the straining truck crested a small hill, he saw below him the first small hamlet. It was nothing more than what in America would have been called "just a wide place in the road," but it was much more than that for Jack — it was the first test of his ability to pass and to escape notice. Even in the cab of the truck, wrapped up as he was, he felt naked. Rubbing his hand across his mouth, he felt the stubble of beard. Would the Afghan drivers have so much hair on their faces? No, he realized, they would be nearly hairless, but he had no way to shave. After years of admiring blonds, he was now grateful for his dark hair and swarthy complexion. Not so dark as the Mongols, of course, but he could improve on that. He took one hand off the wheel and wiped some of the accumulated dirt and grease from the dashboard and rubbed it onto his cheeks and nose. Hardly professional makeup, he thought but it would look less European, more like a regular trucker.

But, how should he go through the town? The road led in and out, he could see from the hill. No worry about getting side tracked or lost. The real challenge was that Qol Khan and his crew, who must have passed this way every week, probably had a routine. Did they stop for tea? Did they get diesel fuel here? Did they at least wave to certain people they knew? He had no way of knowing. He would just wave back if anyone greeted him and keep moving.

The real danger was the possibility of a roadblock. Where the checkpoints were, of course, Jack could not predict. Usually when you least expected it, he reflected you would suddenly come across one of the long steel "telephone poles" of the security police stretched across the road. A small sign, usually so worn by the sun and wind that you could hardly read it, warned you in Persian or sometimes in Russian and English that you would be shot if you did not stop. That was what he had seen at the crest of the Hindu Kush three days – no, it could not have been only three days before. Always in the past, when his car was armed with diplomatic plates, he had regarded barriers as just a time-consuming nuisance. Not now. He remembered with a start the ostensibly hospitable remark of the officer who manned that mountaintop barrier, "You shall not pass by here again without staying with me." He hoped it was not an omen.

What to do? He let the truck coast to a stop to consider. He decided that if there was a check point, he would slow down, as though he were going to stop, like a normal truck would have, and then at the last moment accelerate right through it.

The pole would hit the engine and smash the lights, perhaps even cave in the radiator but the motor would hold and the pole would bend aside. That is, unless, up here by the frontier, they had put cement blocks in the road. But, doing that was hard work, and he doubted that the guards would take the trouble. They would probably be sleeping or drinking tea. In their surprise — like those soldiers at the Hindu Kush pass — they would have to run to get their guns. That would take a few moments and by the time they got them loaded, he would be a hundred yards or more down the road. 'What was the effective range of the Kalashnikov?' He wondered. Would the guards have had much training in firing them? Probably not much, he comforted himself. Ammunition was said to be in short supply and certainly was expensive. He could expect some shots but, unless a stray bullet hit a tire, they probably couldn't stop him.

And, unless they had a Jeep, which he figured was unlikely in such a small hamlet, the guards would have no way of pursuing him. Nor were they likely to alert the next police post. Probably no one in the town had access to a telephone or telegraph. 'God knows,' he silently rationalized, 'it is hard enough to make a telephone call even across Kabul so up here it must be impossible.'

Anyway, he had no choice. If he stopped, the Security forces would arrest him. No chance of bluffing or bribing even if he had the means to do so. And he didn't have a penny with him. All thanks to Smith! But, anyway, no Afghan would take the risk of letting him through even if he were flying the American flag and offered bags of gold coins. This was the forbidden zone. To stop was to end his run. Or maybe…he shuddered.

Leaving the motor running, Jack climbed out onto the running board and gazed down the road behind him. Anything moving would have kicked up a plume of dust. There was nothing in sight. That direction was safe for at least ten miles, maybe more. He then turned and looked at the village. Nothing unusual that he could see. And beyond, as far as he could see down the road ahead, there was nothing moving. Climbing back in the cab, he engaged the gears and began to coast down the hill. It was hard to keep the speed of the truck down to a safe limit. The truck had almost no brakes and he didn't want to make more noise with the motor than he could help. But, above all, he didn't want to have a tire blow out here.

It seemed to him that it took an eternity to get down the hill and up to the first building. As he approached it, he kept his head bent down as though examining the almost nonexistent instruments and controls. Then, as he passed the first group of men, he observed out of the corner of his eye that no one even glanced at him. In fact, few people were on the road. The heat of the late morning had driven everyone home from the teahouse which, as far as he could see, was the sole local industry. He looked straight ahead and just kept going. Mercifully, there was no roadblock. In a few seconds, he was again on the open road. Again alone, again safe.

The first test had been easy. Maybe too easy. Worse lay ahead. Faizabad, the only real town before Kunduz, would be a different matter. Faizabad prided itself, he had read, on being 'modern'. It even had a newspaper. It was the headquarters of the province of Badakhshan and a major police headquarters.

He managed a faint smile, thinking that Faizabad was a sort Afghan version of Cody, Wyoming in the Wild West of the 1870s. Lots of active and suspicious people and not much to do. It certainly would not do to try to make it through town in the early evening when everyone would be walking about or drinking tea. Then the townspeople would be hungry for gossip. His coming through would be an event. He could almost hear the conversations,

"Did you see that truck? It looked like Qol Khan's."

"But that wasn't old Qol Khan driving it."

"Where were his boys? It looked empty."

"Is he now so rich he just rides around empty for fun?"

"Why didn't he wave to old Mohammed like he always does?"

"And he didn't bring the eggs he promised Tareq."

"Strange. Do you think he is all right?"

"Some peculiar things going on up by the frontier, I hear."

"Maybe we should tell the police."

"Better keep away from them!"

"Yeah, I don't want to get involved either."

"But, if they ask us why we didn't tell them, we'll catch hell."

"You're right. It's safer to inform them. Come on, let's go."

No, hearing those voices in his imagination, Jack realized he couldn't risk approaching the town at gossip time. Better pick a time when everyone had just rolled over for a half an hour more sleep. Not midnight, when some people would still be awake or even later, when everyone would be suspicious of a truck on the road, but first light. That was a time when a trucker might be legitimately on the move but everyone else would be fighting for a little more warmth under the blanket or making babies. Caution was better than speed. Better a tortoise than a hare. Hounds don't bother much with tortoises…he almost chuckled for the first time in as long as he could remember.

Bending over the wheel, listening to the steady ping of the engine, he tried not to think about the truck. Obviously, it was nearly worn out. He could not have made more speed even with a better road. Better not to strain the antique engine or what was probably a transmission in the last stages of decay. Anyway, a moderate speed would also keep the fuel consumption low.

'Fuel?' he suddenly thought with alarm. With all the other problems, he had not even considered that. There was no fuel gauge, unless a small cracked and darkened disk of glass, unreadable to his unpracticed eye, was one. The Mongols would have known by long experience when to add fuel. He didn't. So, about an hour out of the little hamlet, he found a place where he had good observation up and down the road and pulled off to check.

Keeping the engine running, he took the opportunity to look over the truck. He decided not to raise the engine hood. For his own peace of mind, he thought it was better not to know what the engine looked like. Probably it would be missing many things he would think essential and be all patched together with bailing wire. Better not to know about that. But fuel was another matter. That he had to see to.

Strapped on the side of the platform, Jack was relieved to find several Jerry cans of fuel. They were the essential things now. He untied the rope that held them in place and pulled the first one off the rack. Unscrewing the cap, he smelled it. Horrible stuff, it struck his nose as a mixture of gasoline and oil with a liberal dash of sheep dung. But, he figured, that was the truck's approved diet or at least all Qol Khan could afford. So he poured it in the main tank. Looking around the cab, he found a long metal rod on which a stain about half way along the shaft showed that it had been used to check the fuel level. He inserted it into the tank. Then, pulling it out, he saw that the new stain was lower than the old one; so he added another can of fuel. Checking again, he saw that it was still too low. So he added another can. Finally, the two stains more or less matched so he assumed that the tank was now as full as it ought to be.

Then he checked the water in the radiator and topped it up from a Jerry can that smelled about as bad as the diesel fuel but was lighter in color. 'God,' he thought. 'I hope I don't have to drink *that*!' Finally, he walked around the truck to examine the tires. Most of them were worn almost through and one had a large bulge along the side. He certainly should change it, he realized, but he didn't want to stop any longer than he had to. It was a hard choice: he couldn't afford a flat in the wrong place, he thought, but could he do it? He looked for a toolbox but found nothing. As he was about to give up, he found a tire wrench but no spare tire. 'Nothing to be done,' he shook his head and climbed into the cab.

Back out on the highway, he kept the truck to a steady slow pace, except once when a particularly rough section forced him to less than five miles an hour. Then, the anguished motor almost stalled and began to overheat. Fortunately, just then, a slight incline enabled him to coast. Each mile was an agony, each pot hole a trap, each ping of the engine like a faltering heart beat.

The hours slowly passed. Dazed from the fumes of the engine he snapped to full alert when he saw a truck parked on the side of the road. Its crew was partly hidden underneath, changing a tire, repairing an axle or just sleeping. No one waved. He stared straight ahead and kept going. Increasingly tired and numb.

Gradually, the sun sank toward the West. When he judged it to be about two hours before sundown, he estimated — guessed? hoped? feared? — that he would be fairly near to Faizabad, maybe ten to twenty miles. He would have to stop soon.

Looking for a place to pull off the road, he came upon a hard, flat plain cupped between half a dozen small broken hills. As he slowed, he could see the remains of campfires, blackened cans and charred rubbish and a few worn out tires. Apparently, this was a 'normal' stopping place. So truckers or any other passersby, if there were any, would not think it strange if they happened to see his truck.

With great care, thinking as he did constantly of the bulge on the left rear tire, he pulled off the road and eased the truck down into a gully. The bed of the gully was smooth gravel and on it he was able to drive about two hundred yards into a secluded spot from which he could not be seen from either the road or the camping ground. He coasted to a stop.

What about the engine? He pondered. If he turned it off, could he start it again? When he had topped up the fuel tank, he had left it running, but he could not let it idle the whole night. It would make too much noise and would probably use up all his remaining fuel.

So, with a sinking feeling, he pulled the bare wires apart. The motor rattled and died.

For a few moments, he just sat in the cab just enjoying the silence. He stretched his arms wide, cracked his back and twisted his head from side to side. Then he reached over and picked up the thermos. The water was tepid and smelled of sheep wool but it was wet and felt soothing on his dry throat. He drank carefully, swilling the water around in his throat, washing away the dust and grit he had breathed in from the road.

Reaching inside his jacket, he pulled out "Percy's" 7.65 mm Czech automatic. It would not amount to much in a land full of Kalashnikovs, he knew, but having it made him feel a little bit safer.

Needing to urinate, something his lack of water had not forced for many hours, he pushed against the cab door. It was stuck. He pushed his shoulder against it again. No give. Sliding across the seat, he pressed down on the door handle and banged it open. His legs were stiff and he paused a moment before opening it all the way. Then, just as he was about to climb out, he *felt* rather than *heard* the rush of bodies against the cab and something rip down his leg. With a scream, he jerked the door closed just in time to stop the onslaught of a wild dog.

Looking out the window, he could see a dozen of them. He knew about them from gruesome stories he had heard and was terrified. Run-a-way sheep dogs, they had established themselves at this campground, and, accustomed as they were to human beings, they had lost all fear of men. Often starving, they laid in wait to eat refuse, to grab a sheep if they could or, when they happened upon a man alone and unwary, to attack and devour him. As Jack recoiled in shock and looked out at the circling silent pack, he realized that he had run into an ambush as deadly as those that had already killed Percy and Qol Khan. Once again, and this time by an even smaller margin, he had just missed death.

Thwarted in their first rush, the pack tried to break into the truck. Jack just got the window up as another beast, a shaggy white male who was missing all of one ear and half of the other, scrambled onto the motor hood and was trying to twist around into the cab. The hate and fury Jack saw in those eyes, he thought, was more than hunger. While Jack had gaped into the eyes of the dog on the hood, the others were deploying around the cab. Like professional assassins, they made no fuss about their work but just moved silently into position for the kill.

While Jack was focused on the white dog, another dog was trying to find a way into the cab on the other side. With surprising agility, he managed to climb up on the running board and had got his head in the window before Jack noticed him. Then it was the dog's hot breath that warned him. He had no time to roll up the window. Anyway, the handle was practically in the mouth of the dog. In a few more seconds, Jack realized, the dog would be in and on him.

Instinctively, Jack whipped out his automatic and, pulling back the hammer with his thumb, thrust the gun almost into the mouth of the dog. He pulled the trigger. The concussion of the explosion, confined in the small cab, deafened and stunned him.

Recovering a few seconds later, he leaned across the seat and began frantically to roll up the window. As he did, he looked down and saw the dog, a canine image of Qol Khan, its face blown away, lying contorted and broken on the gravel.

It could not have been more than a second or so later that the pack, cheated of its meal of Jack, fell upon the still quivering body of the dog and began to tear it to pieces. Jack shuddered at the horror he had just missed and in his mind's eye saw himself borne down in a rush of snapping jaws. As he watched, he thought grimly, 'they wouldn't have wasted an ounce. They would have eaten me, shoes and all.'

Furious and unnerved with terror, he pointed the automatic into the snarling cannibal mass. Just as his finger tightened, his rational mind took over. He had only six bullets left and he could not, in any event, risk another loud noise. The first had been confined by the walls of the cab. Another, fired in the open, might bring down upon him an even more dangerous kind of animal. So, passively as in the scene at the truck, he watched in horror as the dogs, as speedily as any butcher, dismembered their fallen comrade. As each one tore off a limb or a rib, it ran aside growling to chew. The leader of the pack, the one that had lunged at Jack from the right side of the cab, got the lion's share. Several of the younger, smaller dogs got little and were driven off each time they approached the pitiful remains of fur and bone. Apparently giving up, they disappeared from Jack's view and, a few minutes later, he could hear them in the hooded body of the truck, tearing apart the bloody, rotting skins, searching for bodies beneath. Jack felt surrounded, engulfed by the pack. Although safe in the cab, he was trapped. But, exhausted from his long drive, the walk, sleeplessness, and terror, he slumped forward onto the wheel and passed out.

Fitfully sleeping in short gasps, he was beset by nightmares. From the last, he awoke with a muffled scream. Shaking with exhaustion and fear, he rubbed his eyes and looked about him. It was now completely dark outside. He urgently needed to urinate, but he dared not go out of the cab. So, gingerly, he raised himself up kneeling on the seat, rolled the window down part way and managed to empty his bladder without getting out...or getting mobbed. Again, he rolled the window up to within an inch of the top. The cab was stuffy and smelled of years of men's sweat and diesel-oil-stained clothes. Even in the penetrating smell, however, he took some comfort for it meant safety.

Settling down again in the warmth of the great coat, he leaned against the wheel and dozed rather than slept. Waking up from time to time, he would check his watch. That was the one stable point in his life, he thought. It seemed neutral, safe, impervious to the alarms of the day, unaffected by the elasticity of experience. Finally, the hands contrasted with the green luminous background to indicate that the hour was 3:30 A. M.

Danger or not, he would have to get out of the cab to refill the fuel tank with the last of the Jerry cans.

Soon, he must plunge through Faizabad. It was crucial, maybe even literally vital, to hit the town at first light. As he had surmised, true night would be suspicious and sunrise too late. He had to be almost exactly on time, but how could he judge?

He didn't know how far away the town was or what the road to it was like. Better to get in place too soon rather than too late. The town couldn't be far and if he hit it sooner than expected, he imagined – hoped – he could find a place to pull off the road and wait again, dangerous as that would certainly be.

But, first to the chores of the truck. No matter what, he had to take care of them. So, with eyes now accustomed to the night, he gazed out the window and then cautiously rolled down the glass half way. The night was deathly silent. He clapped his hands. Expectantly and fearfully, he awaited a growl or at least a rustle of gravel. None came. He whistled. Still no response. Then he took a greasy wad of rag from the floor of the cab and threw it out beside the truck. Still nothing moved. Gingerly he pressed down again on the door handle and forced the rusty door partly open…that was the point at which he had been attacked before. He waited. No movement. He counted to fifty. Still no movement. Taking Percy's automatic in his hand and cocking the hammer with his thumb, he swiveled on the seat and dropped his thumb onto the safety catch. Then, pushing the gun before him, he opened the door and thrust out a leg. Again he waited. Then, cautiously, he climbed down.

His legs were stiff and he felt cramped, but he froze to listen and look around him. Just as he had in the cabin the night before.

'God!' he thought. 'Could it only have been the night before? A lifetime passed since that cabin.'

All around the truck the night was not just still; it seemed dead, not so much reassuring as sinister. With one hand still on the door handle so that he could steady himself and, if need be, leap back into safety, he thrust the pistol into his pocket and picked an empty Jerry can off the running board rack. He swung it as far as he could off into the night. It clattered on the gravel but brought no response. Then, he let go of the door, got his pistol back in his right hand, bent over and, with his left hand, scooped up a handful of gravel. He tossed it off into the blackness and it rattled against the stones and dry leaves. A twig cracked in the dark and his hand flew upright with the pistol. Bending over, he picked up another handful of gravel and threw it toward the sound. Nothing moved. Cautiously he put the pistol away and reached behind him toward the truck with his eyes still on the pool of darkness in front.

Fumbling as he tried both to see in front and feel behind his back, he found the remaining Jerry cans. Then, turning slowly, he picked one up. It was full. He unscrewed the cap and smelled. Good thing he did. It was water or, horrible though it smelled, it was not diesel fuel. If he had poured that in the tank...but, he stopped, better not to imagine new danger. He had enough.

So, he tried the next can. It smelled right. To be sure, he stuck his finger into the liquid and tasted it. Revolting taste, it almost made him vomit. But it confirmed that it was the same sort of gasohol, probably mixed with dung and grease, he had smelled before. He carried the can over to the main tank, and pulled out the rag which served as a cap. In a few minutes, he had filled the tank or, at least, used up the remaining jerry cans. This was the end: when this lot ran out, the truck would stop.

Prudently, he thought he would check the back of the truck, just in case there was one more can. As he walked back, he saw, scattered all over the bottom of the gully, the remains of the rotting skins with which he had communed so miserably two days before. They had been torn to shreds. Tufts of hair and bits of skin were all over the ground.

No cans were in the back, but as he continued around the truck, he found another rack with three more. These he smelled, and tasted as before, and added to the main tank. When he knocked on tank, it sounded full, but, when he stuck in the metal rod, the fresh stain was well below the old stain. That was a bad sign. Kunduz, he figured, was still more than 200 kilometers down the road and he had no idea whether or not he could get close with the fuel he had. Probably the truckers had some regular stop on the road, but, of course, he dared not go near that.

So, climbing into the cab he pumped the gas pedal several times. He hoped that would prime the engine. Then, reaching down below the wheel, he twisted them together. But nothing happened. There was no spark. . He began to sweat. He crossed and recrossed the wires. Still, nothing happened. He began to curse at himself. "Damn fool," he said aloud. "Screwed it up... screwed it up! God damn it to hell!" Then, with a shock of relief, he realized that he had not twisted together the main wires. And, groping under the dashboard, he fished out the main wires, and twisted them together. This time, when he tried the starter, he got the usual explosion and the motor turned over. With a sigh, he realized he had passed the first test. The second might be much harder.

Now the trick was to get out of the gully without breaking an axle, blowing a tire or getting stuck. What a fool he had been not to use the daylight to get into position or to give himself a margin of safety by parking the truck on an incline, like he had done the Jeep for Nora. Then, he could have started it by rolling. Exhaustion led to sloppiness, he cursed himself. At least he knew that luck was still with him, even if his wits were not. Leaning out of the window to see, Jack backed cautiously out to a place where the gully widened and flattened out. There, easier than he expected, he was able to turn around. Without lights, he found the way he had come in and, in a few moments, was again on the flat camping ground. A dark shape, looking vaguely like a truck, seemed to be parked at the far end, but Jack didn't look too closely. Probably, if anyone was there, the sheep dogs, now his allies, kept the driver and his crew inside. In a few seconds, Jack was out on the road.

It was pitch black and he was unsure what to do about lights. Indeed, he didn't know whether he had any or not. But before he checked, he considered the odds. Turned on, they might attract attention, but, driving without lights would make him seem to have something to hide and thus perhaps attract even more attention.

Besides, without lights, he could not see the potholes or the piles of stones. He was sure to have a blow out if the aged and bulging tire hit a stone or break an axle if a wheel went into a pothole. So he switched the lights on after he had cleared the first hill away from the camping ground and settled down to what seemed to be the cruising speed of the truck.

Mile after empty mile went by with no sign whatever of the town. Had he miscalculated? The town should have been quite close. He looked at his watch again. It was 4:15. First light would come in a few minutes. He tried to pick up a little speed. At 4:30, there was still no sign of the approach of a town. Then, at 4:35, he crested a hill and suddenly right below him was the sleeping town. Off to the East, the first hint of a pale yellow and orange colored the horizon. By sheer luck, he had hit it just right.

The town presented a face of blank mud walls. Gates and doors were tightly closed against the night. On each side of the road, a line of spindly poplars marched along the customary *jui*, the combination open sewer, gutter and water main. No lights interrupted the dark and, so far as he could tell, no people were as yet on the street. The call to prayer had not yet sounded. When it did, the male population would, grudgingly, rise to greet the day in the name of God, but now, each man was buried under his blanket or in the arms of his woman. For all this, Jack was grateful.

The road led into a square which, he imagined, a few hours from now would be crowded with peddlers and animals, with merchants sitting silently in their makeshift stalls awaiting their customers, like spiders in their webs, while auctioneers marched about yelling the bids for rugs and chickens. Now, the stalls were shuttered against the curious and the lawless. The presence of the feared security police was indicated only by bundles of blankets and rugs under which they were sound asleep.

Unchallenged, probably unnoticed, the truck rolled on through the town. The road narrowed. There, just ahead, Jack saw the checkpoint. But the pole was standing upright on its weighted end. It was unmanned. In a moment, Jack was past it. He was on the Kunduz road. Only the town of Khanabad lay between him and it.

Twice he passed through little hamlets, but they were almost deserted. He wondered if he had lucked into a holiday or a day of national mourning. He didn't know, but he was grateful. Only twice did another truck approach, from the front, and each time, the driver waved. Looking down, Jack gave a perfunctory wave of his arm in return. Then, when the other truck was past, he peered out. Neither truck stopped or seemed to slow down.

Finally, about noon, he guessed that he would be nearing Khanabad. What to do? He was torn. The truck had saved his life. And maybe even his mission. But, he knew, it would not be wise to press his luck any further.

Khanabad was too close to Kunduz, the provincial capital and headquarters of the police. Out here, even if the police learned that he had passed Faizabad, which seemed unlikely for at least a few days, he could be almost anywhere. Badakshan Province was a vast and nearly vacant area.

But, if he were observed going through Khanabad, the security police could pinpoint him. So, he decided, reluctantly, it was better to hide the truck somewhere off the road and walk the last stretch into Kunduz.

Just ahead, as he was pondering what was the least dangerous course, the road turned and off to the side he saw a small but deep gully. It had been scoured out by the spring flash floods and was less smooth than the other gully, with boulders scattered along the bottom, but, with extreme care, he managed to make his way nearly a hundred yards before the boulders stopped him.

He leaned out of the window and was relieved to find that he could not see the road. Here, no one would notice the truck unless he was searching for it. And, even the little that might be seen from the road was so covered with dust as to be virtually camouflaged. With luck, it would be a day or even two before the police were notified. By then, he should be in Kunduz.

Not that Kunduz was salvation. 16,000 feet and 200 miles of rugged mountain and deep valleys separated it from Kabul. He could never hope to make that. Alone and on foot. And, as he had seen, on the drive up with Nora, the only road, the Kabul road, was blocked by at least one security police checkpoint. However sloppy the guards might look, they didn't have to be very formidable to stop an unarmed, exhausted and, by then, probably starving man. There was no way he could avoid them or sneak passed them. Off the road, even if he knew the way, it would have been impossible to cross that range in less than a week. So, without a pack animal and supplies, it would be impossible. As he sat, he rubbed his chin and thought: could he get a donkey and food in Kunduz? But he had no money. "You won't need any. Don't take any." Smith had ordered. Perhaps he could steal a donkey but doing that would only make his situation worse. The owner and his friends would be hot after him. To steal a car would be still worse and would solve nothing — he could not get around that checkpoint at the mountain pass. No, unless he could find a way to make contact with Smith. Or, the idea suddenly popped into his head, perhaps with Nora. Without some help from them or someone else, he would have to admit that the Hindu Kush was the Red Queen: he would be checkmated.

Still, he had to try. He had no choice. It wasn't, any longer, after the murders he had seen, 'get there or give up' but 'get there or die.' He climbed down from the cab, taking with him the thermos, now filled with greasy water from the Jerry can, and, still wrapped in the greatcoat and head cloth, made his way back to the road. Now, he would have to worry both about wild dogs and wilder people. He bent over and picked up three large, jagged rocks to throw at any dogs he might encounter. The rocks wouldn't have stopped the dogs he met last night, but, for ordinary dogs, they might work. As a last resort, he could shoot to defend himself. But, shooting was really a last resort and probably wouldn't work anyway. His best hope was to move rapidly.

So, he set off on his now stiff and aching legs. This new effort quickly showed him just how exhausted he really was. And, no wonder. He had got almost no sleep for over 48 hours. 'Christ,' he thought, 'when had he really slept?

It seemed weeks.' And, while he was too frightened to worry about food, he was weak from hunger. Realistically, he would have to get some rest or he would collapse. So he began to be on the outlook for another sanctuary with a 'fox hole' so he could 'lie up' again. Someplace where he could oversee the road...

Road! That was it. Road. The AID people were building a road up here! Why hadn't he thought of that? That must have been why Smith had been talking to Crownover. Crownover was the AID road man, was always out in the rural areas building roads. Now, Jack had heard him say that he was up here, near Kunduz. Working on a culvert, he had said. Then, thinking back over their meeting, he remembered that it was thanks to Smith that he had met Crownover. 'Curious that,' he mused. 'Had Smith, who never did anything casually, meant for them to meet – and at his office. As though to signal without actually saying it that Crownover was somehow involved, maybe as a fallback, a refuge, a bolt hole or a new lease on life if the operation went sour.'

He hadn't thought of it at the time, but more or less by accident – or was it an accident? – they later met at Nora's house for a drink. Their meeting had been arranged by Nora. Had Smith told her to do it? In a long chat, Crownover told him a lot about his work on the Afghan roads. What he said hadn't made much of an impression on Jack at the time, but after the experiences of the last few days he mulled over their conservation. Of course, Crownover had not said much and was embarrassed when Jack tried to draw him out, but the gist was clear – what Smith and by inference what Nora and Jack were doing was destructive, a violation of trust and would get a lot of people hurt. Being very 'people oriented,' as he copied the fashionable phrase, Crownover was deeply disturbed by the idea that what they were up to was not good.

But if he really felt this way, was it conceivable that Crownover could be part of Dirhem? Or was his talk also a sort of cover? Could he have been planted to give Jack a way out – a way back to Kabul -- in case he needed it?

142

Not very likely, Jack decided. But, then, everything so far was unlikely. Still, Jack did not have many options and even if Crownover was not involved, or even hostile, Jack did not have the luxury of overlooking him. Now giddy from hunger and exhaustion, Jack rushed to embrace even a faint hope. 'Maybe I can talk him into taking me to Kabul in one of the AID vehicles. I'm not beaten yet!' So energized he was by this new hope that he jumped up and started off down the road again in a sort of slow dogtrot.

A DIFFERENT CONTRONTATION

AS HOUR FADED INTO DISTRAUGHT HOUR, throughout the nights since Jack had been due to return to Kabul, Nora had lain awake. In her battle with sleeplessness, she felt as though her whole life was passing in review. And it always came to a head on the question of the mission. What was it all about? Even more, what was it all *for*? Was Jack just a pawn in a chess game? And what was the game, anyway. As she went over and over all she had been able to find out, it all seemed so senseless. Almost worse, so badly planned, no sloppy in execution and so needless. As the hours faded into one another, she became more and more sure that Jack was being sacrificed -- and maybe not even for a red queen but for the vanity, even the stupidity of one man, her boss, Thomas Smith.

On the third – or was it the fourth – day, she had decided on a dangerous course of action. Something the training courses had alluded to as almost unthinkable. But still acknowledged as a requirement in an absolute danger, a danger not to one's self, but to the service and its obligation to act in the preservation of the country. She would have to confront Smith, whatever the consequences might be.

Would such a reckless action save Jack? She realized that whatever happened in the cozy nest of Kabul would probably not affect what might happen – indeed, what was probably already happening – far to the north, beyond the vast mountain range. Worse, for her, his doubts rang in her memory:

"…I really don't understand it."

"…To buy a *kelim* from the nomads. What a joke."

"…I don't relish the idea of trying to get by here again. I hope Smith has this covered."

"I wouldn't like to test Afghan hospitality … hidden in the back of a trader's truck."

She had scoffed at him. "Don't talk like that, Jack…Smith is a real pro…You told me yourself that he is going to have you picked up in Kunduz and that you'll be back in Kabul the day after I get there. You just get a kick out of being melodramatic."

But she also remembered thinking, even then, 'The whole mission didn't make sense.' The very words echoed in her mind. 'The mission violated all the tradecraft she had been taught. Why two obvious Americans? Why not local agents? Why way up there, so obvious? What was Jack supposed to do anyway? As a foreigner, he would be immediately spotted. And why such a silly cover story? With Kabul full of rugs, why would anyone drive up here to buy one?' Even to her, not knowing all the details admittedly, the plan seemed full of holes, gaps so large that even a novice in operations could hardly have made them. And whatever else he was, Smith was no novice.

'Then there was the barrier. How could Jack get to Kunduz? He had to pass this way. And that barrier was real.'

Memories of these thoughts swirled around in her mind, driving away all hope of sleep but building a growing determination to confront the source of the danger, Smith.

So it was that the next morning, Nora silently pushed open the door to Smith's office.

Jumping up from behind his desk, he almost ran toward Nora, thrusting out his hand. He was surprised at how strong her grip was. "Ah, Nora," he laughed, "I feel you are in good health!"

Nora did not laugh but stared intently into his eyes.

"I was about to call you," he continued, not noticing her look. "I have good news for you.

"I was very impressed by your report on the Communist party in the University. It was far and away the most complete and balanced view I have seen. And, I asked you to come in to tell you that I have sent it Langley with a recommendation for a commendation for you."

As he looked into her face, he expected a smile, but it did not come. Only, and without emotion, came the words, "thank you, Mr. Smith."

"Yes, it was really an eye-opener, full of detail. We have had nothing like it. My hearty congratulations."

Nora still did not smile. "Mr. Smith, I didn't know you wanted to see me. I had asked your secretary for this appointment. I have come here to talk with you," she said.

"Well, by all means, sit down. Would you like a coffee?

"No, just a few minutes of your time."

"OK, shoot," he laughed.

"It's about Jack and the mission you sent him…us…on."

"Well, before we start, I have to tell you that I cannot say very much."

"I don't want to ask you…you know …about the objective. I want to talk about the procedure in which I was involved."

"Nora, you are highly trained officer and you know that object and procedure often get entangled. So I warn you, I probably I won't be able to satisfy you."

"Ok, I know the limits and I won't ask you what I don't think you will want to tell me.

"Not to be rude, but I don't think you can judge that. You see, this is a code word operation…extremely tightly held."

"Can I ask if Jack knew its purpose?"

"Well, let's just say that he knew what he needed to know."

"I understand that to mean 'no.'"

Smith spread out his hands, shrugged but did not reply.

"Did he know why you had him…us…doing such bizarre things?"

"Look, Miss Adams," he said, suddenly formal. "I told you he knew what he was supposed to know…what he had a need to know. That is all I can say. I think we had better stop on that note."

"Well it is not so easy, Mr. Smith," Nora noticed that she was no longer 'Nora' but in the changing temper of the talk, now 'Miss Adams.'"

"Nothing is," Smith replied testily.

"What I mean is that what has been done violates all the training I ever had and I think that is very serious."

When Smith didn't reply, she went on. "First, there was your decision to use an identified American officer when all the people who taught me would have said that was stupid. After all we have local assets…paid Afghans who would not be so obvious. You couldn't have made Jack more obvious if you had dressed him in a tuxedo and had him carry a flag. After all, he's a lot bigger than the Afghans. He would have been spotted for an American a mile away. Can you comment on that?"

Smith slowly shook his head, "No. I warned you this is an operation in which you are not involved. Your role ended when you came back to Kabul," Smith said, getting annoyed. "I told you, I really cannot go into this further…"

Ignoring his reply, Nora went on. "And the silly reason you had us put out for the trip, 'to buy nomad rugs.' That was almost like hanging a sign out, and of course in this little town everyone latched onto it to say something big must be afoot. You have not been here as long as I so maybe you don't realize how gossip-hungry the foreign community is. For them, this was a feast. Every remark, every guess, every explanation was naturally overheard by their friends and of course by their Afghan servants. Many of them, we know to be working for the Afghan security. I can only guess what the Afghans told *their* friends or their handlers, but I know more about the diplomatic set. As the tidbits of the story made its way from cocktail party to cocktail party, they grew into monstrous size. The ridiculous cover story of our rug-buying expedition has grown into the preparation of a raid by the 82nd Airborne Division into Russia or China."

Smith laughed.

His laugh infuriated Nora who coldly said, "I wish it was a laughing matter, Mr. Smith, but it isn't. I have reason to believe that at least some senior Afghan officials are also speculating about it.

" And one more thing. Jack is overdue, according to what he told me. Do you even know where he is?"

"Of course, I do. And, as you know, Jack is an able officer, experienced, well-trained and smart. He is in superb shape, I am told, jogging every morning and taking care of himself. He is OK. Of that I can assure you. Now, if you will pardon me. I think we have said all we can."

"Not quite," Nora replied. I was sufficiently upset by the way this has been handled that I felt it my duty to report it to the Agency's Inspector General."

Smith jumped like he had been slapped. Then, after a pause, while rubbing his chin, he responded, "I wouldn't advise that. There is much that you cannot know and a report like that will look bad on your record."

At that allusion to her record, which she took as a callous and self-seeking remark, Nora also started back. "My record is not my primary concern now, Mr. Smith. I think you have jeopardized our whole operation – certainly my whole operation here – I will almost certainly lose my contacts in the university and God knows what this will mean for my colleague, jack. I hope and pray he is safe."

"Of that I am absolutely sure. He is okay and your *colleague* will be back here right on schedule. It is all planned…"

Catching what seemed to her a smirk, Nora went on, looking him steadily in the eye. "Yes, Mr. Smith, my colleague. Also my friend but nothing more than that, Mr. Smith. This is a professional matter. I resent your suggesting that it is a private and emotional matter." With that, Nora stood up and headed toward the door.

Smith got there first and opened the door for her.

Without a word or a backward glance, she passed by the desk of Smith's secretary, Jane, to whom she smiled but did not speak. Then, still in full flight, she sallied out the door that led into the Embassy.

Stopping at the desk of his secretary, Smith silently watched her go. Then, when the outer door closed, he turned to his secretary, saying, "Miss Paterson, did my recommendation of Miss Adams go out in the pouch?"

"Yes, Mr. Smith, it went out in the diplomatic pouch just after you gave it to me, this morning."

"Hum…" Mused Smith, scratching his chin, "can we call it back before the plane takes off?"

The secretary shook her head, "No, I really don't think so, Mr. Smith."

"Are you sure…no, I guess it has gone. Is that…oh, then, please take this message and send it by top priority to the Station Chief in Pakistan."

As was his custom when he was dictating, Smith began to pace back and forth as much as the cramped reception room would allow,

"Dear Ed, I sent a message to DDP by pouch regarding one of my staff, a young woman named Nora Adams, this morning. The pouch has already left Kabul but will be transferred in Karachi to the flight from Delhi."

He paused in his pacing, looked up at the ceiling and continued,

"I need to call it back. Would you please intercept it and send it back to me.

"I know this is unusual, but I will explain when we get together next week.

"In just a few words…"

"Not so fast, Mr. Smith," his secretary interrupted.

"Oh, sorry…where were we? Oh yes, I will explain…

"I will explain when we get together next week, but just in a few words… make that read, 'in just a few words… let me just say that Miss Adams has started behaving erratically, seems to have sort of lost her balance…to put it baldly, has been acting the way I hear women's libbers act, you know acting like they know everything and start interfering in things they don't know about."

Smith did not notice that Jane winced as she wrote down his words.

"I am in the midst of an operation I cannot discuss now, but the way she is acting, she could abort the whole plan. I have to stop her.

"Like I say, the dispatch I put in the pouch must be stopped.

"I will be in a position to explain all this when we meet, but in the meantime, if you could get my dispatch out of the pouch and return it, I would be most grateful. Yours as ever, etc."

As though waiting for an opening, the secretary put down her pencil and spoke out, "Mr. Smith, obviously this is not my business, but I'm an old hand and I know the procedures. I doubt that anyone, even the station chief in Karachi, can break the seal on the pouch without a big set-to by the people in Security."

"I can take that risk," said Smith, "but thank you for your advice."

Jane failed to detect any gratitude in his voice. And with some malice she continued, "And, knowing how delighted you were with Nora's – Miss Adam's – work, I also sent your letter of commendation to Langley by cable. It has undoubtedly already reached Personnel."

Smith wipes his hand across his forehead, frowned and mumbled something indistinct. "Well, that's that...Okay," he continued. "That'll teach me for trying to protect her from doing something that might hurt her career."

Jane also frowned but said nothing.

Smith abruptly turned on his heel, went back into his office and closed the door with as much of a slam as the well-oiled hinges would allow.

Jane's eyes followed him out, not surprised but annoyed as she muttered to herself, "a hellovaway to protect Nora. Protecting his ass is more like it..."

KAZAN KHAN

AS JACK SET OFF ON THE ROAD oward Kunduz, he had felt a burst of energy born of hope. The idea that Ernest Crownover was working on a road nearby might mean salvation or at least the salvation of his mission. But his energy waned rapidly as the minutes went by. Still, he doggedly swung down the road. One hour went by and then a second. He guessed that he had covered about eight or nine miles. Kunduz, he guessed, was at least fifteen more. Five, maybe six, more hours, if he held out. But, anyway, he could not go into the city during daylight. Even hidden under Qol Khan's greatcoat, his clothes -- especially his shoes -- would mark him off as a foreigner. Within minutes, he would be spotted and arrested.

He would have to sneak into the city at just the right moment when people were indoors but not watchful for robbers. Just as he had passed through Faizabad. Neither day nor night. The best time for a man on foot, he thought, would be dusk. He would not be so evident and everyone he met might think it natural that someone coming in from working on a road would be grimy and dirty and searching for the American camp. Or so he hoped. He realized that he was beyond rational decision and was becoming disoriented. He was just too tired to be able to evaluate the risks and form a coherent plan. He simply had to get some rest. It seemed years since he had left that ghastly scene at the cabin. The vision of the disemboweled Qol Khan faded into the memory of the faceless wild dog; the inhuman scream of pain of the Mongol boy faded into his own terror at the attack of the dogs.

A small hill just off the road seemed to offer a vantage point and perhaps a shady place to rest until late afternoon. Nothing in this barren land offered any hint of anything to eat. So Jack turned off the road south toward the hill. He guessed it was about a half a mile away. His mind drifted and he was stunned to find himself suddenly at the base of the hill. He was not aware of having walked to it. Dazed with exhaustion, he was even more aware of fear: how long had he walked? He was no longer counting the segments of hundred paces. He had not checked around himself. Was he followed? Had he been seen? He dropped to the ground to peer around himself. But his eyes refused to focus. The whole earth spun around. If he relaxed now, he knew, he was gone. He slapped his face as hard as he could. It stung and woke him momentarily, but, now again wakeful, he realized his danger. He might have walked right into the arms of his hunters. He simply had to sleep. With a last effort, he picked his way from rock to rock up the sides of the hill and, as best he could, once more scanned the countryside. In his last coherent moments, he had a vivid view. The land was not just bare. It was bonelike: even the soil was gone. It was like a carcass picked clean by vultures. Nothing remained but the bone of the long spine of the Hindu Kush. No one could exist, he thought, on this wretched land. Then, just as he was about to settle down into the dust, he saw at his feet the sign of a nomad prayer site. Drawn crudely in the sand, dust and gravel, and marked with small stones, was a shallow furrow. In the middle of the line, pointing West toward Mecca, was a half circle, the prayer niche to orient the worshipers.

Although not a religious man himself, the prayer niche gave Jack a curious feeling of purpose, even of hope. Hard to believe, but even in this dead land, at least some men had found the energy and purpose to think beyond food, drink and murder. He dropped to his knees and ran his fingers along the furrow. It was not an act of piety but of prudence -- he wanted to know how long it had been since others had been on this site. In the desert, he knew, time was measured not by days or hours but by winds and sand. The bottom of the furrow, to his surprise, was still moist and little loose sand had blown into it. Someone, probably a group of sheep herders, had lined up to pray just hours before. So, with one part of his mind, the weakening part, he said to himself, 'be careful. Probably even those men who tortured those wretched Mongols to death rushed away afterwards to pray. And the Muslims who live in China and Russia in their millions went right on, like the Italian Communists, being both religious and Communist...' But, in that other part of his mind that dealt with sleep and hunger, Jack just no longer cared. Suddenly, the whole world went black.

How long later it was that Jack awoke, he had no idea. Slowly, as though rising through depths of fog, he sensed the acrid smell of an unwashed human body. As he painfully opened his swollen eyes, he looked right into a Mongol or Turcoman face. With a start, he tried to sit up and his hand flew to his pocket where he had put the dead man's pistol. Squatting almost on top of him and staring intently at him was a tiny boy.

As Jack moved, the boy jumped -- almost hopped -- out of reach and cried out like an animal in fear.

Jack looked at the boy and then hurriedly looked around him, trying to focus his eyes in the westering sun. He could see no one else. The boy was alone, and except for a slingshot, unarmed. Jack dropped his hand from his undrawn gun. Then, as quickly as he could on his stiff and cramped legs, Jack stood up and, turning away from the boy, peered down the hillside. There was no one in sight, but, off in the distance, he saw a flock of sheep. That explained why the boy was there. He was just a little shepherd. How hard it was, Jack thought, to adjust any more to normal life, normal people doing their daily chores. Everything had become sinister, every man a potentially killer.

He looked back at the little boy. When the boy caught his eye, he retreated a few feet further, carefully keeping his distance. 'Wise fellow,' Jack thought. 'I'm the dangerous one here. I guess life hasn't been easy for him either.' Then, to relieve the boy, he buttoned up his jacket to hide the pistol. "*Salaam*", he said. "Peace." It was the customary greeting in all the languages used in Afghanistan. The boy stared impassively and silently at him.

Surprised by his lack of response, Jack examined him closely. Almost anyone would respond to that greeting. The boy had about him more the look of an animal than a human. His hairless face seemed utterly impassive and his eyes were dull. Jack guessed he would be about fourteen, but his body was painfully thin, almost emaciated. On his legs, he wore the long, supple boots of the *chapandar*, the Mongol horseman, but they were thrust into thick slippers, made of castoff truck tires. Leather was too valuable for walking on rocks and gravel. His baggy pants were tucked into the boots. It was difficult to say what color the pants were since they had been patched and re-patched so many times that red and blue and yellow had mingled and absorbed dust and grime to form a sort of dun-colored tweed.

As Jack looked at him, he mumbled more to himself than to the boy, "A regular Joseph you are, with those 'many colors' aren't you?" The boy cocked his head and stared uncomprehending into Jack's eyes. His yellow, flat face was crowned by a rough cap made of scraps of karakul. He gave off the ripe smell of sheep. He even looked like a young sheep. His only really distinctive piece of clothing -- so tentlike on him that it must have been a castoff from some adult -- was the typical nomad coat, a sort of inside-out sheepskin, with the remains of gaudy embroidery on the leather. Jack said its name, pustin, to watch if the boy touched it or made any response. Then he would know if he spoke Pashto or Dari. The boy just stared at him.

If the boy was away from his home, tending his sheep, Jack considered, he must have some food. Jack was now desperately hungry. So, since the boy did not respond to any language Jack knew, he tried a sort of basic sign language. He pointed to his stomach and hunched his shoulders and frowned. Then he pretended to put food into his mouth and to chew. He smiled. "Please," he said in Dari and then in Turkic. The boy cocked his head, Jack acted out a little skit of a man getting a bowl of food and eating. Infuriatingly, the boy just stared at him. Impatiently, Jack tried again. The boy remained impassive. "Christ, you must be the original Mongolian idiot," Jack said aloud in English and stepped forward. At this apparently threatening gesture, the boy darted back out of reach.

"Oh, shit!" Jack blurted out, and slapping his dusty clothes, sat down exasperated. The boy advanced to his original place. Jack pretended to ignore him. He lay down and closed his eyes. But his hunger and frustration forced him to try again. The boy must have some bread and cheese with him. Perhaps he would understand a trade.

He reached into his pocket and pulled out a pencil. Then, holding the pencil toward the boy with one hand, he pretended to eat with the other. The boy shrugged his shoulders. 'Aha', thought Jack. 'Some progress. Maybe he wants to haggle. Pencils may not be worth much, but I'm near the bottom of the barrel.' He felt around in his pockets and pulled out what was almost his last possession, a small note pad. "Now, how about this?" he said in English. The boy shrugged again. Then, on an impulse, he pulled out his pistol. The boy jumped to his feet terrified. "I guess that tells me something about the quality of your life," Jack sighed sadly in English.

He nodded, smiled and motioned to the boy to sit down. The boy sank onto his heels but with the tension of a cocked spring. He was ready to leap and run at any suspicious move. Jack pretended not to notice and, on a whim, extracted the clip from the automatic and pulled back the slide to eject one red-coated bullet. Then, shoving the clip back into the butt of the gun, he dropped it into his pocket. He looked up at the boy, now staring intently at him, and with a flick of his arm tossed the bullet to the boy. The boy jumped back but then advanced and picked the bullet off the ground. He looked at it, turned it upside down and smelled it. Then, to Jack's horror, he jumped to his feet and, in a bound, was off down the hillside running hard.

Almost before he knew what he was doing, Jack had pulled out his pistol and was aiming at the boy's retreating figure. Fortunately, he had not put another bullet in the breech. With a shudder, he lowered the gun. "God!" He said aloud. "What am I coming to...reduced to killing retarded children." And, another, less humane, voice within him warned that a shot would make too much noise. He felt like he was coming apart, drained, exhausted, beaten. He watched the retreating figure of the boy and again slumped to the ground. He knew he should move, try to find a new hiding place, but he was just too far gone. 'Not defeated by the Hindu Kush, not shot by the Security Police, not eaten by wild dogs...caught by a retarded child,' he shook his head.

He felt himself slipping again into a void...not even fear could overcome his exhaustion. How long he slept, he didn't know, but as he again struggled upward from an abyss of narcolepsy, Jack again felt himself being watched. Again that smell. More in instinct than with thought, he rolled over slightly and moved his hand carefully and in what he thought was the way a sleeping man might to the pocket with the automatic. Then, fully awake, he quickly opened his eyes.

As his sleep-blinded eyes focused, he saw squatting in front of him the shepherd boy and with him were two heavily armed men.

For a few moments, Jack just stared. He was stunned. Was this the moment he had been dreading? Was the mission ending like this, in a whimper? To pull out his gun was to court death. From the boy -- and the bullet -- they would know he was armed. He looked from face to expressionless face. Like the men in the truck, they gave no hint of emotion. He waited for one to speak. Neither did. They just stared at him. Finally, he could stand the tension no longer and said,

"Salaam." They merely stared back.

He glanced down at the dust around him. Footprints were everywhere. They must have been there for a long time, perhaps an hour or more; that was a good sign. If they wanted to, they could easily have bound him or killed him.

Slowly and as gracefully as his aching joints would allow, he began to rise to his feet. The men matched his moves. The oldest of the men bowed slightly and pointed down the hill. As Jack cautiously peered down, he saw three horses, little nomad ponies, like the *chapandars* rode in the *buzkashi* rodeos. They were saddled and hobbled, contentedly eating from nosebags. He looked back at the older man. The man nodded and made a sweeping gesture with his arm.

"Okay, if you insist," Jack said in English and in Turkish "*Teshakur ederim*, I thank you." 'Perhaps,' he thought, 'they will feed me...anyway if they wanted to turn me in, they could already have done it.' So he shrugged his shoulders and started picking his way down the hillside toward the ponies.

The men followed close behind him while the boy sat down on a rock the edge of the hill, staring silently after them, near his resting sheep. When they reached the ponies, the men took off the hobbles and motioned to Jack to mount the largest. He tried, but he found it surprisingly hard to climb on, even though the pony was small, so stiff and sore was his body. His bones seemed unable to flex, and the pony, smelling an unfamiliar scent, shied each time Jack got his foot in the heavy iron stirrup. Finally, one of the men grabbed the pony's mane and all but lifted Jack onto the saddle. Then he and his companion effortlessly leapt onto theirs.

Putting Jack between them, they began to trot toward the south. Jack looked at his watch. To his acute disturbance, it had stopped. He felt like the one secure part of his existence had been withdrawn. He unlatched the strap and tried shaking it. The two men watched him impassively but intently. He shrugged his shoulders and dropped the watch in his pocket. He would try to set it later.

The minutes passed slowly as they rode toward a distant hill. Very quickly in this unfamiliar seat, Jack became aware of a new ache. Between his legs, his trousers creased on the rough, hard leather of the saddle and rubbed relentlessly. He tried lifting one leg and then the other. The horse, already suspicious, shied and neighed; so he just shrugged his shoulders and tried not to move again. But it was no use. The pain was insistent. He would have to ask the men to stop. He turned to the older of the two men, the one who had helped him onto the horse and said, in Turkic, "I must stop." The men looked at one another and then at him. The older man shrugged. Aching, Jack just pulled on the reins. That got the message to his horse at least. Laboriously and awkwardly, he climbed down.

The two men sat on their horses watching him. Jack handed the reins to the younger man and, as he knew he should, he walked over behind a small bush and squatted as though to urinate. That, at least, people everywhere here understood. And, once squatted, when he knew the men would not be looking at him, he ran his hand down his burning, wet legs. They felt like a tomato held over a flame. The outer skin was raw. He took the now useless head cloth, which he had removed from the body of Qol Khan, tore it in half and wrapped each leg with a piece. Then he pulled up his trousers and buckled on the belt. Even more awkwardly, in his new padding, he walked back to the horses. This time, it was harder to get on but, just as one of the men was preparing to get down to help him, he managed to haul himself onto the horse.

The horsemen resumed their trot and now, in less pain, Jack was able to look around him. He saw that the ground was surprisingly broken. What had appeared from the hill to be a featureless plain was, in fact, rutted and gouged by wind and snow. And, in a sunken plain between folds of eroded cliffs, where just a few moments before he had seen nothing, they suddenly came upon an encampment. Six round yurts -- the traditional Turcoman and Mongol tents -- were lined up along the bank of a deep flood channel which retained enough moisture to support a small patch of dense green vegetation.

Suddenly, they were engulfed by a swarm of children and dogs, and his two escorts flailed into both indiscriminately, sending them flying for cover. In front of the largest of the yurts, they reined to a halt and jumped gracefully off their horses. Jack, now very stiff and sore, gingerly slid off his. In front of him, at the door of the yurt, appeared the bent but still graceful figure of a very old man. Dressed in a striped red and green robe, which flowed down over baggy black trousers, he seemed immensely tall. His yellow face was wrinkled, almost furrowed, and, like the land itself, eroded by the passage of many seasons. It was framed by a sparse, white beard below and above by a high black karakul hat of the old design. Around his waist, a magnificent yellow Kashmir scarf was knotted and thrust into the middle of it was a bone-handled dagger.

Obviously the patriarch of the camp, the old man eyed Jack momentarily and then mumbled a word. Immediately, one of the young men rushed to his side and lifted up the brick red carpet which hung over the door. Then, the old man bowed and elaborately beckoned Jack inside.

Stiffly, Jack tried and failed pathetically to duplicate the graceful bow of the old man and ducked into the twilight of the yurt. Soundlessly, the men followed him and dropped to their knees around a fire pit. Immediately, as though in response to some unvoiced command, a small glass of sweet tea was thrust into his hand. The scalding hot glass almost made him drop it. He saw that his audience had observed his pain. But, then taking it lightly in both hands, he smelled the cardamom and smiled at his host. Gratefully, he sipped. The tea burned its way down his throat into his empty stomach. Another glass immediately appeared. Now with a nearly cauterized esophagus, Jack gulped it down. He could not remember how long it had been since he had drunk. So far, no one had spoken but everyone stared at him, intently inventorying his dress and his every gesture. A third glass of tea appeared. This time, Jack forced himself to drink slowly, as he knew politeness required, with a loud sucking noise.

As he drank, he looked from face to face. Minutely he examined the space within the yurt. His first thought was of an exit. If he had to bolt, could he get out? The only opening was the one through which he had entered. No point even thinking of escape, he realized. The only way out was with the leave of the patriarch. Lest his anxiety become evident, Jack scanned the walls of the yurt as he took another sip.

The walls, he knew, were just a woven wicker frame covered in a thick layer of felt to keep out rain and cold. But, to break the drabness, they were hung with carpets, whose brick colored red backgrounds were offset with white and black 'elephant foot' or flower patterns which seemed to glow in the dim light. While he had never before been in a yurt, he knew that the carpets had been made by young girls for their dowries. Where, he wondered idly were they hiding? Probably peeking in under the flaps. Other carpets and bags covered the saddles which rested along the wall and now served as arm rests for the men. The center piece of the room was a huge brass samovar that gave off clouds of steam and the aroma of tea.

As he finished his tea, the glass was taken from him. Another was offered but, although not satisfied, politeness forced him to refuse. Placing his hand to his brow, he said in what was conveniently both Turkic and Dari, "Salaam" and then in Turkish, "*teshakur*...[thanks]." He wasn't sure what language he should speak. Anyway, he wouldn't have much to talk about with them. Just drink, eat (if possible) and be on his way. But, he knew enough about tribal customs to realize that taking their hospitality would give him, also, their protection for a little while. For a day or so, he would be safe, he hoped, if they had kept to the old ways of their people.

All the while he had sipped the tea and looked around him, the old man had examined every detail of Jack's appearance and manner. Finally, responding to Jack's thanks, he slumped slightly from his rigid upright posture and, bending toward Jack, said in halting but distinct English, "You...are...welcome."

Jack jumped as though he had been slapped. English? Here. From this old man? He looked quickly again at the door and then, with terror written on his face, back at the old man.

"Fear not...you are my guest." The words came more easily as though, having searched in his memory, the old man had found the part of his brain where they were recorded.

Jack stared at him with his mouth open. Then, after what seemed minutes later, he managed, "Do you speak English?"

"You will decide," laughed the old man.

"Where did you...how did you...I mean..."

"Hurry not." And then, in a mixture of English and Turkish, he continued. "We both have questions. But, as a host should, I shall satisfy yours. Then you will speak or not as you wish.

"You are hungry and tired. We will slaughter a sheep. While it is cooking, I will tell you my story. But, first, as your people do, I shall tell you my name. It is Kazan. I am khan of this people and this land and these yurts...and, as your people do..."

162

He rose on his knees and held out his hand to shake Jack's. Despite his aches, Jack jumped up and took Kazan's hand. The old man's fingers as he gripped Jack's hand were long and tapered, thin but almost painfully strong.

"My name," said Jack, "is..." But the old man held up his hand to stop him. "Your name is yours. Here you are my guest. You will talk later if you wish. Now, I will set your mind at rest."

Both men settled down and more tea, this time also for the old man and his sons, was passed around. One of the sons refilled the pot on the top of the samovar from its boiling water, and the other, catching a sign from the old man, went out, apparently to arrange the preparation of the sheep.

"I am an old man, and no more than you, I did not always live here," began Kazan. "I was born far to the north where my people, who are Ersari Turcomans, used to live. "We are Turcomans of the Oghuz-khan, cousins of the Salor, the Sariq, the Tekke and the Yomud. And this land, as far as you can ride in a month, was ours from the time of Chingis Khan or even the time of Oghuz. About all this you will know nothing. But know you, my guest, that my people were the lords of the deserts and steppes of Asia from China to Russia. In our time, we were lords of the Earth. Our ancestors conquered China, India, Persia, Russia and defeated all the armies of the Arabs and the Europeans." As he spoke, Kazan Khan had gazed, with that unfocused look of the nomad, off into the distance to scenes of memory and tradition beyond the walls of the yurt.

Then he stopped, looked at the fire before him and shook his head sadly. "But that was long ago. When I was born, God had abandoned us. Our people were being driven from our pastures and villages

"We fought the Russians since...since times that men have

forgotten. Our ancestors were strong men and brave...But, in the time of my father's father, the infidel Russians tracked us across the great river and beyond the mountains into our towns and camps and pastures. They hunted us down. We fought and we died.

"Oh, we were never many and they came like sand before the wind. Our fathers fought as they always had, as brave men do, but the infidels brought cannon and killed us before we could reach them. They fought as cowards, from afar...fearing to taste the steel of our swords and daggers.

"And they fought, not as men should with honor, but killed the women and the children...and even the animals." Kazan Khan wiped a disgusted frown from his face and spat into the fire pit. "When my father was a young man, they had driven us from most of the lands of his father. And they used our cousins against us so that we were beaten in front and broken behind.

"It was at that time that we first met your people, the English. We liked them because they hated the Russians. But we liked them too because they came among us. We laughed when they put on our dress and tried to speak our tongue. Silly people, they thought they fooled us. But we liked them for what they tried to do. We enjoyed them. We humored them. And we honored them...for they were real men. The Russians were just brutes...we hated them because they were cowards and they fought as cowards do.

"And we hated them because they took our lands. Ah, we loved those lands. They were not as these lands, mean and dry. There we had grass and water. We loved the clean air and the mountains and streams where even fish lived...Ah...those lands where I was born." He gazed vacantly away with a smile on his face. Then he scowled. "Like the sands, they came...they filled our tracks. They dishonored our women. But they were not the worst...The worst came after their *inqilab* their, how do you say, their revolution.

"They killed us with their talk. They corrupted our young men and even conquered our language and split it into parts so we could no longer talk with our cousins. They found us a great people and made us into many little peoples. For death we could forgive them, but for making us a little people, we will always hate them...hate them." Kazan Khan's whole body shook as he slammed his right fist into his left palm. "I am an old man and I have seen much...too much," he sighed. His shoulders slumped forward and he seemed drained, exhausted by his memories.

The room was silent except for the whistle of the samovar. Then, after a few moments, Kazan Khan continued.

"We fought them when we could and ran when we could not. "The English helped us a little...not much. We are not grateful. We are not beggars. And then, when the knives were hot and wet, the English left us...left us to the Russians. Some of the English...did you know Charles Beg? Ah, no, you are too young." He eyed Jack critically. "Charles Beg was a major. He could ride like an *ifrit* and he had eyes like an eagle. When he shot...finished. And, when he gave his word, finished. He was a lord."

Again he fell silent, dredging up memories of that long-ago time of bravery and daring. Then after a long pause, "Charles Beg was my friend...he was a man. But England!" He spat again into the fire. "England had cannon. But England ran from the Russians all the way from Merv and Samarkand back to India...Charles Beg, with tears in his eyes, as brave men have, told me that they had ordered his column to retreat and to leave us to them...

"Of course, I could not stay. I had killed many Russians. I was known...ask about the name of Kazan Khan. They will tell you. Many widows I have made. A price...a treasure...was on my head." His face beamed with pleasure. "No, I could not stay. My name was whispered with fear. So I went with Charles Beg to India. He was my friend. While he stayed, I was treated with honor. But, as the English do, he left.

"I spent nearly twenty years with them. That is where I learned their...your language. But they were bitter years. Me...a warrior, a khan, for whom the Russians would have paid a fortune. Known from Khotan to Baku for my sword. And do you know what they made me become?" His face contorted with agony and shame. "A groom for their horses!

"Oh, of course, I was at first a soldier, but then they cut back the army and all the old men, the men who knew me and knew my worth, left and the young came. They made me a groom for their children. They kept me like a pet dog. They tried to break me. Break Kazan! Ha! I spit on them. It was undignified. It was unseemly. So one night, I took the biggest and the best two horses and a rifle and a blanket...and I left.

"I was not a thief...I was a warrior, and I took what I needed to fight. But their arm was long and they caught me as I tried to cross the frontier. "They took me back in chains! In chains! Can you see? They questioned me, but I refused to speak English and would not answer their questions. They beat me, but still I would not speak. Finally, they threw me in a miserable jail with filthy Indian peasants... peasants... *chomur*...and me a lord of the *chorva* ! It stank. They stank. Worse, they made me a slave, an animal behind bars in a cage! And me a man of the steppe, born with a bridle in my teeth and a rifle in my hands. A Turcoman of the Ersari!

"So I waited. God orders us *sabr*. To be patient, waiting for His will to become known. But *sabr* does not mean giving up. It means getting ready."

He paused and smiled, fingering his dagger handle. Then he stretched out his arm, as though pushing aside a curtain. "One night the Hindu guard came too close." Kazan Khan's long, bony fingers clinched together. "I took the keys from his body. Then, to show those wretches how a lord lives, do you know what I did? I released those filthy Indian peasants. Dogs of Hindus that they were! And I got another rifle, a better one.

"Oh, the English lost when they tried to put Kazan in a cage! And three horses I took. And that time, I rode like a devil, on one pony after another. I drank the blood of the horses…like we used to do. I never stopped except to let the horses drink water from a stream.

"One horse died and then the second, but I rode on and on. Finally, I crossed the frontier and found myself among the Pathans. Of course, I had learned their tongue when I fought with the British and I made myself their guest. When I told my story, they honored me. I lived with them for many moons. And we feasted and rode and shot and sang poetry. The Pathans are not like the English. They know how to treat men.

"Finally, when my time came, they gave me a new horse and a dagger. And I rode north again, north as close as I could to my old lands."

He slumped back against a saddle, tired from his memories.

"My story then became long. But, with the help of God and my cunning, I crossed the frontier of the Great River. I found some of my people. A wretched bunch of sheep they had become under the heel of those devils. And I led them out of Russia, out of our old home, across the great river into this land. But we did not just leave…no, that was not the way I had learned from my father and he from his. As we went, we took back from the Russians all we could carry -- for it was ours -- and we killed as many of their soldiers as we could on the way. In those days, rifles sold for many sheep and so we carried off all their rifles...enough for a whole people. So that is how we came to be here.

"Now I am old and my sons and grandsons are leaving me to work in the cities. The others have all drifted away. The old life is ruined, blown away by the savage winds. The Russians have grown strong and we have become like women. We can no longer fight. Even the British have left except for a few like you." He threw his arms apart in a gesture of despair.

"I am not British," Jack shook his head gravely. "I am American."

"It is all the same," sighed Kazan. "You are white of face and speak as they spoke. You have the same ancestors even if your tribe is sometimes at war with their tribe. You are like us and the Salor or the Yomud. To an old man, it is all the same...all the same." He shook his head slowly and, picking up a pinch of earth from the floor, let it pour through his fingers.

"But to us, it is often very different," said Jack in Turkish. Bitterly he thought of the cabin and the truckers. "No, Kazan Khan, we are as different from the English as you are from the Tekke who drove you from your pasture long ago or the Mongols or the Kirghiz. To us, it matters...matters as it does to you."

The old man, annoyed at being interrupted in his story, shook his head stubbornly and went on, paying no attention to Jack's comment.

"My four sons and my granddaughter, Gul Jamal, are all that are left to me. Of sheep, we have few. Of yurts, only these you see. Once we were rich. Once we were strong. I have lived too long. It is bitter...

bitter to remember. I lived in the wrong age. I was meant to ride and fight in the free air on the endless steppe...Not to be cooped like a sheep in a pen waiting for the knife."

He sighed, his eyes wet from the smoke of the fire and the bitterness of memory. Only the bubbling of the samovar broke the silence.

Lost in thought, mentally chewing the feast of Kazan's memories, Jack gazed around the walls of the yurt at the tent carpets. His eye was caught by a particularly fine *Pardah* hanging over the door. 'That must be the hand work of the grand daughter, Beautiful Rose, *Gul Jamal*,' he was musing when he caught Kazan Khan's eye on him.

"Ah, I see," said the old man in Turkic. "You are not a barbarian! British though you may be. You were admiring the rugs, but were polite and did not say so. Well, these are the last rugs of my people. There will be no more, ever. Who could make them now? But I see by your eye that you know them. You shall have one. Which do you choose?"

"Oh Khan," said Jack gravely in Turkic, as he knew he should for such an offer. "You do me great honor. But now I must ask your mercy."

"Mercy?"

"Yes, mercy. For now I am as you were when you left the British in India. Or when you left the Russians in your ancestors' lands. I can carry nothing but my life. And men are now trying to take even that from me."

Kazan Khan looked at him gravely. He had never heard a Westerner -- or an Englishman, as he insisted -- speak words like Jack was then speaking.

"Of mercy I have little, but protection...well of that I have little as well, but what I have is yours."

"I do not wish to bring my troubles upon you."

"Troubles of others enable one to gain honor."

"But my troubles are very great."

"Then the honor of helping you shall also be great."

"It would be best if no one knew of my being here."

"No one shall. You have my word, the word of a warrior."

"I can only bring you trouble...no honor."

"I do not wish to invade your privacy but in order to help you, perhaps you can tell me, are you then escaping from prison like I did? Did you kill the guards?"

"No, Kazan Khan, not from prison?"

"Then from vengeance?"

"No, not from vengeance."

"Ah, my son, if you do not wish to speak, do not, but to help you, perhaps it would be best if you care to tell me from what or from who then?"

"My story, like yours, is long and difficult."

"Ah," he nodded, "then tell no more. I asked only to help...But you are our guest. I have done wrong. Tonight you will eat and drink and sleep in safety. Tomorrow you will rest. Then my grandsons will ride with you to where you will. Even to India!

"Now we will have more tea to clean our throats of these evil words before we eat." With that the old man awkwardly turned and uttered one soft sound, hardly even a word. At once, the tent came alive. The four young men leapt to their feet and the old man struggled to his. Silently, they stepped to the door of the yurt and, one after another, disappeared into the black night outside. As he stooped to go out, Kazan Khan turned, in a sort of half bow toward Jack and said simply, "*salat*...prayer." Jack knew it was not an invitation, just an explanation, and he slumped back against the saddle. He closed his eyes. How delicious it was just to lean back. How safe and secure he felt in the womb of the yurt. Still exhausted, he felt himself drifting again. But, just on the edge of sleep, he was caught by a heavy, penetrating sweet smell. Musk! He jerked his head around and his eyes caught the intense black eyes of a young Turcoman woman. She had silently come into the yurt and was kneeing beside him to hand him a new glass of tea.

Astonished, Jack reached out for the glass. His hand brushed hers. The glass tilted and the hot tea spattered on her hand. She gave a little cry and her eyes opened wide like a frightened gazelle as Jack took her hand in his.

GULJAMAL

A FEW MINUTES LATER, the Hashlu rug covering the opening of the yurt was lifted and in came the austere figure of Kazan Khan. The old man had no sooner squatted beside Jack than his sons began to carry in platters of food which they placed on the ground beside the two men. Finally two of them carried in a large tin tray on which a whole roasted sheep was lying, surrounded by a mound of rice which, in turn, was decorated with almonds and saffron. Suddenly the air of the yurt was permeated with the conflicting scents of cardamom, ginger, cloves and cinnamon.

Kazan's sons, diffident and respectful as they were, could not help licking their lips and gazing longingly at the feast as they squatted wordlessly near the door flap. For them, such a sight was at best a yearly happening, on the great feast day following the month-long fast of Ramadhan. Such a meal was ruinously expensive since their flocks were small and their lives depended upon the production of lambs for the karakul fur market. But, as Jack had often been told, the Turcomans would gladly kill their last animal to do honor to a guest.

The old man took out his dagger and cut into the lamb. Then pulling back the sleeve from his right arm, he plunged his hand into the steaming roast, twisted it toward him and ripped the most flavorful piece from the spine. "Eat!" He commanded. "Eat in the name of God. You do us great honor, oh guest. But I am ashamed that we can offer you no more than this mean repast."

Then, as his practiced eye found each prime piece, his long fingers would dig into the roast and gouge it out; momentarily weighing it in his hand, he would toss it onto the bed of rice on the platter next to Jack. Meanwhile, Kazan himself ate nothing. It was a ritual, strictly prescribed by an ancient social code, and Jack knew at least that part of its rules. His host would continuously urge him to eat more. But, Jack realized that this luxurious platter, so overwhelming to one person, must feed the whole encampment. After Jack had finished, his host would eat, then as the two men withdrew, Kazan's sons would settle by the trays. Finally, the trays would be carried out to the women and children. The scraps and bones, well chewed by that time, would find their ways to the dogs. Nothing would be wasted.

So, having praised his host and thanking God for His bounty, Jack tore off slivers from the long sheaves of unleavened bread resting on the sides of the tray and scooped up rice and meat in little parcels, like tortillas. Starving from his long trek, he ate hurriedly and with relish. Then, after an almost indecent consumption – he could have gorged on twice as much – he rocked back on his heels and sighed, "thanks be to God...may God grant you long life."

"And you, my son. But here, eat!: Kazan again plunged his hand into the roast and pulled off another piece which he threw onto the platter. "Is this mean dish not to your liking. Here! Perhaps this piece is better. Ah, all fat and gristle...a mean dish...unworthy!" The old man shook his head in mock sorrow.

"No, oh Khan! I have eaten as ten men. Of the best. I will surely burst if I eat one more bite!" Jack said as he allowed the old man to force one last chunk of meat upon him.

"For my sake, you must eat," insisted the host, but his eager voice was not matched to the urgent, hungry looks of the young men who perched silently in their places.

"No...no...I cannot. You will kill me with your generosity," said

Jack as he wiped the grease from his hands on a leaf of bread. "No, this is the end." Then he ate the bread and washed it down with a long drink of kumiss.

Kazan finally allowed himself a few bites of meat and rice and then also drank deeply of the kumiss. "Ah," he belched. "God is generous. Thanks be to God!"

Seeing Kazan stop, Jack rose and stumbled backwards on his still stiff legs. He circled around the fire pit and the trays and walked over to the door flap of the yurt. There, from behind, a woman's hand appeared, holding a water jug. Jack stuck out his cupped hands and, receiving a jet of warm water, rinsed them. Kazan, watching him closely and admiring the way Jack had respected the nomad customs, followed and rinsed his hands also. Then, with one finger of his right hand, the old man washed his teeth as well. Meanwhile, the young men had fallen on the tray like wolves. Silently, they gulped down balls of rice and strips of meat. In their turns, they quickly rose and washed their hands and teeth. Then they carried the still warm trays outside to the waiting women and children. In just a few minutes, this great extravagance was only a memory.

"Now you will sleep," said Kazan. "Fear not, for no harm will befall you here with my people. I see in your eyes, my son," he said in a kindly voice, "a tiredness I too have know. A man on the run can be recognized by those who have known fear. But, tonight at least, you are safe and can sleep. Rest in safety. My sons will seize the horizon."

To reassure himself, Jack asked, as casually as he could, "Oh, Khan, are there many of you here?" The old man looked at him sharply for a moment and then laughed. "No, my son. Not many. But enough. You have met my four sons. They are strong and skilled horsemen. My son-in-law, who should have been here...a cousin who married my young granddaughter, left us to earn his fortune in a truck and was killed when his truck went off a cliff. The rest are women and babies. No, we are not many. But so long as we live, you are safe. Be sure, my sons will let no living man near tonight."

Jack nodded and mumbled his thanks, hoping that he had not been followed or observed. If he had been, he thought bitterly, not only could these few gallant people not protect him but his very presence might spell ruin or death for them. One more glass of tea was offered to cut the grease of the meal, and Jack was led out to a smaller yurt where he found a fur cape spread on the felt floor.

"May God keep you!" said the old man and dropped the door flap of the yurt. Jack found himself gratefully, contentedly, safely alone. His head had hardly touched the ground before he sunk into a black oblivion.

In the middle of the night, from his dreamless sleep, Jack was aroused. The many glasses of tea had worked their ways through his body, and he found that had to urinate. For a while, he tried to delay. The thought of going out into the black night among the guard dogs he had seen was not inviting. But, after a quarter of an hour, his intestine would brook no further delay. So, as silently as he could, Jack slipped through the opening of the yurt. Once outside, he was dazzled by the brightness of the stars. He had not realized how dark, how womb-like, was the interior of the yurt. He looked around him. The camp was deep in sleep. Far off in the distance, he could make out a faint glow on the horizon. That would be the city of Kunduz or, perhaps, the town of Khanabad. He checked the North Star. Just below it, about thirty miles from the Soviet frontier, would be Qizil Qala. No lights there. Danger lay like a shroud on that wretched little border hamlet. Further south, perhaps thirty or forty miles away, another faint glow announced Pul-i Khumri, on the way to Kabul and safety.

Now oriented, Jack stepped around to the side of the yurt, to a

175

decent but still safe distance, and quickly squatted, Turcoman fashion, to relieve his bladder. He heard the dogs whine and one or two growled; so as quickly as possible, he crept back to the door of the yurt.

As he was just about to bend down to go inside, a figure suddenly loomed before him. Alarmed, he jumped back and his hand again flew to his automatic pistol. Then, in the starlight, he saw that the figure was that of Gul Jamal, "Beautiful Rose," the granddaughter with the gazelle eyes who had brought him tea while the men had prayed. He bowed slightly, not knowing what he should do. To speak to her might awaken the dogs or Kazan and then she would be compromised and embarrassed.

Gul Jamal answered his silent question by touching her lips with her finger, commanding silence. And, looking into his eyes with a forthrightness he could not have imagined among Afghan city girls, she reached out and took his hand in hers. Half turning, she led him silently through the opening of a small yurt next to the one in which he had been sleeping.

As he stepped inside the felt-womb, his eyes, blinded by the stars, were momentarily useless. Slowly and carefully, he put one foot before the other and, responding to the insistent pull of her hand, inched forward. Then the girl's hand stiffened. He stopped. She pulled her hand from his and placed it lightly but firmly upon his shoulder, pushing him down. He bent his knees and sank onto the ground. Beside him, as he felt with hands, was a fur cape and a sort of pillow. Gul Jamal's hand now stole up his chest to his neck, propelling him backwards against the pillow.

Jack was astonished. Was this a dream? Could this really be happening. He was excited beyond anything he had ever felt. Was it the danger, the silence, the soft strength, the overpowering scent of musk? Perhaps it was all of them together. He did not know what to do. Danger, as real as with the killer dogs, lurked in that girl. If he were found here, he would certainly be killed by a dishonored brother or father. But he felt more keenly alive than ever before. Unable or unwilling to heed the danger, he reached out for her.

The girl pushed his hand away and knelt before him. Deftly, she unfastened his jacket and removed his shoes. Again Jack reached out and felt her hand. This time she did not push it away. His hand then rubbed up her arm. What was she wearing? The meeting under the stars had been too fleeting to know, and here he could see almost nothing. His fingers brushed against her sleeve. She stifled a laugh. Further his hand advanced, found her shoulder and neck. Rubbing against her cheek and eyebrows, it crept down her breast to her waist. She was wearing, he now knew, only the soft under-gown of the Turcoman woman. Pulling her towards him, he felt for the snaps or buttons of the gown. What would it have? Again she smothered a laugh and pushed his hand away. He felt as he had not since he was a teenager on a "heavy date." As he felt her arms move, her skillful hands took over the task of unhooking, untying and un-looping the bangles and badges of her outward beauty and brought them silently and secretly down to the thick felt of the floor. Gul Jamal then slipped out of her bodice and loosened her long hair. Now only a shift covered her young body.

With growing excitement, Jack reached out and ran his hand down the stiff weave of the silk. His fingernails scratched in the stillness of the night. Her hands touched his lips, and he stopped, taking her gesture to mean that he must be quiet. Outside, as he listened, the dogs stirred again and the wind rustled the sand.

In a moment, she had slipped out of her shift and was lying before him in unseen but imagined and urgent beauty. His hands smoothed down her flanks and rose to her breasts while her hands began to unbutton his shirt. Then she reached inside to his chest. As her fingers felt the hair on his chest, she paused and then withdrew her hand.

Jack pulled back. Had the hair on his chest repelled her, he wondered. Hair, he reflected in that moment of pause, is such a varied and yet deeply evocative convention. Turcomans were nearly hairless on their faces. But did the men have hair on the chests? He realized that he had never seen a naked Turcoman. Would she be as turned off by the hair on the chest as he would have been by hair on her breast? It is all so different. Americans shave the hair under their arms as unsightly, but Italian women think it arousing; Germans, Arabs and Indian women often shave their pubic hair, but American women think hair there to be natural and beautiful. And, on legs…

These momentary flashes of thought were speedily banished by the musky scent that arose from the secret places on her body, stifling his mind, enveloping his every sense, and she answered his unspoken question by pushing him back against the rug and running her lips and hands down his body, feeling, examining, tasting, exploring. The very alienness of each was overwhelmingly erotic to the other.

Neither said a word. Jack hardly breathed. Do Turcoman women kiss, he wondered. If so, how. He would try. His mouth sought out hers. Eagerly, she returned his kiss. His tongue wandered down her body. His hand picked up her breast and conveyed the nipple into his mouth. To his surprise, it was wet. Then he remembered that old Kazan had told him that her husband had been killed in a truck accident. She must have a new baby. Idly but only fleetingly, he wondered where it was. Nearby? In this yurt? Even beside them? Guilt, or was it excitement, coursed through his mind.

His hands found their ways down her sides, across her belly and toward the lips of her vagina. Would they be bare, clean shaven or plucked. He paused, wondering, almost fearing. Then, he jumped his hands to her thighs, pressing them open. Gently, he stroked her inner leg and, with mounting excitement and curiosity, lifted his fingers into her vagina. It was as silky as her shift, soft and already wet. She too had been excited by the danger and the adventure. And, poor girl, he realized with a momentary pang, she must be desperately lonely.

Rising to his feet, he pulled down his trousers and then lowered himself onto her body. His penis was throbbing and wet, and he feared that he would have an orgasm the second he penetrated her or even before. Suddenly sober, he realized that he must not make her pregnant. Gul Jamal must have thought the same at that moment too for, silently as a wraith, she pulled away and was gone. He lay waiting for what seemed hours. Then he smelled her. Behind him. Her fingers kneaded his shoulders and gently rubbed his brow. Slipping under his arm, she dropped gently to the floor and slipped her body under his, pulling him down onto her. He trust deeply into her as she arched her back and pulled his head down onto her breast, biting his earlobe. Slowly at first and then faster and faster, he plunged into her. Her breathing came deeper and then spasmodically and finally in gasps. His ear, he thought would soon be in shreds, but that, at least kept him from ejaculating too soon.

Then, just as he felt himself coming a climax, he heard a soft whimper beside them. The baby! The baby was stirring. Gul Jamal went rigid under him. Her hands pressed hard against his shoulders. She was stopping him. "A second, just a second," he whispered in English...I'm nearly..." but her strong arms were like a brake. He stopped and was about to pull apart from her, but, to his surprise, she only guided him slightly sideways from her body. Then she half rose, reaching out and pulling the baby toward her breast. Placing its mouth on her nipple, she smoothed its head and whispered little cooing noises to it. With her other arm, she pulled Jack back against her body and, moving her hand down to his buttocks, forced him again deeply into her body. Jack plunged into her once more, feeling as though he had never before known a woman, and, almost before he realized it, he exploded inside her. Even the baby gasped and cried out. Jack was utterly spent. He collapsed upon her.

It was nearly dawn when Gul Jamal gently but firmly shook him. The baby was still at her breast. Jack quickly sat up, rubbed back a shock of hair and then, bent and started to kiss her breast, but Gul Jamal modestly pulled away and covered herself with the shift that now lay beside her. He smiled, "vanity, even in a yurt, thy name is woman…" She looked puzzled but her face dissolved into a smile and her sparkling white teeth and jet black hair appeared to him as the most beautiful things he could remember.

Urgently, she pointed toward the door. Neither he or she could afford to have him found in her yurt. Jack nodded and rose to his feet, quickly slipping on his clothes. Turning, he blew her a kiss. She looked puzzled again, but then smiled once more and mimicked his gesture. And, like a shadow himself, he slipped out of the yurt and, after making a detour to where he had urinated in the stillness of the night, he stood upright and walked nonchalantly back to the guest yurt. He had only, he told himself, done as men do, relieving himself in the night. All else was but a dream.

Jack slept late into the morning. When he arose, old Kazan, he thought, looked at him carefully, appraisingly, but his voice was matter-of-fact. "The dogs growled in the night. Wolves must have been abroad. But my sons kept watch on the distant hills, and no man came to disturb your sleep. I hope that you are now refreshed, my son, and ready for what God may decree for you."

"Turkish, especially Eastern Turkish or Turki," Jack's instructor had told him in the language school, "is not a subtle language. Everything is either black or white. No fooling around." But in each of Kazan's phrases, Jack read or thought he could read a potential double meaning. If Kazan suspected anything, he was unsure or did not wish to face the dilemma suspicion would create. Obviously, he knew nothing for sure or Jack would probably not now be alive. But, then, as he had said, and as Jack himself was learning, the world had been turned upside down and the old life, with its rules and customs, was dead or dying. It was a curious thought, one that would have fascinated him at other times, but then he had no time for such speculation.

Kazan had told him that one of his sons would ride with him to where the road builders' camp was located and leave him a discrete distance from it so that he could make his way there safely and quietly. Unsaid perhaps even unthought by Kazan was the absolute imperative Jack felt that Kazan's little group not be compromised if, indeed, it was not compromised already. Realizing the danger as much for them as for him, Jack was determined to take no risks beyond what was absolutely necessary. He also thought, idly but fondly, that once this pall of terror had passed, he would return bearing a sheep to make up for the terrible drain he had caused to their livelihood. No, he thought, that would be taken badly. He would have to find some way, indirectly, discreetly, even delicately to reward Kazan. But more urgent demands called upon his mind: taking his hand, Kazan led him to where the little Mongol ponies were saddled and hobbled. He turned to look deeply into Jack's eyes, remembering no doubt his own departure long ago from the Pathan camp when he rode back into the danger of Russia, and said gravely, "may God be with you and keep you safe."

"And you, great Khan! You have shown me generosity, keremiyet, beyond any I have ever experienced, for you truly are one of the last of the kerimler. I shall always be grateful and, were it safe to do so, I would sing your praises to the whole world. Alas, it is best if we both pretend that we had never met. There are those who wish to still my voice and to do so they might also still yours if they knew. Never mention my name. I will not mention yours, but I shall ever guard it in my heart. May your days be long!"

Kazan nodded. "I do not know your name. It is better thus. How mean are these days in which we live. As you flee from the hand of man, trust no one, least of all your own kind. Of this, I know."

Then, without further ceremony or words, the patriarch, suddenly seeming older and more bent, bowed and turned back to the yurts.

Sadly, Jack watched him go. He would not forgive himself, he realized, if he had been tracked to this encampment. Only desperation had demanded the terrible risk he had imposed upon these gallant folk, this pitiful but proud remnant of a once great people. The thought passed through his mind that he knew no friends or colleagues who would have taken such risks or who would have so generously, even eagerly, jeopardized their very lives to divide with him the little that remained to them. But the young man was already mounted and impatient to ride. Seeing the urgent looks of his guide and the other sons, Jack hurried to his pony and, even more painfully and awkwardly than the day before, just barely managed to mount. Would Gul Jamal be watching? Laughing at his awkwardness? Crying at his departure? Or just indifferent? Had their encounter been real or just a fantasy? He would surely never know.

Then, as quickly as a dream, the camp disappeared from sight into the heat waves of the high-noon mirage. The miles and hours filed past in tandem. Sunset came more quickly than Jack could have hoped. His legs were now scalding hot and sore beyond pain and, in riding toward the west, his nose and eyes seemed to have been broiled by the sun. Grateful as much for softening of the gathering dusk as for the sight of the town, he saw Kunduz begin to materialize before them. Silently, the young Turcoman led Jack from one hillock to the next, avoiding the roads and paths as much as possible and then skirting around the houses that began to sprinkle the town's outskirts.

Nervous that they would be seen together, with who knew what consequences for the young man, Jack reached out and took hold of his companion's arm. "Dur," stop, he said in Turkish. Just point me the way. The young man shook his head and said, yok, no, not yet. Touched but worried, Jack acquiesced, saying "teshakur," thank you, and impulsively, as a gesture, took off his wrist watch, which, unexpectedly had begun to function again, and pressed it upon the unwilling young man.

Finally, the Turcoman stopped and, pointing to a low collection of buildings and an unmistakably American house trailer, spoke his first word of the day, in Turkic, "May God be with you, American. There is your goal."

"If only it were," muttered Jack.

ERNEST'S TRAILER

JACK KNOCKED SOFTLY. Jack knocked softly. Then louder. He looked back and saw the swinging lantern of the advancing night watchman. It would not be a minute before he would be seen.

"Who's there?" sounded a welcome American twang from within.

"Please open quickly. This is an emergency. Please hurry," whispered Jack. From inside came the noises of a man getting heavily out of bed, scraping slippers onto his feet and fumbling with the door knob.

"Please hurry," whispered Jack again, more urgently this time, as he watched over his shoulder the steadily advancing watchman. The knob turned and the door opened a crack. On the other side was the sleepy face of Ernest Crownover.

"Why, I'll be Goddamned...Jack Farnsworth...what in the devil? Wait a minute and I'll get this chain off. I'll just get my lantern."

"No, please, no light...no light, please. Just let me in quickly and I'll explain. There has been an emergency."

"An emergency...someone hurt...a car accident? Just a second."

A highway accident was the one thing that could make Ernest Crownover move quickly in the night. The chain rattled and the door creaked open.

Jack almost dived in and pushed the door closed with his back. The two men stood staring at one another for a few seconds. Jack had pressed his head against the door and was listening for approaching footsteps. Satisfied, he turned and stared at Ernest -- what would he do, knowing nothing of

Jack's mission and obviously stunned into disbelief at the apparition that Jack must have seemed. Even without Qol Khan's headcloth and the great coat, he knew he was a shocking sight. His clothes were stained and filthy, his face was burned from hours facing the sun, his eyes were bloodshot, and his hair uncombed... Finally, on his face was the stubble of days of beard.

Ernest could hardly believe his eyes. He sized Jack up and decided that he was not drunk but thought that he must have been in an accident anyway.

Stunned and speechless, Ernest sank down on his bunk and, with his chin, indicated the other bunk for Jack to sit on. He eyed Jack critically but said nothing for a few moments. Finally, he smiled and said, "funny time to come calling. What can I do for you, Mr. Farnsworth?"

"Mr. Crownover...Ernest...this is an emergency or I would not be bothering you, certainly not up here and not at such an hour. But I'm at the end of my rope. I'm absolutely exhausted. I'll tell you as much as will convince you to help me...and as I have the strength left to talk. But, first, could I have a drink?"

"Sure...I'm always good for a drink. Can I turn the light on now?"

"Please don't. I'll tell you why in a minute...then you'll understand."

"Oh...er... well...ok," he stammered. "I guess you are in trouble... must be hellova...Are you on the run...Did anyone see you come in?" The words poured out in stunned disbelief.

"I'm pretty sure your night watchman didn't see me."

"Blind ol' fart. He couldn't see his pekker in a pisser."

Ernest's Oklahoma gibe broke the tension. So as he usually did when there was nothing else to say, Ernest laughed. Then he heaved himself up off the cot, walked over the sink and fumbled through the dirty dishes of the evening meal. After what seemed to Jack an hour, he located two tumblers.

After a perfunctory rinse, he wiped them off on a napkin and filled them to the brim with whiskey. Then he set the glasses down on the table and squinted at his watch.

"A bit early for me to go to bed, but it has been a long son-of-a-bitch of a day, and we start early up here."

He paused, looked appraisingly up and down Jack's clothes, then laughing again, he shook his head, "Boy, I must say you make it quite an occasion. Now, if it were anyone else, I wouldn't blink an eye, but like I told your Mr. Smith..."

"Let me tell you there isn't much love in my heart right now for my Mr. Smith either."

"Hum," said Ernest eyeing Jack carefully.

"What kind of trouble are you in, my friend?"

"Nothing...personal, Mr. Crownover. Let's just call it official trouble."

"That's what I was afraid you'd say. Hell, I wish't it was something easy like a girl or even a holdup." He tried a laugh but there wasn't much mirth in it. "What you guys do 'officially' gives me the willies. I don't want no part of it."

"I understand."

"Like I told Mr. Smith..."

"I really don't blame you. But, could you just accept it that we are fellow Americans, and I am in some sort of trouble you don't know about... and I need your help?"

"What sort of help...to do what?"

"...what?" Jack blurted out. 'What could he say, what could he ask for?

"Yeah, help to do what?"

"Well, as you can see, I'm beat. The first thing I need is to sleep. I really haven't slept in about four days and I've covered a lot of country in that time."

"Hum," Ernest said. "I guess I don't really want to know too much, but I can't help asking what are you doing up here anyways? Near the Russian frontier...Well, I guess I just answered my own question, didn't I?"

"Yeah, that's it. Can we just leave it at that?"

Earnest paused, looked away, shook his head and then evenly and carefully, like he would speak to a man who was about the pour the cement the wrong way, spoke, looking directly into Jack's eyes.

"Well, it's not that easy. Really it ain't. Like I told Mr. Smith. And you too when that friend of yours, Miss Nora, got us together after my – what should I call it, 'interview' with Mr. Smith. I mean, I'm over here to build roads. I don't understand what you fellows, and Nora too, are doing. I don't think I like it much either, but that's neither here nor there. Fact is that I'm here to work for AID. And AID is here to work for the people of this country. We can only do our job...I can only do my job...if they trust us. They trust me, I think, and you guys are trying to cash in, it seems to me, on their trust and for things I don't understand but I don't think are right."

"Ernest, I think you may be right. I'm not sure. But, in the state I'm in, I can't do a very good job now even of thinking, much less arguing with you about American policy or national interests or things like that. Do you think you could let me have that whiskey now?"

Ernest looked at the two glasses of whiskey on the table. "Oh, I'm sorry, Jack. Got to thinking. I'm one of those dumb bastards, like Lyndon Johnson once said, who can't walk and fart at the same time. Here. Here's looking at you."

"Thanks," Jack mumbled and swilled the whiskey around in his glass gratefully.

"I don't mean to be impolite," Ernest went on. "And let me tell you, I'm no prude. I really understand trouble...don't like not to be of help."

Jack drank a big drought of his whiskey and spluttered and coughed. Just at that moment, there was a knock on the door.

Jack almost dived under the bunk. Involuntarily, his hand crept toward his jacket zipper. Then, looking at Ernest, who had observed both the look of terror on his face and the movement of his hand toward the unseen pistol, he realized that this was the test. If Ernest hid him, he had begun to decide to help him; if not, the game was up.

"Who is it?" Ernest shouted. "Whaddaya want?"

A voice outside answered, "Ern Khan...you okay?"

"Hell, yes, I'm okay, Daud. Why the hell shouldn't I be okay?"

"You alone, Ern Khan?"

"Sure...ain't no girls in here with me. I'm just talking to myself. I'm going back to sleep now. You git along, Daud, and check those fences, like I tol' you. If any of those tools disappear, I'll skin you like a jack rabbit, you hear? Now git!"

Both men waited silently, staring at one another for a few moments. Then Ernest eased the door open a crack and looked out into the darkening night. About fifty paces away, he could see the retreating figure of the watchman, swinging his lantern.

The two men continued silently to look at one another. Both realized that the first decision had been made for them by Daud. Jack relaxed slightly and slowly drained his glass. Then he tried to lighten the mood. "Isn't it funny how our names come out...You have become 'Ern Khan' and to my man who everyone calls 'Old Abdul', I guess I will always be 'Jack Beg.'"

Ernest nodded but he was not led astray. To be polite, he said, "Want another one?"

"Would you mind?"

"Hell no. That's one thing we share at the Embassy. Cheap booze." Ernest filled Jack's glass from the Scotch bottle.

"That's the easy part. Now let's get down to business. What do you really want from me?"

"Like you said, that was the easy part."

"Okay, let's hear the hard part."

Jack looked him straight in the eyes and slowly said, "a ride to Kabul."

"Why don't you just catch the plane?"

"I can't."

"I don't see why not. You're a…a diplomat, ain't you. I mean officially, whatever else you may be. All you have to do is to show your fancy black passport and get on the plane. Or call up Smith and get him to send up a car. Got lots of 'em down there, doing nothing…lots of people just setting around."

"It's not that easy."

"Hum…I don't see…"

"How much do you want to know?"

"We already talk about that…" Ernest seemed tired and discouraged. "As little as possible."

"Okay, then just take my word for it. I just can't do it. I'm doing something…something official, something I didn't ask to do, which has a lot of people after my hide. I don't mean to be dramatic, but…"

"You're doing a pretty good job of being dramatic, if you don't mind my saying so, bursting in here in the middle of the night, looking like you just killed someone and he damn near killed you, and scared out of your wits when the stupid ol' son of a bitch of a watchman knocks...I call that pretty dramatic."

"Well, okay. I have something with me that's very important, maybe even vital for the security of our country. And I have to get it to the Embassy as quickly as possible...and secretly. That's it...as simply as I can say it."

"Only problem is that it ain't that simple.

"I know."

"No, I don't think you do," said Ernest shaking his head.

"Well, I realize you don't want to get involved."

"Hell, it ain't that I don't want to get involved. I ain't worried about me being involved. I'm an old man. Not too many things either scare me or surprise me any more. That's not the problem."

"I didn't mean to sound personal, Ernest."

"It ain't personal...you see, the problem is, like I tried to tell your Mr. Smith and was just about to tell you when Ol' Daud came to the door. I mean, I know you're beat and I'll try to make it short so you can get on your way or...or get some sleep. Whichever you want."

"If that's an invitation, I'll accept gratefully."

"Well, I'm not sure it is. Listen first and we'll decide that later."

"Sorry. Go ahead," Jack sighed and put his glass down.

"You see, I believe that in my own little way, I'm doing something to make the world better. I don't mean to sound big or important or even like a goodie goodie, but this is a time to say it like I see it. It's not much, I know, what I do, and crooks can drive on highways just as easily as honest folks.

But with roads, these poor farmers out here can get their crops to market. And if they get them to market, then people will get something to eat.

"Hell, I don't mean to sound like a Sunday school teacher." He paused again, searching for words. "But, I guess I do. Well, okay, I guess I have to say like I feel it. I really believe that's God's work. I think it's serious. I think it really means something. And that's why I'm over here doing it."

"I understand."

"Maybe you do, maybe you don't, but let me finish," said Ernest waving Jack down like a speeding driver. "But, if these people here think that's all a smokescreen, that what we're really doing here is to throw dust in their eyes, to use them against the Russians or the Chinese or some other damn people, then the whole thing'll fail...and that's what you guys are trying to do, use us...use me." Ernest shrugged his shoulders.

Jack nodded his head. "I really do understand," he sighed.

"Now, if I had a car of my own up here, why, hell, I'd drive you down to Kabul in a New York minute. I wouldn't care. Not me personally. But I ain't here 'personally' any more'an you are. We're both here 'officially'. It's just different...your official from my official."

Jack nodded and looked down at his nearly empty glass.

Ernest went on, "and hell, I don't even own a car of my own any longer. If I was to drive you down to Kabul, it would have to be in an AID vehicle and I just don't see how I could..."

Before Ernest could finish, Jack slumped down on the little bench that served as a table. He had simply passed out from fatigue, relief and whiskey.

"Poor bastard, I didn't know it was that bad," mumbled Ernest. "Hell, no matter what, I can't throw him out now." Then, lifting him as gently as possible in the cramped trailer, Ernest laid Jack on the bunk and covered him with a blanket. Just as he straightened up and was about to get down his spare blanket, Jack came to and sat up.

"Lie down and go to sleep," Ernest commanded.

"No, let me try to tell you one or two things," Jack pleaded. "I'm sorry. That wasn't fair, passing out like that. I just couldn't…"

"Well, stop when you want to."

"I don't want to embarrass you. And I really do understand. I think I even agree with your position. I'm not sure that what we're doing is the right thing. But let me tell you just enough so you will understand why I'm here."

Ernest started to say something but Jack waved him silent. "I probably won't make much sense, but let me talk."

Ernest nodded silently.

"I was sent up here to get some papers from a man, a foreigner, and when I got to the place I was supposed to meet him, he was dead. And his killer was dead beside him. But, I got the papers." He patted the bulge in his jacket. "I don't know even what's in them, but I was told that they're terribly important. Someone wants them so badly, they have been after me and, I'm sure, they would kill me to get them. Whoever it is who's after them… and me…has already killed at least three other men who were helping me. I saw them do that. Don't worry. They wouldn't bother you. Those men were Afghans…or something else. Whoever is after me wouldn't harm you or I wouldn't have come here. I promise you that."

"I ain't worried about that," said Ernest.

"Well, from what I've seen, it's worth worrying about, I'll guarantee you," said Jack bitterly. "But, me, it's different. To get the papers, they have to get me. So, they'd just wait until they got me on a dark trail and ambush me...then they'd make it look like a truck ran over me. Anyway, Mr. Smith has ordered me to get them back to the Embassy and, Goddammit, I'm going to do it...then, would you believe it, I think I'm going to resign and, maybe if AID'd take me on, I'd learn how to build roads too."

Ernest just laughed. "Pretty good, Mr. Farnsworth. That, I'd like to see!"

"No, I'm serious. I think you're right about helping people. I'm less and less sure what I've been doing with my life really means anything...anything to anybody except us, except giving us a jag and making us feel serious and tough and important. It's a kind of game for big boys." Jack visibly sagged. "Ernest...I'm gone. But I really meant..." his voice trailed off.

"Poor devil," Ernest shook his head and, bending over, covered Jack again with the blanket. "Maybe you do really mean it."

He stood up and took the spare blanket and, covering himself with it, Ernest laid down on the spare bunk for a fitful night of dozing and listening both to the wind outside, afraid to hear footsteps of the gossipy old watchman. Even when he fell asleep, he was quickly roused by Jack's sleep-slurred voice. He was afraid to awaken Jack but afraid himself to go to sleep. He listened carefully. He couldn't understand much of what Jack mumbled but what he made out absolutely terrified him. In his fitful sleep, Jack whimpered, cried and droned on and on about truckers, torture, wild dogs, nomads and all sorts of other things Ernest really didn't want to hear but somehow did want to understand. There was no way he could fall asleep. Finally, his release came with first light. He bent over Jack and felt his chest. His hand started back when he felt the automatic and it rested a few moments on the papers. They had come loose as Jack rolled over. Ernest picked them up and examined them. They were in some foreign writing and he didn't have a clue what they were all about, but they were covered with spots of blood and about that he had no doubts. "Tom foolery, if you ask me," he mumbled. Then, as quietly as possible, he pulled on his boots and work clothes. Taking out a pad, he wrote Jack a note.

Stay here and don't open the door. No one is supposed to come in. I will lock it double. Don't answer if anyone knocks or tries the door. Some food is in the hamper. There's water in the toilet. Use the bucket. And don't make any noise you don't have to. I'll be back about 4 PM. Get all the sleep you can.

Good luck, Ernest

That done, he bent over Jack and stuffed the note in the opening of his jacket. Tiptoeing across the few feet to the trailer door, he let himself out and made sure it was securely locked. Then, turning, he walked briskly over to Daud who had watched him emerge, and, as jovially as he could manage, said, "What the hell do you mean waking me up last night, you ol' coot? I had a terrible time getting back to sleep. I tol' you never to do that. I'm an old man, you ol' devil you." He slapped Daud on the shoulder and smiled broadly.

Daud looked blankly back at him.

Ernest didn't wait for more conversation. Getting into his pickup, he stepped on the starter and drove slowly out of the gate toward the construction site.

THE CHIEFS

"I SAY, IS THAT SMITH?" came the calm voice on the other end of the gray scrambler telephone.

"Smith here," he replied in a low tone into phone. Twisting slightly aside, he absentmindedly fingered the gold tassel on the flag beside him. "Is that Major Crighton-Philips?"

Without bothering to identify himself further, since of course no one but the two of them could be on this line, the British station chief went right to his point. "Smith, that chap of yours, any word from him?"

"No. And frankly, I am beginning to get a little concerned. He should have been at his rendezvous two days ago unless…"

"Well, he has apparently robbed the nest."

"What!" Smith sat bolt upright and dropped the tassel.

"I said, that chap of yours has apparently robbed the nest."

"I heard you. I'm just stunned. He was not supposed to be…uh… maybe we had better not talk this over…even on this…could we meet right away?"

"I think we must. Immediately."

"Your place or mine?"

"I shall come right over."

The phone went dead, but Smith continued to hold it. He stared blankly across the bleak, windowless room. Then, putting the phone back on the cradle, he dropped his forehead into the palm of his right hand and shook his head, "...robbed the nest. Jesus! How the hell..."

Not many minutes passed in the small town of Kabul before the door was silently pushed open by the secretary and in walked a tall, gaunt and stooped man in a tweed jacket and baggy gray trousers. Smith always admired the way Major Hughe Hanbury Crighton-Philips looked, so British, so different from his own neat but standard appearance.

"Thank you so much for coming over...uh...Hughe." Smith always fumbled over the name. Crighton-Philips had never exactly said, "Call me by my first name", but one couldn't say "Crighton-Philips" the way one could say Smith or just Philips. It got stuck in the mouth. But Smith savored the name even when he made fun of it, 'the Brits love that double barreled name stuff,' he affected but secretly he liked to imagine how it would sound to be announced as 'Worthington-Smith'.

Crighton-Philips smiled perfunctorily and limply acquiesced in the vigorous shaking of his hand.

"Thank you so much for coming over. It is not easy right at the moment for me to move," said Smith as his visitor strode into the middle of the room.

Crighton-Philips allowed himself a moment of sweeping appraisal. It had always amazed him, as he had remarked just the evening before to his ambassador, "how effortlessly the Americans combined bad taste and expense to produce efficient ugliness."

"Rather good, that," had been the ambassador's reply. "Of course, as you will remember, that was how the Greeks felt about the Romans; there were the Greeks and the barbarians, and the Romans were on the wrong side of the divide...vertere barbare, you know and all that."

"Have a seat, Hughe. Needless-to-say..."The words came out a trifle too fast. Smith always found himself rushing with Crighton-Philips. Something about him, about all the British, made him uncomfortable, nervous, like a pupil before his teacher. In fact, that was exactly the relationship. The men of Smith's generation had learned their craft from the British. Their secret intelligence service was the model they studied. And the old attitude lingered. Smith and his generation felt that way even when, as he and his colleagues often were these days, sure that the teacher didn't know the answers. But, as he put it to his own staff, they had been around so long and had such a manner of self assurance that they put you -- put one -- off.

"Could I get you some tea?"

"Coffee, if you will, please."

"I got some tea out from Fortnum and Mason."

"Good of you, but I never drink tea for elevenses. Coffee." Another small defeat, thought Smith. No matter how carefully he tried to turn Memphis into Oxford, it just didn't work. Getting the tea from the best place and trying to serve it at the wrong time! 'Damn', he thought to himself. Of course, that was the problem between them. While Smith didn't know it, Crighton-Philips really rather liked things and people American. He just couldn't bear what he called the 'near-miss' Anglo-Americans. That was how he thought of Smith. 'Funny,' he laughed to himself, 'that Smith didn't hyphenate his name: Farmington-Smith -- or whatever -ington-Smith? That would have suited him just fine. Then he would need a coat of arms. He could see it now, a dollar rampant on a field of...'

Meanwhile Smith had unlocked the door again and called out, Jane, would you please make it two coffees?" And over his shoulder to Crighton-Smith, "Black, Hughe?"

"White, please." He said, sitting down on the sofa.

"One with cream, please Mary."

Rejoining Crighton-Philips he said, in a whisper of confidentiality, "we'll talk in a few moments, when the coffee arrives."

As though taking him literally, Crighton-Philips began examining his fingernails with minute care, one by one, placing each one carefully between the calipers of the thumb and index finger of the opposite hand.

Smith was just on the point of jumping up to find out what had happened to the coffee when the secretary walked through the door with two white paper cups. She knew Smith would have preferred the china cups with Crighton-Philips, but savoring revenge for the way Smith had tried to recall his praise of her friend Nora, she pretended not to notice and, setting the cups down on the table, turned and walked out, pursued by Smith's frown.

Smith followed her and bolted the door. Then he turned to the still clinical Crighton-Philips who, by then, had thoroughly surveyed every particle of his finger nails. "Hughe, it was very good of you to rush over here..."

"Rather important task, you know."

"Yes. Hellishly awkward. I really don't know..."

"Well, let me tell you what I have been able to find out so far."

"First, Hughe, I think we ought to set the ground rules."

"Ground rules?"

"Yes, as you know, the Joint Intelligence Committee..."

"Oh, bugger the JIC."

"Well, we've had a lot of trouble in the past by..."

"Look Smith, that chap of yours is somewhere out there either dead or alive with all that stuff we have worked months to set up. The bloody JIC can't do a thing to help out now."

"Well, Hughe, let me put it to you frankly."

Crighton-Philips sighed impatiently and dropping his eyes toward the table, reached for the coffee cup. "Right you are. Carry on then."

"Frankly, since the defections of your chaps, we have had to be..."

"Of course, I understand that you must be careful. We all have to be careful," Smith began.

Impatiently, Crighton-Philips shook his head, "We more than most... but, I understand. " He sighed, "That is the nightmare we live with." Then after a pause, he went on, "But surely there is nothing in this business we don't both know. Or is there?" He looked sharply at Smith.

"To be frank, Hughe, I really don't know what we know. I know what I know. That may be something different...or even less than you know. But, at least, it would be good if we could established agreed procedures...so we could figure out how to discuss this and how to help one another and Farnsworth. Procedures matter."

"Pro-ce-dures?" Crighton-Philips' pronunciation almost doubled the length of word, coming down hard on the 'ce' so that the end of the word shook like a tail. In his mouth, it had become an obscenity.

Smith had taken up his pencil and was rolling it uncomfortably between his fingers. He resented the way Crighton-Smith made him appear like a petty bureaucrat, but he wasn't sure how to deal with Farnsworth's mission, wasn't sure how much of the onion he could or must peel. "Yes, I am sorry. Procedures," he reasserted.

"Right," sighed Crighton-Philips with the air of resignation a brave man might affect when told that the firing squad had forgotten its ammunition but that someone had been sent to fetch it.

"The 40 Committee has instructed me to refer to JIC all the issues affecting the Chinese and the Uzbeks which, as we both know, you are to handle without reference to me."

"I know all that. I am a sort of blind drop between the Super Powers."

It was Crighton-Philips' first vulnerable point and Smith, the old committee man, seized his opportunity. "Oh, Hughe, don't play Little England now. You understand why and what I meant."

Crighton-Philips shrugged his shoulders and again began to examine his fingers. "Go on, if you will, please."

"To put it frankly, the point is that since the defections, and since you are acting in the...shall we say delicate, role with the Chinese and the Uzbeks, I am required to talk on this issue within narrow limits." As Smith spoke the familiar words of his instructions, his confidence grew and, he noted with some pleasure as he let his eyes wander over Crighton-Philips, that his collar was frayed and that a button was missing from the sleeve of his coat. 'Tarnished glory', he silently gloated. Then, determined to retain the advantage, he plunged on. "With that chap of yours working in Moscow, we don't know what they may know of your procedures or even if he has the names of your locals -- like Qol Khan -- or, worse, if he or his new friends have left a sleeper behind."

Crighton-Philips sat impassively with downcast eyes.

"And, as I am sure you know, many of our senior men believe that the split between the Russians and the Chinese is not real. We really don't know why the Chinese agreed to get involved in this operation with us. If they really did. Or even know about it. So, Hughe, you see, it really is a bit more complicated than I would like it to be."

He paused and, seeing Crighton-Philips struggling with the rapidly wilting paper coffee cup, he said, "Wouldn't you like me to get you a proper cup?"

"No. Thanks awfully. I always drink coffee in paper cups. Like it better that way."

"We have some china cups right here..."

"I'm sure you have."

"Well," retreated Smith, "let's talk through the operation, keeping within what we are supposed to know together, shall we?"

"Isn't that rather a waste of time, now, Smith?"

"No, I don't think so. Perhaps we can pick up the thread and put everything back in place. But, perhaps you are right about priorities. First tell me, if you will please, what you have found out."

"Right," replied Crighton-Philips, seizing the chance to avoid a textbook recital of the procedures of their calling and a summary of what they both knew. "It seems that your chap actually found the cabin and got the papers."

"Hum...found the cabin. That night? Are you very sure?"

"Yes." Crighton-Philips nodded. "Absolutely."

"Were the men there...were they dead when he arrived or don't you know?"

"Oh, yes, they were both there, both dead. Of that I am quite certain... quite certain. The way he said it precluded further questions. Smith really didn't want to know what lay behind the 'quite'.

"And did your chap Qol Khan drop him off at the right spot?"

"I believe so. I should tell you at this point that Qol Khan is dead, but one of the chaps who was with him dropped off, himself, at the first village after they had dropped Farnsworth, and made contact with us."

"So he confirmed..."

"Yes. We received his message. He confirmed that the first part of the operation had gone as planned. Your man should not have found the cabin. That is, if he followed instructions. But we don't know any more...and probably won't from our man. He was subsequently picked up and we don't know what has happened to him. Bought it, I imagine."

"Was Farnsworth...was he dropped right at the cabin as planned?" Smith asked as innocently as he could manage.

"I ought to say, just to clear your mind, Smith, that I know the real intent of the mission." Crighton-Philips shrugged.

"What do you mean, 'real intent', Hughe?"

"That he was not supposed to find the cabin...you know 'Scimitar' and all that."

"Hughe, this is a most sensitive subject. If we are to discuss..."

"Let's not discuss it. I am simply telling you that I know. I say this not to ask you anything but to let you know that I am sure of the location where Farnsworth was dropped off."

"Is it possible," Smith asked, dropping his reserve, "that the instructions got garbled or that the driver went wrong."

"Anything's possible, of course, but that's immaterial now. Whatever went wrong, Farnsworth actually got to the cabin and, as I am now certain, got the papers, 'robbed the nest,' as I said.

"The question at this point, I should have thought, is what we can do to retrieve the situation and effect Scimitar."

"Well, I guess we are on the same wave length. As you say, damn the Washington Committee. Let's go back to the beginning. I'll fill you in. As you probably know, our fellows managed to get hold of an up-to-date list of the Russian, or more correctly, the Uzbek and other Russian minority security officers in Central Asia. There wasn't much of anything in it, really, no details, no bios, and even the names were in no apparent order. That seemed to make it valueless, but in fact it turned out to be the best part of the whole thing. At first, however, the specialists in FE started down the wrong track, trying to identify all the people. As it turned out, that didn't make any difference."

"Curious remark, if you don't mind my saying so, not caring who was on it and why."

"That was what FE thought. So the Moscow and Hong Kong and Ankara stations, along with some of our codebreakers in Pakistan and Iran, tried and actually managed to correlate a few names with radio intercepts. But that was the end of the road. So the materials and the fact of their existence were passed along to the JIC. I presume your chap in JIC informed MI6 in London. Anyway, somewhere along the line, an idea came up of how we might put these scraps of information to work…"

"I have been reliably told, Smith," Crighton-Philips broke in, "that the idea was yours."

"Well, you know how ideas come up."

"How very modest of you," Crighton-Philips nodded his head, delighted to get the talk back to the substance and to ease Smith's mind. "All our chaps agree that it was a brilliant stroke."

"Well, as we both know, ideas are cheap. But, what really counted was the way your fellows and ours got to work on it.

"Making it appear, as I have been told, that about a third of their Security chaps were disaffected and…"

Smith glanced nervously at the door and broke into Crighton-Philip's sentence, "...in contact and ready to make a deal with us...not specified, of course, but, from their point of view, none-the-less treasonable."

"Absolutely exquisite," complimented Crighton-Philips. "A great credit to you and to your Service, grand in conception, bold, well, just jolly good."

"Well, thank you, thank you very much. Coming from you, that is very gratifying.

"The beauty of it, as I said," Smith continued, "was that it didn't make any difference who was on the list or what each person did. Just the fact that his name was there would put him on the rack. Being suspicious, the senior men – that is those senior men whose names were not also on the list -- would assume that the named men, and here was a neat feature. You see, they were a real rag-bag. Surely many of them didn't even know any of the others, but because they were all on the same list, it appeared that they had some sort of connection, that they were all working together. So the Russian counter-intelligence would have to spend months tearing apart their own service to try to find the connecting links. And, of course, since there weren't any, they would just tear it apart...futilely. Better than we could ever hope to do. But the trick...the trick was or is to get the list back into their hands, in some way that they would believe, and not think it was a plant, so that they could commit suicide with it."

"Ah, that is so often the trick in life: let the other fellow have a proper shaft on which to impale himself."

"We spent a lot of time worrying through that problem."

"Again, as I understand it, 'we' translates to you."

"Well, several of people came into the act..."

"Ah, your heavy battalions."

"Hardly battalions. Just a few people."

"As you wish." Crighton-Philips waved his hand dismissively, "In our poverty, even four seems rather heavy, you know,"

Ignoring him, Smith went on.

"We were enormously helped, of course, by the fact that the Russians have accepted our notion of the domino effect."

"The domino effect?"

"Yes, you know that at the end of the Second World War, Prime Minister Smuts convinced Churchill that if the Communists took over Greece, it would fall against one after another of the other states in Europe so that they would be knocked over like a line of dominos. Of course it didn't happen, but Secretary of State John Foster Dulles picked up the idea or at least the analogy and convinced almost everyone in our government that the same thing would surely happen if we let Ho Chi Minh triumph in Vietnam. And, the funny thing is that the Soviets also believed it, not for Communism of course, but for nationalism. Apparently, or at least our fellows in Moscow are convinced, that they feared that the Muslim minorities in Soviet Central Asia were all lined up and ready to fall like dominos at the slightest touch."

"So you gave a push?"

"Well, it wasn't that easy or straightforward. We just wanted to help them do it. We got a Chinese fellow – from of their Turkish Uighur minority -- who works with us out of Hong Kong to make contact with a known double agent in...well. It doesn't make any difference..." Smith's voice trailed off in the realization that, despite his initial caution, he was now rather carried away.

"Not my business."

"Well, not mine either, Hughe."

"You fellows are so security conscious, I sometimes wonder if you even talk to yourselves."

"Well, security pays off. At least we don't often have any really bad blows...like Philby. I'm sorry to keep bringing this up but he is rather like the skeleton in the closet, you know. And if there is another mole -- and I assume there must be a number of them in every service, ours as well as yours -- well, then he won't get more than a sort of mole's eye view."

"That is a long and philosophical discussion we can have some other time if you wish," said Crighton-Philips wearily. "Let's get on with the case before us, shall we?"

"Well, the double agent passed along word that we were onto something really big, something that he couldn't get hold of but had heard about, more or less reliably. Not much bait on the hook, just a smell. Too much and they would have distrusted it. But, from that source, it got attention. Sorry, we really don't need to go into that. Suffice it to say that the fish was willing to bite. Then we let the line go slack for a while. Next our Uighur chap disappeared. Said to have retired or maybe 'was retired.' We put out a sort of alert, all very discrete, you know, but enough to be noticed. Finally, we arranged to have him surface in Pakistan and from there to make contact, still very distant and discrete, with one of the names on the list. He demanded a guarantee from three other names on the list, refused to discuss anything without their being involved. A nice touch that, if I may say so."

"Brilliant."

"We made it look like he got into contact in Karachi with one of the chaps who, earlier...but not much earlier...had tried to contact us and on whom we had blown the whistle, blown it to the Russians, if you follow."

"Yes. I follow," Crighton-Philips frowned.

"Well, we got word back to the Russians that the fellow was going to collect something at a remote frontier post."

"Which fellow?"

"Our Uighur."

"Oh."

"Just where, we didn't let on. But we let clues begin to be found. And, finally, our Chinese, that is our Uighur, was observed with one of their fellows...a fellow we had turned. We let out just enough line to get them really excited. Then we had the Chinese fellow disappear again. Finally we leaked a message referring to Afghanistan in an old code which we were sure they had broken. Again we let the trail go cold. That's when we asked for your help. I have only an outline of what happened then."

"Well, then it is time I told you," said Crighton-Philips. "Nothing so grand or elaborate as your tale, of course. As you know, we have inherited the rather ram shackled remains of our old apparatus. The apparatus going back, some of it, to the Great Game long before the First War. Most of it is by now only a memory. Other parts are really patrimonies..."

"Patrimonies?"

"Well, sort of fiefs of men whose fathers or even grandfathers we set up long ago and whom we have helped in a minor way over the years. But, for reasons you know well, we have not been able to do much for a long time. Almost nothing that required money. From what I understand from my reading on America we have become what you would call the 'lace curtain Irish' of the Intelligence world.

"When we got in touch on this matter, we arranged for one of our locals, a courier, who had died of more or less natural causes to get found with things he should not have had on him. Among others was a map of the Wakan Corridor with the little cabin..."

"Marvelous, isn't it, how we all assume that the other fellows are so much more efficient than we. I imagine that we would have lost too many of the clues before we had..."

"My dear fellow," replied Crighton-Philips, "Inefficiency is the final redoubt of honest men. Perhaps we just assumed that they were not so honest...But let me go on.

"Then we arranged to feed a fellow we knew was in financial trouble and who had passed along bits and scraps of information to others before for money. We gave him a few details whose importance he shouldn't have known...but which he would try, of course, to peddle elsewhere. Among other things was the note that a strange fellow, not one of us, was meeting someone from the other side and we had to get him up north. Not much more than that."

"When do the Russians really get in?"

"Ah, the Russians," snorted Crighton-Philips. "A bit later, really, but we can skip lightly over the details and get right to them. The Russians had to join in, thinking at first no doubt that the real culprits were the Uighurs and so they could rely on their Chinese cousins, but your chaps..."

"Well, obviously, we had to treat them with more than casual care."

"We too, old boy. I say, you know we have been around this track a few times ourselves."

"But, in this case, you were freer than we."

"Perhaps. At least we were not so hung up on the question of whether or not there really was a split between them and the Chinese. We just assumed that they would each pursue their own national advantages. This brings us to Vasili Maximovich."

"...and his merry band of thugs."

"Oh, he is really not so bad a chap, you know. A professional. One can talk with him."

"How well do you know him?"

"Ah, there you go again. I really am no St. John Philby, my dear chap."

"I didn't mean to imply."

"Perhaps you didn't. But I did infer. Sorry. The nerve is more exposed than I like to think...the nightmare with which we have to live. But, let me tell you about the story relative to Dirhem. Vasili Maximovich is a senior man in his Service, roughly the equivalent of a major general. As you know, he has a big station here. Clearly Russia takes Afghanistan very seriously. Our fellows in London are convinced that they regard taking over Afghanistan as their logical next step."

"Your chaps have thought that for generations."

"Well, yes, but then the Russians have too. They have moved continuously south. And long before the Communists took over. Remember that much of the population of northern Afghanistan is made up of refugees from the Russian push into Central Asia. It seems logical -- and I am told that your people in Washington agree with our assessment -- that they would follow up, eventually try to take over the country. It makes strategic sense if they want to make India do what they tell it to do. And, of course, Russian control of Afghanistan would put Iran in a vice."

"That assessment doesn't seem to be reflected in your country's policies."

"Well, India is no longer ours to lose. Apparently, it is now yours to protect. Like almost everywhere else."

Smith winced. "Back to Vasili..."

"Yes, Vasili. As you know, he is a very experienced fellow. Long career. When we first got onto him, he was already quite senior. Seems to have spent many years on Central Asian stuff. Apparently went to the language schools and to the Institute of World Economy and International Affairs of the Soviet Academy and, presumably, to various staff and command schools.

Survived the various shakeups and purges along the way. I don't know about his Party affiliations, but I would wager they're minimal. Must have kept his head down. We have put various Afghans onto him and found that he knows Pashto, Farsi and presumably also Eastern Turkish. I have met him socially and he spoke perfect English."

"In short, the usual Russian -- eight feet tall," laughed Smith. "I can't think of a single one of our fellows who could speak...or be spoken of...like that."

"Well, not to worry. This is their back garden, so to speak. It used to be ours. Our chaps used to handle..."

"That just makes us seem more retarded...None of us could handle Spanish, Portuguese and a couple of American Indian dialects."

"Hum...well, be that as it may..." He stopped, sat back and looked inquiringly at Smith, " I say, what do you have on Vasili?"

"More or less what you do, I imagine. But, one personal note you did not mention -- he is said to be a keen photographer. Went to any amount of trouble to get a new Nikon recently. We gave him some help, indirectly... to whet his appetite, you know stuff about all the lenses and expensive peripherals."

"What?"

"You know, all the extra filters and flash and close-up equipment and all the stuff that bankrupts an amateur."

"If you don't mind my saying so, how like you!"

"Consider it a compliment. We also hear that he is married and has two sons, one of whom is a cadet in the military academy. He sends parcels home with some regularity, some even through the open post. He lives modestly here in bachelor quarters. He likes soccer, as a spectator, but appears to read a great deal about the country. Really quite an Afghan buff. At third country cocktail parties, he often tells stories out of Afghan history and has been known to recite Persian poetry. Delights the Afghans, of course, although I guess he scares the hell out of them too. We have never tried to run an operation on him to the best of my knowledge."

"Hum, curious summary of a man. I hope I never fall afoul of your fellows!"

"I hope not too, Hughe," Smith was even more deadpan than usual.

Crighton-Philips looked sharply at Smith but said merely, "As agreed, Vasili is to be dealt with by us."

"That's what the instructions say, he's all yours."

"What about the Chinese? Neither of us has a role with them, I gather. They have more or less played their part in this operation. No?"

"If you mean the ones here," Crighton-Philips replied, "the answer is no for my part. After all, they are really the new boys. Nothing like the same caliber as the Russians, at least not yet. Small outfit in Kabul. But, one must assume that just beyond the Wakan Corridor, they have legions. And what we used to call Chinese Turkistan is their back garden. Maybe some of them are specialists on Afghanistan. I would be surprised if they weren't."

He paused and gazed off. "Wakan Corridor...now there's a place. I've been all over it in my younger days, when I was briefly with the Scouts. And let me tell you that it is rough country, unfit for man or beast. If I were Russian or Chinese, I would be delighted to leave it as it is, in Afghan hands...Incredible country. The mountains rise to twenty thousand feet. You've seen the maps -- or do you only use U2 photos these days?"

Smith did not respond to the gibe, and Crighton-Philips went on, "Well on the maps, it looks like its name, a corridor but on the ground, it is less that than a sort of plug. Really as much a barrier as...as, say, the

Maginot Line. So I guess the Russians and Chinese feel relatively secure about Afghanistan.

"But, what neither feels secure about is Turkish Central Asia – the areas around Bukhara, Samarqand and Chinese Turkestan or Sinkiang as it is now called. That is what will rouse their interest. Anyway, it was agreed at JIC that we would fit that piece into the puzzle...the dominos as you put it.

"Each was more or less willing to help us...well, not exactly us... but at least not to help each other because, as much as they fear Turkish nationalism, they really intensely dislike and distrust one another. The Russians were delighted at something that would weaken the Chinese and the Chinese were more than happy to reciprocate. Remember that they had fought several big battles against one another up north, even while pledging eternal brotherhood. So, they had something to gain by more or less, perhaps unwittingly, doing or at least not stopping a limited deal with us -- just like we are now doing..."

"Our 'special relationship' is thought to be a little more stable," Smith shot back.

"Right you are. But until recently, everyone thought theirs with the Chinese Communists was too."

"Anyway, what was their deal?"

"Ah, the deal. Well, it was rather simple at that stage. The Russians staked out the little hut. Not much of a challenge, that. After all, there couldn't be more than a dozen or so huts in that desolate area. And that is where we found their fellow when we needed him."

"You...uh...found him there."

"Precisely. He was the other man of the two."

Smith nodded, "I really don't know how our Uighur chap got up there from Pakistan. I lost him there."

"Well, not to put too fine a point on it, your whole Service did too. He was picked up, by agreement at the top, mind you, by one of our fellows and conveyed to the little hut where, by pre-arrangement, he met with the other fellow and let us just say that they were both neutralized.

"Timing was, of course, crucial since the Russians and, by this time, the Chinese had a pretty good idea of who was where and the Afghans, not exactly altruistic themselves, and for once at least were paying attention. So they were also keeping an eye on the hut."

"Expensive piece of real estate, that hut!"

Ignoring the remark, Crighton-Philips went on. "What we had to do was to get your fellow, not a proxy, but one of yours, to lend credence, near the hut at the right time...*et voilà.*

"Well, we got him to your Afghans."

"Yes, I know. Old Qol Khan. A third generation friend. Reliable chap. He was waiting, I happen to know for sure, at the pick-up point and met your man. From there on, I have only one report, by a younger man whose reliability is not so good as Qol Khan, but who was...I should have thought... trustworthy."

"But, you said you do know that Jack found the hut."

"Oh yes, I know the end -- or nearly the end of the story. But I don't know exactly what happened. I just know that Jack... what's his name?"

"Farnsworth."

"How charmingly American...Yes, Jack Farnsworth...found the hut."

"You see, Hughe, my colleague thought he was *supposed to find the hut.*"

"Ah, the high cost of 'security'." Crighton-Philips raised his arms in mock supplication.

"Well, we had to do it that way in case he got caught. He had to think..."

"Pardon my saying so, but time after time I have seen your colleagues get into a pickle because, when you really get down to it, you don't trust one another. I understand it is because of the immigrant problems." He laughed.

Smith didn't smile. "That is one difference between us, admittedly, and each way has its costs."

"Oh well, hardly for us to decide, what?"

"But, if your chap indeed dropped him at the right place and if he did as he was carefully and repeatedly told, he would have missed the cabin and by morning would have found the truck, probably by then under observation by the Afghans, been arrested, questioned, given his lame excuse and been sent back here to be expelled."

"Well, evidently, it didn't happen like that. Apparently, he robbed the nest and is somewhere out there with the papers. So we...or rather I...simply have to get them to find him."

"What?"

"Of course. My dear chap, we have gone this far. We have lost at least one very good agent and spent a great deal of money...we've become cost conscious, you know, and..."

"But, if he has got the papers and got away, and they track him down... to get the papers, they'll surely kill him..."

"Oh, I don't know. We cannot predict...but probably you are right. I certainly would have."

"Hell, Hughe, he is an American…"

"I am fully aware of his nationality."

"We cannot just…"

Major Crighton-Philips turned up his hands and shrugged.

Staring at him, Smith blurted, "I mean, it's one thing to knock off Afghans and Chinks but he is one of…"

"My dear boy, there is no 'us'…that is what you were going to say, isn't it? Occasionally…just like the army, men and equipment get wasted. I've sent men to more certain ends than this."

"But that's dif…"

"How, different? It's a mission. Bad luck. Might have been you or me. Nothing personal. Part of the game."

Smith looked anguished.

Sighing, Crighton-Philips went on. "If he hadn't tried so hard or if you had briefed…"

"That's a can of worms. Don't open it up. I did exactly what I was ordered to do, told him exactly what I was told to tell him…"

"Precisely."

"…and no more."

"Precisely."

"Well, I carried out my mission. It is finished."

"Precisely."

"And now you want…"

"No, I do not want to do anything. I simply don't think we have any choice. My instructions are to be sure that the papers reach the Afghans." He looked evenly at Smith. Then he continued. "As you say, your part of the mission is finished. This part is ours. Or to be blunt, mine. I believe the JIC instructions make that very clear. Or have I read them wrongly?"

"No, you are essentially ri..."

" Essentially? In what respect am I not right?"

"No. You are exactly...precisely...right." Smith sighed.

"But, I don't want anything to happen to..."

"Neither do I want anything to happen to...er...Farnsworth. But, frankly, I am less concerned with him now than that the papers get where they are supposed to go."

"Can't we think of..."

"Smith, you know very well, we are not free to improvise. There may be parts to this show that neither of us knows. We might, in actual fact, do exactly what Farnsworth has done, blow the whole game by mucking about with the scenario, if I may use one of your words."

"But the chances are that Jack will be..."

"That is a chance we must all take. Part of the game, my dear fellow."

"Yes, that's true." Smith sighed.

"So, I must now ask you to stand aside."

"Well. I really have no choice given the JIC directive, as you say, short of getting in my car and driving up to try to find him..."

"I have no objection to that...provided that you do not find him."

The buzzer on Smith's desk rang. Smith went behind his desk and picked up the telephone. He listened intently with the ear-piece pressed tightly to his head. "Yes, thank you. He can take it here if he likes or we can give him the spare office. Just a minute." He turned to Crighton-Philips. "It's for you. Your office. Do you want to take it here or shall I give you another office where you can be private?"

"How private would that be?" Crighton-Philips laughed. "I'll take it right here."

Smith ostentatiously turned aside and walked back to the sofa.

Crighton-Philips casually picked up the phone, looked at it for a second, and then put it loosely up to his ear as though making sure that Smith would see that he didn't mind being overheard. He listened and then, after a soft click, said, "Are you there, Edward? Do you have something for me?" He listened but said nothing for two or three minutes, injecting, only "right," or "right you are" and "go on," are you sure...say that again, please and finally "thank you very much...yes, in half an hour."

He hung up the telephone and turned to Smith. "We now have confirmation that Farnsworth got the papers and has disappeared. He did not make the second contact with Qol Khan. The Afghans did. They made rather a mess of it, I'm afraid. Possibly scared him off, if he were nearby. As far as I know, the Afghans got nothing from Qol Khan but one of his boys, rather young I gather, was induced to tell them that they had seen an American 'hippy', as I understand you call them, and gave him a lift. Before they finished with the boy, he described Farnsworth. Then, I understand, they all were...they all were shot."

"Are you sure?"

"Yes I am. I may as well tell you, to confirm what I say, that we have a fellow who was at the truck, one of the Security types who passes materials on to us from time to time."

217

"And he watched your agents get killed?"

"He did not know, of course, that they were ours. Possibly he thought they were yours...or the Russians' or maybe even innocent drivers. Anyway, he is not really 'our' man, just a dealer with whom we occasionally trade. But, a reliable chap."

"And no word of Jack?"

"No word of Jack." Crighton-Philips paused and then continued. 'Well, that's not strictly true. What my number two, Edward just said, as I guess you heard, was that fter they got the drivers to talk, or maybe it was before, I'm not sure, they went to the cabin. There they found the shoulder harness – the device that had been fixed up to hold the documents. It was cut so that the pouch was missing and, nearby in the dust, they found an American pocket knife. I know we didn't put it there. Did Farnsworth have a knife?"

"Yes...or I suppose so. I think I have seen him with a little pocket knife."

"Well, I assume that is one more bit of evidence that he was there."

"Would this 'dealer' have told you if they had found Jack?"

"Absolutely. Of that, I have not the slightest doubt."

"We can be sure, then, that he has not been apprehended?"

"No, of that we cannot be sure. We can be sure that he had not been apprehended by this particular group of Afghan Security....as of the day after."

"Of course, now, everyone will be after him. Every bloodhound in the north will be on his trail, Afghan, Chinese, Russian..the whole pack. The Afghans by now will obviously have concluded that something unusual is afoot, probably something big, and I am sure they will try to seal off the entire area."

"I'm less worried about them," Smith replied. "Don't you think we can pretty well disregard the Afghans in our calculations, Hughe?"

"No. I shouldn't have thought so...not by a long shot."

"You surprise me. They don't even know what's up. This may sound condescending or, you might say, 'American', but they don't really figure, do they? I mean, after all, what is this country? Just a stage for the Russian assault on the West. They won't even know what it is all about until one of their chiefs sees a way to make a pile in some Swiss bank by selling the materials to the Chinese...or the Russians, the shuravi, as I believe they call them."

"Don't get carried away, old chap. This is, after all, their country. They know it. Some of them even love it."

"But they have no capacity..."

"I shouldn't write them off, no matter what you think. We did once. Of course, that was a long time ago, before the Sepoy Rebellion in India. We thought the same as you, that the country was just a stage for our war with the Russians. And they gave us no end of a lesson. We lost a whole army up in these mountains. In a few days too. More than seven regular regiments of our best troops. It was the worst disaster we had in the Nineteenth century. And it wasn't the end. The civilians and the remaining troops, nearly sixteen thousand of them, tried to walk down this short road to our lines at Jalalabad. Not very far, mind you, and all down hill. Relative to what your chap Farnsworth faces, just an afternoon outing. The Afghans hung on them like hounds on a stag and finally bore them down. Out of that sixteen thousand, only one man reached our lines alive. One man. No. I shouldn't think it prudent to write them off. Not by half."

Crighton-Philips had stood up and paced across the room as he spoke.

Smith stood impatiently, shaking his head. "But that was guerrilla warfare. This is entirely different. A matter of brains."

"Well, they have stayed alive and independent -- from us and from the Russians -- a long time by using their wits."

"But they are completely corrupt."

"Of course they're corrupt. That is what we are banking on, but I think we should be making a mistake to regard them as stupid. And, after all, they know their country as we never shall. One of us, like your chap Farnsworth, sticks out like a sore thumb. Where can he hide? They know every spring, every well, every drinking hole -- and he will die without water. I have been there...been thirsty... How could he get across the mountains, alone, without supplies, with everyone looking for him."

"I admit the physical odds are almost impossible."

"Well, all I am saying is that we have to assume -- as I intend to do from here on -- that the Afghans will play the role we want them to play, and play it fairly well. The only question is whether this new wrinkle, your chap's having made away with the goods, will Scimitar work or will he ruin it. My hunch is that he will delay it a day or so, but not much more. One thing I am sure of. Your chap won't get far without food or water and some means of transport. I know that country. Rode over it on horseback a long time ago. Wonderful for birds fleeing Siberian winters. But certain death for men on foot. Particularly for men alone. He'll be begging them to arrest him shortly."

Smith stared off into the eternity of a blank white wall. Then he shook his head and said, "Hughe, I guess you were right not to discount the Afghans. But don't make the mistake of discounting Farnsworth either. He's a good officer. He will try hard...very hard."

"Much the worse for him. He would do us all a favor to turn his ankle and limp into the nearest village."

"If he does, you can be sure he will have hidden the papers."

"Hum…" said Crighton-Philips thoughtfully, "good point. That we cannot have him do. They must make him produce them one way or another."

"I don't want to talk about that."

"Right. My job. Not pleasant to think about. They certainly will not be gentle."

Smith frowned and sighed, "then, of course, they could not let him live."

Major Crighton-Philips again shrugged. Then he continued, "So, what do you think he might try to do?"

"Well, there is just a possibility that he might try for the AID camp at Kunduz…where they are building some road works…to try to get them to give him a lift or something."

"Unlikely. I doubt that he could ever make Kunduz."

"If he doesn't, your twisted ankle scenario will work then."

"Hum…not so good as I first thought, that. If he hides the papers and is arrested…" Crighton-Philips paused a long time, staring up at the ceiling. Smith watched him intently. "I must think this through…but…if they know about the papers, which they probably do from their search of the hut and the harness they found, and they arrest him, someone is apt to decide to make him talk regardless of his diplomatic status. That would be serious and you would have to take offense. If you knew, that is. But…" he paused again and then looked at Smith. "But, if they made him talk, I think you are right, they really couldn't afford to let him go afterwards, could they? If he is a tough, serious officer and doesn't know the real intent of the plan…"

"He doesn't. Of that I am sure."

"…as seems apparent, then he won't talk easily. They will have to make him, and it won't be pleasant, and then they will have to kill him. And, even then, he might lead them astray or might not even talk at all."

"I am sure he would resist to the very end."

"That would ruin the whole show...hum...no the twisted ankle scenario is unacceptable. He has got to have the papers on him when..."

"Hell, Hughe, we can't keep him from twisting his ankle..."

"No, but we may be able to keep him from hiding the papers."

"I don't see how?"

"First, of course, we will have to find him."

"Everyone is trying to do that, as you say."

"You mentioned Kunduz and that is a logical goal."

"Well, if I were in his shoes, that is where I would be headed. North is *Russia, East is China, south are the bare mountains. Where else is there?"

"Right you are. Let us consider Kunduz. I understand you have an AID mission up there. Will your AID people help him?"

Smith thought a moment and the face of Ernest Crownover came before his eyes...the memory of the discussion they had right in this room. "No. There is only one man there. I don't think he will get much help there, even, which is unlikely, he even knows that there is an American there. And how could he ever find the AID camp. Why he would have to have a sixth sense or an up-to-date map and a compass."

"Did he have either?"

"No, I made sure that he had no equipment, no map, no field glasses, no compass."

"Well, he couldn't have got any of those from the bodies in the hut. Of that I am certain."

"And I don't think he and Crownover, the AID man, ever exchanged more than a hello. He probably didn't even know Crownover was up there." Suddenly he sat bolt upright. " Wait a minute! He may have. Let me just check." With that, Smith picked up the telephone and pushed the intercom button. After a moment's delay, he said, "Please connect me with Nora, I mean Ms. Adams."

A moment later, he said, "Nora, Smith here. I have just one question, did Jack see Crownover after he left my office. What. You did. Oh, no, it's all right. We'll talk about it later...later, I said. I cannot talk now." Then he put the phone back in the cradel. And looking at Crighton-Philips, he said, "well, it turns out that they did meet. Nora, my number three, had the two men over for a drink before she and Jack left for the North. So I am sure Crownover would have mentioned that he too was going up north to Kunduz. He was going to supervise some road work. And just in passing, he could hardly have avoiding mentioning it. But, that is not to say that Jack would know where he was even if he had an idea he was near Kunduz."

"But, it is a contingency we should note."

"Well, yes, I guess so, but not likely."

"Contingencies never are. What else can you think of, as you put it, if you were in his shoes."

"Well, if he gets turned down in Kunduz, he would have to figure that he couldn't get over the mountains to Kabul on his own. He might try to contact our local 'friendly' in Kunduz."

"Yes. I had thought of that. I must ask you to identify him to me."

"Well, Hughe..."

"My dear fellow, you really must, you know."

"All right. But you will go easy..."

"Just watch. Not touch. My word on that. What else can you think

223

of...could he think of?"

"Well...but...no, that is not a real possibility. He would never make..."

"Let's just inventory the possibilities, not try to rule them out in advance. What were you thinking of?"

"Hughe, I am not supposed to tell even the members of my own staff..."

"For God's sake, man, must I go to the JIC for authorization on everything?"

"No." Smith shrugged in resignation. "I guess, under the circumstances, you have a need to know about this. Anyway, it is a contingency so remote..."

Crighton-Philips waited, blue eyes fixed firmly on Smith's. The seconds almost sounded from their watches.

"All right." Smith nodded. "There is an old 'final emergency' plan dating way back, long before I came out here. Each successive station chief was told of it, but there was a gap between me and my immediate predecessor so the information was entrusted to Jack. I know that Jack knows because he briefed me on it when I arrived.

"You see, at one point in the past, there seemed a possibility of an uprising against the central government when all the usual protections would break down. And, since we had certain things here we absolutely had to get out uncompromised, we worked out a plan with an American super-secret organization called the Special Rescue Group, not part of the Agency, for a site, a highly unlikely site, in the wrong direction...toward the Russian frontier since the way south would, in that kind of emergency, presumably be cut.

"At the site, we or rather they, laid down an emergency ration, a long-life ultra high frequency pre-coded radio, jam proof, and operating so short a blast that it would be practically untraceable, to call in a rescue turbo helicopter from Pakistan."

"And it is still maintained?"

"Yes. It is part of the automated world-wide...well, the short answer is 'yes'."

"Where is it?"

Smith looked down at the pencil he held between his fingers. He paused, opened his mouth and took a deep breath...then slowly, almost painfully, he rose to his feet. Crighton-Philips watched him closely. Neither man spoke. Smith rubbed his hand across his face and worked his jaw. Finally, shaking his head, he spoke. "I will immediately inform..."

"Of course, you must, and I will immediately confirm to the JIC receipt of the information."

Without another word, Smith walked over to his safe and, putting his body between the combination lock dial and his visitor, began to twist the dial to the correct numbers. He moved quickly and the dial was silent. No clicks. Suddenly he yanked open the door and, reaching behind all the files, pulled out a sealed manila envelop.

Walking back to the sofa, he sat down beside Crighton-Philips and put the envelop on the table. Crighton-Philips could make out a centered white label on which was written in large red letters, apparently by a magic marker

'DO NOT OPEN STATION CHIEF ONLY'.

Smith tore it open, dropped it on the table and turned slowly to Crighton-Philips. In his hand was a folded white paper on the back of which was also written, but typed this time, in large lettering,

TOP SECRET * NOFORN * CODE WORD MATERIAL *NOFORN *TOP SECRET

Deliberately he unfolded a map. Laying it down on the table in front of them, he pointed first to Kunduz on the far right hand side.

"If he could get to Kunduz, and get through the town without being arrested, he might try this."

His finger moved toward the left, west from Kunduz, along a deceptively straight red line toward the town of Mazar-i Sharif, just south of the Ab-i Panja river and the Russian town of Stalinabad.

Crighton-Smith bent over the map and followed Smith's finger with his own, pausing at each topographical note. Just short of Mazar-i Sharif, Smith's finger stopped.

Bending over closer to the map, he looked carefully. Then, nodding, said, "yes, here..."

"What?" Crighton-Smith looked puzzled.

"That pin hole in the paper."

"Oh, I see. Clever, that."

Then his finger moved south along a winding road, little more than a pathway, according to the map, into the Hazarajat, the central mountain-locked valley which was the final redoubt of the southern army of Chingis Khan's Mongols. There his finger stopped. He looked up.

"I don't follow," said Crighton-Philips.

"The scale is too small," said Smith, picking up a small white envelop that had rested next to the map. This he tore open and pulled out a rough, hand drawn sketch map and a typed sheet of instructions. Unfolding it, he said, "Here is the village of Haibak. And here is a sheep trail up out of the valley toward the flat top of a mountain. The map doesn't show any detail but the sheet has instructions. Jack knows them by heart. As he put it, when he briefed me on it, shortly after I took over, 'the only way is up; no need for a map, really.'

"So, if Farnsworth got that far, he could, assuming the weather conditions permitted, call in a helicopter and get lifted off."

"Would your station in Pakistan or wherever check with you?"

"No. The deal is that they would not. The assumption would be that something had gone very wrong here, and they would immediately go in and get whomever was there before asking even Washington. Frankly, Hughe, I have violated my instructions by revealing..."

"Not to worry, old chap," Crighton-Philips replied, "not a chance in hell that he could make it so far. If you don't mind my saying so, this is the most unlikely lifeboat I have ever heard of. If any of your fellows -- in a real panic -- could get way up there, they bloody well wouldn't need a helicopter -- they would just fly out on their own wings!"

"Yes. I agree. I have always doubted the value of the plan, but I just inherited it. Anyway, now you have it, the most remote possibility. So we must just wait."

"Rather. I appreciate your frankness. Now, if you will excuse me, I had better get back to my own shop. Perhaps all is not lost yet."

Both men stood up and walked to the door. "Would you mind awfully if I go out through the Embassy way as I was seen to come in?"

"No, of course. I'll have you shown out past the Marines. Please keep me informed," Smith almost whispered.

"Of course," replied the major, now putting on his most distant manner. In a second, he was through the door, and it closed behind him.

Smith turned and walked back to the desk. He stood for a moment vacantly staring at the papers scattered on the coffee table. Then, shaking his head slowly, he said aloud, "Shit! I'm not sure...not sure at all..."

THE END GAME

JACK AWOKE LATE IN THE MORNING and sat up on the bunk, disoriented and confused. The events of the last days tumbled in his memory like clothes in a washing machine, all twisted and shapeless but still recognizable. Painfully recognizable.

The central issue was distinct — he felt for his jacket under his head where he thought he remembered putting the packet of papers for which 'Percy' had died and for which the whole venture had been launched. He bolted upright. The packet was not there. Frantically he groped around in the dim light of the shuttered trailer. Then he realized that he had his jacket on. He felt the pockets. In one was the dead man's 7.65 mm automatic. Its black steel was warm from his body heat — he had been so exhausted he had not even felt it under his body.

Then, he felt for the papers. They were not, he was sure, where he had left them. They were not under his shirt but also in a pocket of his jacket. The memory on which he prided himself was obviously no longer reliable.

Anyway, Percy's papers like the automatic, his only two real possessions, were reassuringly present. He didn't take them out to look at them. He had never examined them since the first few seconds after he found Percy. There was something sinister about them, something he didn't want to touch or to know about. All he cared about was to get them into Smith's hands.

Then, as he sat up, his eye fell on Ernest's note. He read it hurriedly. Ernest had been kind, maybe too kind for his own good already. Jack doubted that he could talk Ernest into taking him to Kabul. He wasn't any longer sure he even wanted to try; in fact, he was nearly sure he didn't want to.

Even though it might be suicidal, it seemed to Jack wrong, even obscene, to try to subvert Ernest, particularly in his pursuit of things that ought to help people and, he agreed with Ernest, things that just might, even in some vague way, make the world more the sort of place that decent people could live in. Maybe even make it safer.

How could anyone sort out these conflicting imperatives? Jack concluded that he could not, but it worried him that he might compromise the evident value of Ernest's work for the dubious value of his own. That thought bothered him, but he didn't have the energy or willpower to think it through then. He decided that whatever else the mission had accomplished, it had given him tools – if he lived to use them – to rethink his life.

He crumpled up Ernest's note and started to throw it away. Then, thinking better of it, he smoothed it out on the tabletop, trying to unwrinkle the paper. Turning it over, he wrote very carefully,

Dear Ernest, I have thought a lot about our talk last night. And I have decided that you are probably

He crossed out 'probably'…

right. I shouldn't compromise you or AID any further. I am deeply grateful for your taking me in last night. Someday, maybe with luck, I can repay your kindness. For now and for your own safety, I urge you to forget that I was here. Don't mention it to anyone. I can't tell you, and you wouldn't want to hear, any more. But there are some people — I don't know exactly who they are — who will stop at nothing to keep me from getting to Kabul. I don't want to be dramatic, but if you get any hint that anything suspicious is happening around you, please do me a favor and go home to Kabul for a few days until this all blows over. Just to make my point, I'll just tell you that in the last few days, I have seen five men murdered. Be careful and thanks again. Jack

I hope the old devil believes me,' Jack thought as he put a glass on top of the note to keep it from falling on the floor. Then he went to the refrigerator and got out all the food he could find, ate some bread and luncheon meat and drank deeply and repeatedly from the water bottle. He used the toilet and even used Ernest's razor to shave. His hair was matted but he combed it as well as he could.

Feeling refreshed, Jack suddenly reflected that he had not even peeked out of the windows. The trailer seemed so cut off, so shuttered from the world, so safe.

He went to the window nearest the door and lifted a corner of the curtain. That view showed nothing but rubble and trash and, about fifty yards away, a high wire fence. Then, turning around and twisting his body, he stepped over the opposite window. Again, he lifted a corner of the curtain.

Immediately he dropped it.

What he had seen there made him gasp. Parked outside the gate was the pair of Russian Jeeps he had seen at the truck stop. He recognized one of them by the police symbol and the number 29 written in Persian on the side.

Cautiously, he again lifted the corner of the curtain and slowly panned his eyes along the fence line. To the left, at the gate he had entered, was the old Afghan night watchman talking to three men in the baggy uniforms of the Security Forces. Then, as he watched, an officer walked up and group turned to face the trailer. They seemed to be arguing amongst themselves. Finally, the officer started back to the Jeep and the others ran to take their places. The old Afghan started after them, but, with the same scream of motors and gears Jack had heard on that awful early morning, they were gone in a cloud of dust.

"Christ," he mumbled to himself, "they must have guessed I would try old Ernest. Logical move. Fellow American and all that. But somebody is sure quick off the mark. I've never heard of the Afghans being so efficient. These fellows must have a sixth sense or else whoever penetrated...but, anyway, that settles it. I can't stay here and wait for another visit. They must have gone to get permission from higher authorities to search a U. S. Government installation. But, how the hell can I get out now?"

Jack quickly pulled on his pants and shirt and laced up his boots. He rummaged through Ernest's clothes and found a cap like Ernest always wore. That wasn't much disguise but they might think he was a visiting AID official, he hoped. Then he found a prize, a canteen which he filled with water. Again he drank. And, in a little metal box, he found a few coins and these he stuffed into his pocket too. Returning to his note, he picked up the pencil again and hurriedly wrote,

P. S. When I looked outside, I saw 2 Afghan Security Forces Jeeps. I guess they were just checking and didn't come in. I hope they haven't followed me here. Maybe your watchman saw more than we thought. I sure hope not. But be very careful. And, Ernest, I have borrowed a few things, a canteen, some food and a few coins. With luck I'll pay you back in Kabul. Again thanks. J. F.

Better not leave that note just lying there, he decided. That would compromise Ernest more than anything. So once more he crumpled up the note and shoved it into one of Ernest's spare boots.

Again he went to the window and, peeking out again, he saw the watchman go into his little cabin. In a bound, Jack was at the door and silently unlatched it. Stepping out and quietly closing it behind himself, he walked hurriedly but upright up to the gate. At the corner of the cabin, he paused. From inside, he heard the rattle of pans and a man mumbling to himself. He hoped the watchman was making tea. 'Thank God for tea,' he thought. He peeked around the door and saw the man's back to him. In a stride, he was past the open door and out the gate. A big yellow road-grader was parked nearby and he slipped behind it and climbed into the cab to survey the road before going ahead.

For a few moments, he considered simply hiding in the grader. No one would think to look there. Just then, he was startled to see the two Jeeps, now joined by a larger, more senior looking official car, rushing up the dirt road toward the gate. As he watched, hunkered down in the grader cab, the three cars screeched to a halt and were momentarily hidden in dust. The old watchman rushed out of his hut and bowed low before them.

As the dust cleared, he could see that the four soldiers had out their sub- machine guns and put on a more formal, more martial show before the senior officer than they had in front of their own more junior officer. Immediately, the junior officer barked a command and they ran to form a circle around the trailer from which they also covered the fence line and the gate, guns at the ready. The senior officer said something to the junior officer which, of course, Jack could not hear, turned and got back in his car. The junior officer, in turn, spoke to the watchman and, together, they walked up to the trailer. Again the junior officer spoke and the watchman knocked on the door.

The watchman waited a few moments and then knocked again. Holding out his arms in a gesture of resignation, he looked back at the officer. The officer said something to him that made the watchman recoil in evident fear. All of this was played out before Jack like an old silent movie, with jerks and jumps, followed by gestures but with no sound.

Although Jack could hear nothing of these exchanges it was clear that the officer had demanded the key. The watchman shrugged his shoulders, evidently saying that he did not have a key; so shoving him ahead, the officer, obviously undecided what to do, walked back to the limousine. There the watchman hung as far back as he could while the officer walked up and saluted. Then he bent over toward the car window and talked with the senior man for a few moments. When he had reported and got whatever orders he was to follow, he stood up and saluted again. Turning to the now bent and cringing night watchman, he said something. The man must have objected because the officer shouted at him. He cowered, almost falling on his back and turning, ran back to the trailer. Again he beat on the door. Jack winced. Those knocks would have been the sound of doom if he had still been inside. Then the watchman circled the trailer, trying all the windows and finally came back to the door, knocked again and, turning, raised his arms in resignation.

His gesture was followed by another shout and what must have been a torrent of abuse. The watchman visibly sagged. He turned toward the door and mounting the little ladder that served as steps, put his hand on the knob and his shoulder to the door. Apparently, he had been told to break the door down.

This time, when he twisted the knob, he almost fell into the cabin since Jack had been unable to lock it after himself. With a shout, he turned back to the younger officer and he, in turn, called out to the senior officer. 'It would have been Marx Brothers, if it weren't so terrifying and so real,' Jack winced. The whole group now converged on the trailer, and, with his pistol drawn, the junior officer went inside.

His search could not have lasted a minute and as he emerged, he in turn, raised his arms and the palms of his hands, still holding his pistol, in a sign of resignation. With that, the senior officer now advanced from the immunity of his sedan and, in his turn, he examined the trailer. Emerging, he walked up to the watchman and slapped him viciously across the face with his swagger stick. Without a word, so far as Jack could tell, he strode to the sedan and drove away. The junior officer then screamed at the watchman who ran back and closed the door of the trailer. When he had done so, the remaining soldiers ran to their Jeeps. In another swirl of dust, they were gone, leaving the watchman, hand on his now swollen cheek, staring dumbly after them. Then, with a shake that seemed to course through his whole body, he turned back to his little kitchen and his tea.

Huddled in the cab of the grader, Jack felt a drip of water going down his sleeve and realized that he was wringing wet from the sweat of his fear. He had no doubt that he would now be dead if he had been in that trailer when the soldiers arrived.

As he watched, he saw by the retreating dust trails that the Jeeps and the sedan were far down the road toward Kunduz. He tried to focus on the meaning of his location. If the camp were on the southwest outskirts of the town, he could make a large arc and avoid both the camp and the town. But where would he be then? He didn't have a ghost of a chance of getting to Kabul on foot.

For a moment, he looked longingly at the wheel of the grader. What a sight that would be, driving into Kabul on a big yellow grader, mowing down check points and plowing Jeeps and armored cars out of his path. They would certainly have done it in the movies. But this wasn't the movies. No, the grader had done its best for him. He looked around. Was there another vehicle? Yes, a non-descript truck was parked about fifty yards away, but one look told Jack that it was jacked up on rocks and was missing the two front wheels. No luck there. What if he stayed and 'borrowed' Ernest's pick up when he came home? That was an inviting idea until he considered the problem of the checkpoint...maybe now many check points...between him and Kabul. Even with AID plates, which were somewhat less imposing than diplomatic plates, he would never get through. Anyway, he couldn't stay so near the camp any longer. Obviously, his pursuers would think he was nearby if they thought he had been in the trailer. So, it was likely that the soldiers would come back, carrying with them in their Jeeps the next time dogs to track him. And even if they had no dogs, the old watchman probably did. He would be so scared, he would surely let out his guard dog. So it was impossible to risk staying.

He thought again of his instructions. No clue what to do in this circumstance. Odd, he thought, almost all plans have a fallback position in case something breaks down. But this one did not. 'Chalk up another for old Smith,' he thought bitterly. 'If he had been out to get me, he could not have done a better job.'

But the words 'fall back' triggered another thought.

"In an extreme emergence and if all else fails," he remembered the first station chief he had known in Kabul, who was just leaving when he first arrived, saying, "there is a spot near Kunduz where we have pre-positioned supplies, arms and a special, long-life ultra-high frequency transmitter. It has a pre-recorded half-second beep. That beep will activate a message in the survival center in Pakistan. When that message is received, without any further questions and without checking with anyone, they will send a long-range turbo-jet helicopter and pick anyone at the site up in less than two hours."

Jack had been fascinated. It was the real stuff. Final redoubt, secret signals, unjamable, automatic...ultra high tech. No checking with the Station, Langley or even with the White House. They just came. Questions might be asked later. But, hell, wasn't this just the sort of thing it was designed for? Jack alone of the junior officers knew about it because he had been the one to brief Smith when he arrived. Maybe that was why he had been picked for this mission. He alone had the key to the only exit! Certainly no one outside the mission and only he and Smith inside the mission could have even guessed such a thing existed.

This really was what it was all about, even in the spy novels. It felt like one of those scenes where the hero jumps off a cliff and suddenly a balloon inflates and he sails away from his pursuers. Here was his "balloon." He still had a chance.

Now was the time to move, and quick, he decided. The watchman would be licking his wounds in the cabin, mad as hell at the officer. The junior officer would be getting chewed out by his boss who, in turn, would be waiting for a balling out from his boss who, in turn...God, it was endless, the bureaucratic ladder.

'Now, while everyone is busy getting hell,' he thought, 'is the time to move.' So, as quietly as possible, he slipped out of the cab into the broad daylight. The best thing to do, he decided, was to keep the cab between him and the watchman's cabin, walk about a half a mile straight out and then double back around the camp. He would have to walk upright like he owned the place. Trying to hide would only attract attention. But, he felt as exposed as if he were walking through town naked, even like having a spotlight trained on him.

It reminded him of his conversation with Nora when he described his visit to Leningrad before he joined the agency. But the difference this time was that it was not him who "knew" but them. They knew whom they were looking for; he did not know for sure even who they were. He was really, in the bad sense, not the good sense he had described to Nora, completely alone.

For the first fifty paces, he had an almost physical feeling of a gun-sight on the middle of his back. But nothing happened. And, in a few minutes, he was far enough from the camp that even if the old watchman had seen him, he would not recognize him as a foreigner.

Except for Ernest's cap! He had forgotten that. Removing the cap, he placed it under a large stone and then turned abruptly right to walk due West. As the sun sank it bored into his eyes. Soon he regretted not having that cap, but, of course, it was too obvious. In real pain he decided that he must make some sort of shade for his face. So, squatting down in a small hollow, he removed his jacket and took off his wool shirt. The wool was new and hard to rip, but with his teeth and fingers – how he regretted not having the pocketknife he had dropped at the cabin — he managed to rip off a section and to fashion a sort of brown bandanna. It wasn't elegant, but it kept his skull from cooking and made him look just a little more native... some kind of native, at least, Tajik, Uzbek, or something. Maybe, even like a hippie. But it kept off at least some of the sun.

After he had walked about three hours, he guessed -- since he no longer had his watch -- he sighted a small hillock just before him. Some sixth sense warned him to be careful. As though he had been anything else for days! He dropped behind a rock at the base of the hill to listen. Then, out of nowhere, for the third time in just the last few hours, he heard the high whine of an air-cooled Russian Jeep. Jack pressed against the ground as, not more than a hundred yards ahead, the Jeep hove into sight. Practically on top of him, it stopped and out jumped a soldier. He saluted, and, after clumsily hitching up his baggy pants and adjusting his Kalashnikov, he trotted off toward the base of the hill.

His path to the hill passed only a few yards from where Jack lay, but the soldier, knowing that the eyes of the officer were on him, rushed past Jack so fast that he did not see him. Then he squatted down in the shadow of a boulder to watch over the stretch of country across which Jack had just come.

"Jesus Christ, another near miss," whispered Jack to himself as he froze against his rock. "I must have just about used up all nine lives."

Then, satisfied that the soldier was in place, the officer started up the Jeep and drove toward the South. As he watched the jeep go, Jack realized that the soldiers were staking out the town. 'They must think I am going to try to go for Kabul,' he thought.

They were wrong, but their mistake did not help Jack: he realized that he could not move now without being shot. Then the thought occurred to him that the soldier would be accustomed to a siesta and might doze in the hot afternoon sun. He quickly gave up that idea: from watching the senior officers at work, the soldier would be too scared to sleep. No, he would certainly stay wide-awake. But, there was one small flicker of hope. Jack had not seen any sort of radio so if he managed to get past the soldier, the soldier would have no way to warn his control.

In that ray of hope, of course, was a sinister element: it meant that the soldier was under orders simply to kill anyone coming past. The Jeep was now far to the south and, from the change in the whine of the motor, it had apparently stopped to let off another soldier. In a few moments, it started

237

up again and sped off east as though confirming Jack's estimate that they thought he would be heading for Kabul. 'Good for them,' he thought with grim determination. But, he realized, if he stayed put, he would run out of water and, in any event, they would just tighten the noose around the town. 'Now's the time to move.'

Just at that moment, he heard a rockslide. Then another. The soldier was moving. Just like stalking a tiger, he thought. He crouched and stepped carefully and as silently as possible further behind his rock. A foot scraped. Another rock slid out of its place. The steps came closer. Then, suddenly, right in front of him, he saw the soldier. His back was toward Jack. He stretched, was urinating and peering out over the land on which Jack had been about to walk. 'It's him or me, now,' Jack realized. As the soldier turned half toward him, Jack saw that he was the man who had wiped off the knife after disemboweling the Mongol boy.

Just as he turned full onto Jack, Jack took one step forward and, jamming the 7.65 mm automatic into the soldier's chest, so as to make as little noise as possible, pulled the trigger.

The hammer snapped on an empty chamber!

Both he and the soldier were stunned. For a second, each stared at the other in disbelief. Jack recovered the faster, from the lesser shock, and quickly stepping forward, tripped the soldier who was trying to disengage his Kalashnikov from the strap over his shoulder. The soldier and the gun fell back against the rock and Jack was on him before he could move again. Jack's right hand closed on the man's throat and his left hand grabbed his hair and banged it against the rock. He felt the man reaching for his knife. In desperation, Jack raised up, grabbed a large stone and with both hands brought it down on the man's face. Again he struck and he felt the man go limp under him.

Aghast – was it the shock of the empty pistol? the horror of murder? or the fear for his own life? — Jack stood up, now sweating profusely. Then he bent over and felt the soldier's pulse.

He was dead.

Jack straightened up. He felt no elation or pride. But also no sorrow. It had been a desperate act, a matter of survival. The man would certainly have killed him if he had seen Jack first even if he were just walking away. And, stuck in his mind was the image of the same soldier cruelly killing the young Mongol boy.

No, he felt no sorrow.

Jack then bent over and picked up the automatic, dropped during the struggle, and checked it. Of course, he remembered, he had taken out the bullet to give to the shepherd boy and had never primed the gun again. How stupid. That had almost cost him his life. But, he shook his head bitterly, it kept him from possibly shooting the poor little shepherd boy. One gain and – nearly – one loss.

He looked down at the man. He was crumpled and bloody.

Despite what he had done to the Mongol boy, it was hard not to feel sorry for him. In death, he was a pathetic figure, dressed, almost wrapped, in a uniform that was little more than a gunnysack, but, Jack realized, his survival had been mainly a matter of luck. And luck might soon run out. Probably the Jeep would come back for the soldier at dark. So Jack figured that he now had about four hours to get away.

Then he thought once again, 'How could it be? They had never been far away, those devils. How had they tracked him so easily? Somehow, it was almost too good. Almost as though they knew. Of course, they did. It was simple, he told himself. They knew he was on the way to Kabul. That is where they would expect him to try now. But they would realize that he would know that too. So they would try to catch him doubling back to Kunduz.

Then he thought back to Ernest. Jack hoped he had changed his boots! But, even if he read the note, he would probably not believe it. 'How hard it is to convince anyone,' Jack thought, 'how bad things can really be. That, at least, work in intelligence taught you. Things are always at least as bad as they seem. Usually worse...But no time to think now. Move!'

No one would expect him to head west into the desolation of the Kindu Kush mountains and the Hazarajat. Absolutely nothing up there. Not even a few blades of grass, certainly no trees, and, above all, no water. So that was the way to go. With luck, he thought, he could make about eight or maybe even ten miles by the time that Jeep came back. So, with long loping strides, he set off.

At first he jogged and then walked in roughly hundred pace segments. That way, with a five minute break each hour, even if the trail was not easy, he figured he could make at least five or six miles. But, soon, the ground became so rough that he could not make anything approaching that distance. However, he kept moving.

At sundown, he was in the foothills overlooking Kunduz. The view was so magnificent, he could almost forget its danger. The sun streaked through the saw-teeth of the mountain chain ahead of him, painting with violent reds and purples the hills and plains beyond Kunduz, where he could imagine Kazan Khan and his Turcoman hosts would be gathering their animals and preparing tea.

Looking over this vast panorama, the events of just a few hours ago seemed disembodied, distant, historic, parts of some other life only vividly remembered. He paused for his five minute break and used it to search the landscape. He tried to find the hill where the dead soldier would be lying. But it was lost amidst a sea of hillocks far below. He searched for the Jeep. But, to his delight, he saw nothing move, no telltale plume of dust.

With luck, something he desperately prayed for, the commander would leave his trooper overnight where he had dropped him. He was hopeful because he knew that the Afghan armed forces commanders cared little for their soldiers and treated them roughly and carelessly.

Perhaps he had more time than he realized. While all his training told him that it was not wise to depend on it, he figured, he had an hour and a half of cool half-light. Then it would be too dark to walk.

Getting up, now feeling the beginnings of a cramp in his leg, he struck out again. And, as he alternatively jogged and walked, he searched his memory for all the scraps of information he would need. The redoubt, he knew, was between Kunduz and a little village called Haibak. He would have to cross this range, then go down into a deep valley, cross a flood channel, which roared in the early summer with melted snow and boulders from the peaks of the Hindu Kush but which should be dry at this season. Then he would go up a mountain overlooking Haibak. Once he overlooked the stream, he could pick out the landmarks...he hoped.

Of course, he had never seen the spot. A special team had come out from the headquarters of some undisclosed and very secret military unit in America, by way of Pakistan, to make the drop off of supplies. They had apparently picked the spot from aerial photos. No one in Kabul, not even in the Station, had contacted them or talked with them. The station chief had just got a signal, in the midst of a garbled message on other matters, which read 'incubation' where the word would have made sense as 'installation.' The station chief had told Jack about it just before he left and Jack was the only link — the only 'memory' — to Smith. Maybe, he thought again, that was why he had been picked for this mission. He would have that one advantage over anyone else. He would have the final trump card.

That, and the fact that he was in good shape from his jogging. Thank God for jogging, he laughed. He had needed every muscle in his body. But, he thought ruefully, he sure as hell would never again advertise his jogging.

These thoughts had taken another of his five-minute rest periods and Jack turned again into the last rays of the sun. No one would be up here to watch him, he thought gratefully. Nothing at this season for animals to eat. No roads for officers' Jeeps. And while the Afghans had Russian helicopters, they apparently had not been trained to use them and had no spotter aircraft. He was nearly home free.

He was near the top of the crest now and the sweat was coming down the top of his back and from under his armpits. But it was good honest sweat, not the sweat of fear with which he had been soaked so often in the last days.

Sweat! He suddenly thought in a different light. Would it also soak the papers, even make them unreadable? So, for the first time, he reached into his shirt and brought them out. The little plastic pouch was intact. They would be all right. Weighing them in his right hand, he thought how light and small they seemed. So insignificant to be the cause of so much misery and so many deaths. Carefully, almost with distaste, he put them back in the pocket of his jacket.

Satisfied, he felt for his, or rather "Percy's," 7. 65 Czech automatic, pulled back the slide to be sure that he had primed it this time, eased the hammer onto the bullet, fixed the safety and put it back in his other pocket. Then he began to orient himself for his next leg.

The flood channel snaked between the mountains and, where it formed a sharp jag to the West, he knew he should find a trail leading up and West.

That was all he needed to know.

Now it was time, not direction that mattered most. Better get as far as possible before darkness forced him to stop. So, after another searching look down the valley, he plunged down the hillside as fast as his tired legs could safely carry him. Still smarting from the saddle, he realized that walking down hill, while easier on his muscles, chaffed at exactly the spots that the saddle had rubbed raw. He must keep his mind off pain. 'No winning in this game,' he thought ruefully, 'just different ways to lose.'

As it does in the mountains, darkness fell abruptly with the finality of a curtain so that Jack was forced to halt. Almost from one minute to the next, the wind suddenly turned freezing cold and sweat chilled his body. He sneezed. A tattered wool shirt was the price he had paid for his sun guard. Miserably, he hunkered down into a ball to conserve his warmth. But it was too cold and too uncomfortable for him, even as exhausted as he was, to sleep much. He thought that perhaps there would be enough moonlight to go ahead about 4:00 A.M., but, when the crescent moon crested the eastern ridge, about 3:00 A.M., he decided to get underway. Slowly and cautiously, picking his way among the rocks, he began his descent. He had not gone far, however, before his foot caught a rock and he slipped, almost starting a landslide and tumbling him against a boulder. His ankle twisted and, just in time, he slumped to the ground, grabbing the boulder and skinning his hands. The rocks, dislodged from their accustomed resting places, made a fearful clatter as they tumbled down the mountain. Jack sat stunned and angrily cursed himself, "they ought to be able to hear that in Kunduz."

This time, slower and more carefully, he moved down the mountainside. But the moon was quicker and before he had reached the bottom, it had passed over the western crest and left him again in pitch blackness. Again he was forced to stop and again he used the interval before first light to nap. He would need every ounce of energy, he realized, for the rugged trail ahead. "Thank God," he said quite aloud, "no one knew of it. *They* had been lucky tracking him before, but now there was no more luck, no one could possibly know…" No matter how hard it was, at least he would be safe from the hounds that were tracking him.

Tired as he was, he slept longer than he planned. The sun was near the crest of the mountain when he awoke. Painfully, he raised himself upright.

His body would not take this punishment much longer. But he felt that he could make it. After all it was just over the stream, over the Ab-i panja, the Five Waters, which fortunately was then bone dry. Also, without any cover. So, in the flat light of the early morning, he plunged downward and, after pausing a moment to look both ways, as one might at a busy street, he crossed the rock-filled streambed.

From there on, he remembered, the road would be up. About fifty paces up, he turned and looked back. He froze. He thought he saw a shadow move. But, at this hour, before the rays of the sun had hit, would there be really distinct shadows? He waited. Nothing happened. No movement. He realized that his mind was no longer fully under his control and that he could expect his eyes to play tricks on him. Memories. Nightmares. There were so many stored in his head. Must be seeing things. His eyes must no longer be recognizable, probably they were just red balls. He could feel his eye twitch as another sign of exhaustion.

Now he needed that eye. A few minutes later, winded, he stopped to watch. He put his left hand up to steady his gaze and searched the hill opposite. Again, he thought he saw a shadow move. He waited motionless and watched intently. He could see no movement, no unnatural shapes, nothing suspicious. Was his body just tricking his mind to get him to rest? He shook his head, "Stop malingering! Move, Jack, move!"

With his little store of remaining logic, he considered his situation. No one could possibly have followed him. Only he and Smith knew about the redoubt. Smith! A mole? Impossible. Real paranoia. And Smith wouldn't, couldn't tell a living soul…no, no one could know about this spot, and certainly no one could have followed him over the mountain at night. Anyway, no one could have beaten him up here, unless he had a helicopter, which certainly, the Afghans did not have or at least could not use.

Anyway, the Afghans would have thought he had doubled back to Kunduz to hide…or steal a car or try to reach the Embassy…No one would think of the Hazarajat. That way was certain death. By starvation or thirst. That would have made it too easy for them: they would just have to pick up his body then. Except for the redoubt…and about that they could know nothing.

But, how had they known of the papers? Had they really known about them? Or had they just smelled a big and possibly lucrative operation and once they got involved had to go all the way. Possible but not likely. They must have known something, he decided, to go to all this trouble. Doubt had burrowed into his mind like a worm in an apple, day by day, hour by hour, as he watched man after man tortured or killed.

Something was rotten. But what? Who could have told them? Percy and his hunter were both dead when Jack found them. And, if the Afghans had got there first, they would have just taken the papers. Smith had assured him that the Brits had known only about the truck that was to get him to the cabin.

And, even if they had known or guessed something more, they would hardly have confided in the likes of Qol Khan. So, no matter what had happened to Qol Khan, and it had been as horrible as anything Jack could have imagined in his worst nightmare, Qol Khan had nothing to tell his torturers. Jack shuddered at the memory of Qol Khan and the Mongol boy.

Ernest? He didn't know anything more than that Jack was running.

And someone knew long before Ernest did. It was either the Americans or the Brits. It couldn't be the Americans. Colleagues. Members of the same team. Unless Smith was playing a Philby. Impossible. But, then, it had been impossible for Philby. He was, after all the darling of the British service, a serious candidate for the top position. Impossible, except that he existed. Jack couldn't get it all sorted out. He just shook his head. He was too exhausted to think rationally or, apparently even to see clearly. There were no moving shadows. Nothing on that hill.

The goat trail was covered with sand and dust. Must not be used often, he realized. And that was partly why, of course, they had picked it. No place to go but up. Just follow the trail. But even that was not so easy. His foot caught another rock and he fell heavily to the ground. He rested longer this time, panting as the icy air brought its stingy ration of oxygen into his heaving lungs. His sweat turned instantly icy cold. But, as he looked up, he thought, almost happily, 'it can't be much more, not more than a mile or so... then a rest while I wait for the rescue chopper.'

The goat trail began to peter out and the vegetation became even more sparse. How could it be more sparse, he thought. A maze of almost indistinct paths branched though increasingly larger and larger boulders. Jack paused. He must not lose the trail...A pebble had worked its way into his shoe. It wasn't going to find its way to some safe place, like between his toes. He had to stop. In a step, he was next to a giant rock, a place against which to lean. It was a perfect spot. The boulder blocked off the wind which, strong and icy, was now pouring down the mountainside. It made the gritty gray sand ripple like water at his feet. When he leaned back momentarily against the rock, a trickle poured down his neck. He felt gritty all over. It rasped his skin, yet it didn't seem to soak up the sweat.

He worked off the shoe, found the offending pebble and threw it down the trail.

At that moment he froze.

No longer could he doubt the movement of the shadow.

Just then he was struck by a sudden rush of sand and something hot and horribly painful. With infinite grace, the mountains silently leaned over onto him, blocking out the now-scorching sun, as he slumped slowly, silently, almost gratefully, onto the trail. The whine of the bullet never reached his conscious mind.

THE PICK UP

IT WAS ONLY A FEW MOMENTS later that the first of the shadows materialized. Across the canyon, toward the now rising sun, a man stood and waved his headcloth in signal. Then, a hundred or so paces above where Jack lay, another man stepped from behind one of the hundreds of boulders. The first rays of the sun illuminated his gray *karakul* cap and glistened on his shiny, Western-style suit. It was as much a uniform, in its own way, as those of the soldiers, a mixture of mohair and rayon favored by senior Afghan officials. The man was lean and straight of back but not young. Even from close up, would have been difficult to tell his age or even his position. He could easily have passed in any station of life, but he had an air of command.

The man stood for a few moments as though checking the wind and surveying the trail. Then silently, he strode forth and walked rapidly down the trail toward where Jack lay. Just before reaching him, the man stopped and gazed down at Jack's body. Then he cocked his head to the side and listened. Nothing answered but the wind and the rasp of the sand on rock. After a few moments, he squatted on his heels and stared into Jack's face. Finally, he lowered himself onto one knee and, almost kindly, raised Jack's head toward his own. Supporting Jack's head with his left arm, he wet the palm of his right hand with his tongue and placed it over Jack's mouth and nose. In the cold early morning air, he felt just a lingering touch of warmth on his wet hand.

Then, gently lowering Jack's head back onto the ground, the man quickly and expertly unzipped the American jacket. Thrusting his hand inside, he felt under the arms and down to the waist. What he touched made him recoil. He jerked his hand out of the jacket. It was covered with blood. Silently he cursed in Pashto. Pulling out a silk handkerchief from his pocket, he wiped off the blood. Crumpling the stained handkerchief, he threw it on the ground.

Then he felt under Jack's other armpit from outside the jacket and, after again finding nothing, moved his right hand down the side of the jacket, coming to rest at the pocket holding the 7.65 mm Czech automatic. Standing up, he hefted the little pistol as though weighing it; then he clicked his tongue in disgust. "Silly. What good would that have done him," he shook his head.

He gingerly dropped the pistol back into the jacket pocket and glanced warily around the desolate scene. In front of him, across the canyon, a now-fully-visible soldier stood with his rifle in his arms. The man whistled twice, and two other men stepped into view on his side of the canyon and another, behind him and further up the mountainside, whistled in reply.

Again, the man bent over Jack's inert form. Methodically, he examined the rest of the right side of Jack's body. In the pants pocket, he found a lump of stale cheese and a small handful of coins. Straightening up, he threw the cheese aside but looked quizzically at the coins, weighing them in his hand, laughed to himself noiselessly and tossed them into the dust. He paused a moment; then, with both hands, he gently turned the body over and began examining the left side. The pants pocket was empty. The man shook his head. Then he felt the outside of the jacket pocket. He smiled with relief. Quickly, he unbuttoned the pocket flap and reached his hand inside. From it, he pulled out a grimy and blood-smeared plastic pouch. Eagerly, he opened the pouch and saw that it was full of papers.

Holding the pouch in both hands, he turned it from side to side, weighing it as he had the coins and the 7.65 mm automatic. Then, gingerly, he put the pouch into his own inside coat pocket.

Turning back to the body again, he once more felt the nose and mouth.

After just a moment he stood up straight and shook his head. Almost soundlessly he mumbled in Arabic, "God gives and God takes away. We are all His and to Him we return." Then, in English, he continued, "I am sorry, Jack Beg."

Without another word, he strode purposefully up the trail toward the plateau and the waiting helicopter.

The four soldiers scurried after him.

THE GOAL KEEPERS

IT WAS SOME HOURS LATER when a tall, gaunt figure of a man, dressed as was his custom in a worn but good quality tweed jacket, was ushered into Smith's office.

Jumping up from behind his desk, Smith blurted out, "What has happened? What have you found out? Is Farnsworth okay? And the papers…"

Major Crighton-Philips stifled a laugh. Not so fast, my good man. I will tell you all. But the key point is that the papers are in good hands. The mission is a success.

"Well, that's wonderful news, Hughe. But what about Farnsworth?"
"Farnsworth, I am sorry to say, has bought it. He is dead."

"Are you sure? He is not a captive in some…some Afghan dungeon?"

"No, he is dead. I have it from an absolutely reliable source.

"But the amazing thing is that he really did make it up to your evacuation spot. Incredible feat of endurance, that. Poor bugger. I would have given odds he couldn't have done it. Know that stretch of country pretty well myself. Must have been quite a fellow. We could use more like him in our service. Don't make them like that much any more. Really deserves a decoration. Too bad it was all in vain."

Smith heard this silently, shaking his head. Then he started to ask, "Did you…"

Crighton-Philips cut him off. "That, we agreed, is my part of the show.

You really don't want to hear any more, I should have thought. Just a casualty of war, you know. Better leave it at that. It's all over now."

Smith nodded. "But at least we will have to retrieve his body..."

"No, don't even think of it. You and I don't have a clue where it is or what happened to him. Any hint that we do might jeopardize the whole show."

"But, we can't just leave our man..."

"Your man is dead. What is out there is just a body. Seen a lot of them in my time. Anyway, you will probably – or at least possibly – be able to claim the body sooner or later. I imagine that the Afghan Security will arrange for some miserable shepherd to find the body and then they'll hang him for murder. Then, after they move the body to some more neutral -- or natural -- place, I should have thought that they'll contact you to ask if you want it back."

"Farnsworth had nothing on him pointing toward us, did he?"

"On him? What a question. His body is enough. It is rather difficult not to identify the body. Not many shepherds look like an American. And he certainly couldn't pass for a Chinaman. And I doubt that they would think him a Russian or an Uzbek. Anyway, although we shouldn't go on about this, the right people up there – you know, in the Security apparatus -- apparently knew him. But, I am told, he had managed to accumulate a few things during his run."

"Accumulate a few things? What on Earth do you mean?"

"Apparently, he got a canteen from your road builder. It was stamped 'Government Issue USA' but I feel reasonably sure they won't breathe a word about it, certainly not protest. But sooner or later, someone will probably go to your ambassador and try to use it to get some concession or other. Perhaps they will also get the fellow, what's his name, Crownover, declared *persona non grata…"*

Then I'll catch hell from the ambassador, but that can't be helped. He'll be gone soon. And the Agency will – or at least should – protect me in Washington."

The tall man looked at him sharply, then laughed and said, "My dear chap we are all expendable, you know. Part of the game."

KEEPING SCORE

IT WAS TOWARD EVENING OF THAT DAY that Smith was seated behind the desk in his office, uncharacteristically pencil in hand – he chose not to allow anyone in the station to see what he was writing so it could not be typed. He was putting the finishing touches on the message so that it could be hand-carried to Washington by courier on the next morning's flight. He had just written,

"The mission put a heavy strain on our team. In fact, I have decided that I must send one of my officers, Miss Nora Adams, who had got emotionally

Laboriously, he erased the word 'emotionally,' wrote in "irrationally," sat back a minute and then erased that too and rewrote "emotionally."

"I would hate to ruin her career," he sighed. "A good girl…still, one must…" Then he went on again,

involved back to be reassigned. I had thought that she was more professionally

Again, he paused, shook his head, and then went on again,

dispassionate. But really it was my fault. I misjudged. I think that after a period of time, she will recover her balance. I guess her attitude is a sign of the times, young people, especially young women always think they know more than they do.

He paused and after a moment or so, scratched out *'especially young women.'*

'Can't tell who will read this,' he mused. Then he went on,

254

After all, she had just produced a very professional study of the Communists in the University...

Then he shook his head slowly again, put down his pencil and gazed at the wall. Finally, he crossed out these lines and returned to the text he had been writing on a separate piece of paper, under the paragraph title,

"Among the casualties were..."

"...not only all these men, some long-time and highly valued agents of our British colleagues, but even an entire Turcoman tribal group with whom Farnsworth had evidently sought refuge. That is a curious twist to the story. Those people have nothing to do with us or, I am assured, with the British..."

He paused and then wrote,

but one of them, thieves that the nomads always are, apparently stole the wrist watch of Farnsworth and when he tried to sell it the money lender turned him in...I understand that...

Just at that moment, the buzzer on his desk forced him to pick up the telephone. In the ear-piece, he heard, "Mr. Smith, Mr. Crownover who came to see you last week is out here and insists that he see you immediately."

"Oh, Christ, tell him to come back tomorrow. The Embassy is closed, and I must get this message off to Washington."

He had taken the receiver away from his ear and was putting it down when he heard the secretary almost scream, " ...No, No, wait a minute, Mr. Crownover, please...wait. You cannot go in now. Wait, please Mr. Crownover..."

The soundproof door, carelessly left unbolted, burst open and in stepped the oversized form of Ernest Crownover.

"Mr. Smith. I just had to see you. It's about Jack, about Farnsworth."

The secretary had followed him, with a stricken look on her face, unsure what to do.

Ernest turned toward her, "That's all right, little lady. It wasn't your fault. You did the best you could. I apologize."

"Okay, Miss Peterson. You can leave us now." Smith stepped to the door and pushed it closed. "...something...something about Farnsworth?"

He hurriedly returned to his desk and turned the paper he had just written over so that it could not be read. Then he turned to confront Crownover.

They looked at one another for a few seconds without a word. Crownover blew out his breath and then spread out his big hands in a sort of gesture of defeat. Then he dropped his hands lifelessly and awkwardly to his sides. He paused, unsure how to begin. He was still smarting from the rebuke he had received from the ambassador and angry about the smirks and giggles of the desk-bound Kabul staff of AID who had begun, in that little closed world, to hear all manner of rumors. He had overheard one 'little shit', as he had described him on another occasion, saying, "I told you that big gorilla was not the simple country boy he pretended to be...he was with the spooks all the time."

As the rumors had spread like wildfire, they grew in the telling and his whole life had seemed to come apart. Even his wife, that rock of his existence, had looked kindly but coyly at him and asked, "Ernest, why didn't you tell me? You know we always tell each other..."

So, it had taken a great effort to come to Smith's office. Then Crownover began.

"You see, Mr. Smith, Jack Farnsworth came stumbling into my camp up near Kunduz four days ago. He was really beat. I don't think I have ever seen anyone so tired. It wasn't just body tired. He was tired to his...soul. Really nearly dead. He didn't think he could make it back here and really put the pressure on me, but real gentlemanly like, to smuggle him back. We had a talk, something like yours and mine. Then he just passed out. Slept like a dead man. I guess it was also the altitude, always hits me up there, and he had a couple of whiskeys. But mostly, it was the…well, whatever it was he'd done.

He went kin'a loco. Began talking about how *they* — whoever the hell 'they' were — were after him. How he had to get some papers to you. How our national security depended upon it. Said he had been walking flat out from up near the Russian frontier. And all that kin'a stuff.

"I didn't know what to make of it. If anyone back in Oklahoma had told me a story like his, I would've call'd the men in white.

"Finally, like I say, he just passed out. I put him to bed on my cot. He mumbled away the whole night, must have been having terrible dreams. Of course, I couldn't sleep and I heard the strangest tales imaginable. He was not so much sleeping, I guess, as delirious. He was still like that when I left the next morning. Just plum wore out. I left him a note to keep quiet and stay put. I couldn't stay with him. I had to get out to my culvert. They was pouring cement that morning. Anyway, I figured he would sleep all day. Like I say, he was just plum wore out.

"But I got to thinking about our talks, yours and mine and his and mine. Hell, I thought, I'm just a country boy. What the hell do I know? Like I say, I felt I couldn't take him back in the AID truck. But I really felt lousy about it, like I was letting him down. If I'd had my own car up there, I'd have done it in a New York minute, but I just couldn't do it in the AID truck. Maybe I was wrong, but I…"

Smith stared at him wordlessly. Then he started to say something.

But Crownover held up his big hand and motioned him to listen. "I'm gittin' confused, I know, but let me finish.

"That was the night before. So after Jack fell asleep, I had another drink to think it all over. Even if I didn't understand, I thought I just *had* to try to help him. But, like I say, I was trapped. I couldn't involve AID. It wasn't right...

"So, I thought I had better do like you – and Jack too – would think was smart. And I had to do like I thought was right.

"Jack had said he was carrying these...these very important papers – 'vital' was the word he used, vital to our national security. Oh, don't worry, Mr. Smith. I see it on your face. He didn't tell me much, not more than a few hints, but I figured it out. You can't see the movies nowadays and not know all about what James, what's-his-name, er...Bond and all those fellows in your outfit do. Any kid knows that spies always carry secret messages. I guess it's your badge like a road grader is mine."

Ernest chuckled and then abruptly stopped himself, feeling even more awkward.

Smith again started to speak.

"No, don't stop me, Mr. Smith," he waved his arm and shook his head. "I'm almost done.

"I decided that I would hire out a taxi so it would only be me and not AID if I got in trouble. But, I'm gittin' ahead of myself. You see, it got confusing because Jack was gone when I got back that afternoon, and Ol' Daud, he's the watchman up there, well he told me, but that was the next day, that is the day after Jack arrived. Damn, it all happened so fast. Well, that night, the first night, when Jack arrived and had passed out, I got him partly undressed to put him to bed. Then I saw his secret papers, the ones he was so worried about gittin' down here to you. I remembered what you said about the Russians building their highways thick enough so planes could land on them. I guess that is what it was all about. But, of course, I didn't know. So I got this idea. I might not be able to git Jack down here, but I could help him finish his job.

"So I got out his papers. Couldn't read'em, of course. Didn't want to, to tell the truth. But I couldn't have anyway as they were in some damn foreign language. Maybe they were the fellows who were building those stretches of highway. Well, I got out a list of the workers and their families up there on the project, and they was mostly in a foreign language too, so I figured they would do. I made them into a little roll so's you could hardly tell the difference when I had finished. I even got them a little sweaty. Let me tell you it wasn't hard by that time. By then I was scared shitless myself, what with the stories Jack had told. But, to be safe, I took off the top sheet of Jack's papers, with blood all over it, and used it to wrap up the roll I had made. Oh, don't worry, Mr. Smith, there was nothing written on that one.

"I figured that if anyone came into the trailer in the night, Jack wouldn't get into any more trouble. So I hid my papers, you know, *his* papers, in one of my extra boots. And there was a funny thing. I guess you fellows have things happen like this all the time, but it really shook me. When I came back that afternoon, I mean the next day, I found a note from Jack in the other boot...funny, if he had put his note in the other boot, I mean the left boot, he would've found his papers again.

"But anyway I figured on telling him when I got back in the evening, and then, I'd tell him how I was going to git them – and him too - down here in a taxi. Then, like I say, when I got back, Old Daud, that's the night watch-man, was sitting sort of sullen like in his cabin. Wouldn't hardly look me in the eye. I figured something must have happened about Jack, but of course I couldn't ask him. So when I went to the trailer, the door was unlocked and Jack was gone.

'I dunno where he went, but I guess he'll be glad when he finds out about all this."

Then, falling silent, Ernest reached into his inside coat pocket and pulled out a small, dust-stained lump of paper.

"Here are your papers, Mr. Smith."

www.ingramcontent.com/pod-product-compliance
Lightning Source LLC
Chambersburg PA
CBHW061954170626
46813CB00006B/2640

* 9 780098 293404 3 *